ALEXANDER KENDZIORSKI

Death Will Know My Name

An African Painted Wolf Novel

This book was professionally typeset on Reedsy.
Find out more at reedsy.com

This novel is dedicated to the tireless work of wildlife conservation workers and the rangers who risk their lives in protecting the wild.

All proceeds from the sale of this book will go to organizations serving the African Painted Wolf.

Contents

One

*I*t *will be over soon.*

The dark wolf lay in a vulture's shadow. His breathing was shallow, his body inert. The first touch was gentle, despite the beak being sharp as a dagger. The next nipped his soft furry belly, releasing a red trickle. Half-closed glassy eyes stared, the wolf's jaw agape. Tissue thin as a sheet held in his entrails, and the blood of a lifetime.

The blood of the last wolf.

With a convulsion, his lean body jerked and spun, his paws now planted on the sandy soil. The bullet shaped head was held low, large dish ears angled back. His jaws were parted, baring eager serrated teeth. A deep resonant growl broke through the silence of the morning.

The vulture swept wide its wings and with a single flap was in the air, landing several meters away.

Fur dominated by black with hints of gold and white was tousled by the damp breeze under the high orange sun. His coat was faded, in places worn thin with age, lending the old painted wolf a ghostly appearance. He stood, coiled, every sinewed muscle taut across his slight body. The white of his tail was in the air, narrow hips crouched. Every claw was dug into the ground, eyes dark as onyx flashed with an implacable rage.

"Death comes for us all. When it comes for Blackthorn... *it shall know my name.*"

The white-backed vulture stared at the dead wild dog, now returned to life. Another flap of its broad wings and the bird was aloft to continue the hunt for corpses.

Vibrant leaves fluttered on a giraffe thorn acacia tree, the flattened green crown obscuring the dark red wood and the thousands of paired white thorns covering the branches. From under the leaves came a series of *kuk kuk kuk kuk* calls. Black wings speckled with white fluttered as the red-billed hornbill took flight, soaring over the wetlands. Mixed acacia forest stretched into the distance surrounding the vast flat grass plain, now drenched with the late summer rains. Stands of tall herringbone grass topped with green florets on reddish stalks were scattered across the bushveld between broad pools of muddy water.

Reed cormorants and darters picked through the contents of the pools, while sacred ibis stabbed their needle thin bills into the sand. A baboon family waded through a distant pond, grazing on grass strands and flowers. The mother held her arms above the wet as she stepped gingerly, her balance thrown off by the infant clambering over her back.

Close by, a male hyena skulked around the trunk of the giraffe thorn acacia, head held low by a long neck. His powerful shoulders were hunched forward, black spotted coat splatted with mud. Dark maroon eyes furtively looked toward the painted wolf, down at the ground, and back to the wolf.

The brilliant green of grass seemed to stretch on forever, meeting the sky on the edge of nowhere. Toward the horizon, the spiraled horns of greater kudu danced as a bachelor herd browsed from a thicket. Waterbirds soared, gliding in to alight on the standing water. Steady snoring calls of common platanna frogs filled the air.

A pack could thrive in these lands.

Blackthorn stepped forward, head down, scanning the ground before him. Prints crisscrossed the sandy soil. Deep hoof marks of wildebeest and cape buffalo were mixed with the cattle-like prints of eland and kudu. A single track of leopard prints disappeared into the grass. Scattered clawed paw prints of hyena could be seen stretched between puddles and pools, with occasional white calcified dung middens.

There were no tracks of painted wolves.

Blackthorn looked behind him at the few claw marks of his in the soil, the slight depressions moist, eroding with each raindrop. Soon, they would be washed away.

The only sign a wolf inhabited these lands. A whimper in the storm.

He sensed the presence of another hunter, but could not tear his gaze away from his tracks.

The male hyena ducked behind a tall grass tussock as he approached Blackthorn, who finally turned to face the visitor.

"You are hoping I will join you in the hunt." The dark wolf allowed himself a grin, white teeth gleaming from his parted jaws. "You would do better to follow another." He turned to leave.

Grass rustled to his side. The male hyena had bounded before him. Still with downcast eyes, his long neck dipped beneath Blackthorn's. Nostrils flared as the scavenger sniffed the wolf.

Blackthorn tensed, lean muscle rippling beneath his hide. A quick look about revealed no other hyena in the area. He sniffed, and the strange, acrid smell seared his nose. Foul to him, yet somehow not offensive.

"Your scent betrays no malice." Another sniff. "Your clan has abandoned you, has it not?"

The male gave no sign of understanding, eyes still cast toward his feet as he moved slightly closer.

"You must be lonely indeed to seek a companion in me." He remained tense. "Ill fortune is the only kind I have had."

The hyena took another step with his paw on the moist ground. His pant was ragged, as though he held back a labored cry.

"And you would not hesitate to sate your hunger on my dead flesh."

The head and powerful jaw were nearly on the ground in supplication.

"Perhaps you think me a fool." He gazed across the flood-plain at the distant grazing herds of eland and wildebeest, birds fluttering over their numbers. "And a fool I would be to consider this."

A glance upwards, the dark red eyes meek under a raised brow.

"You do not understand me. Or you are quite mad."

The hyena took a step back, powerful shoulders still hunched.

"So it must be." Blackthorn gave one last snuff, like a sneeze, and straightened up.

The hyena relaxed, and stood by the wolf's side.

"If they could see me—" Blackthorn's voice cut off so abruptly the hyena glanced toward him with alarm. The wolf took a deep breath, closing his eyes, and exhaled long and slow. "If only." He looked down at the stranger, who dipped his head at his gaze. "A curious pair we shall be."

Together they padded across the mud plain, into the acacia brush. The hyena moved with an ungainly lope, mouth hanging open as he tasted the air. The wolf jogged lightly upon the ground, ears folded back, head down, tail out, his dark eyes seeking the first kill of the day.

***

Robust antelope clad in coarse grey fur stood erect and alert on the edge of a broad languid pool. A dozen were at attention, long funnel like ears all directed across the water. Each of the males in the herd held their horns aloft, ribbed and curved upwards to the rear. One took a mouthful of grass, chewing absently.

Blackthorn stood on the opposite bank examining the young male waterbuck ram. He padded along the edge of the lightly rippling surface, peering into the dark waters.

"I see no erosions indicating crocodiles entering this pond." He glanced at the hyena. "Still, we must be cautious." The surface was a smooth mirror, disturbed only by a scattering of bugs. The eyes of the herd watched the wolf intently. As he reached a shallow sand bank that spanned the pond, the waterbuck began to move in the opposite direction away from him.

"I will not escape their attention. Not like—" He glanced back to the hyena, who followed him at a distance. Peering at the waterbuck, he saw they still focused upon him alone.

"Make your way around this pool." He gestured toward the waterbuck herd. "They may not be as wary about you."

The hyena stared at him.

Blackthorn furrowed his brow for a moment. He bared his teeth, which made the hyena recoil for a moment, then he gave a long look to the herd, then back to the hyena.

He looked at the ground, long neck angled down, and he gave a low mooing rumble. He threaded his way into the tall grasses, disappearing from view.

"*Vervloeks*." Blackthorn hissed to himself. "I should not have expected that *oke* to listen to a wolf." He shook his head and looked across the pool again toward his prey. "I can cut you down without a pack to assist me." Loping quickly, he crossed the sand bar. Before he returned to dry ground, the waterbuck herd had splashed into the pool. As he drew closer, the rams all clambered out onto the mud on the opposite side. Blackthorn reversed his course, but before he placed a paw back on the sand bar to cross again, the males had begun to slip once again into the cool water.

"*Bliksem*." He snuffed. The waterbuck continued to watch him without expression.

The entire herd suddenly splashed into the pool again in a panic, one left behind on the bank. His only cry of alarm was a snort, mouth wide, horns high as it stumbled to the ground.

The male hyena chuckled, its heavy jaws clamped on the hind leg of the waterbuck, the staccato crack of bone audible even above the splashing of the herd.

Blackthorn lost no time sprinting around the pool, and bore down on the injured waterbuck. The hyena's eyes were wide, its grip on the flank of the buck was a vise.

With a bound, the wolf seized the snout of the waterbuck, and planted his paws on the mud. Even with the damp he was an anchor, and despite the buck outweighing him by tenfold, it could not move.

The hyena loosed his hold, his eyes slits, his mouth wide, conical fangs and hefty canines on display. Jaws locked upon the buck's shoulder, and it was dragged down.

Blackthorn let go of the snout and ripped open the abdomen, spilling the intestines onto the ground with a gush of maroon that poured into the water.

The hunters eyed one another for only a moment, and each set to devour the antelope's organs at haste. They did not quarrel, nor did they make a sound, each bolting down kilograms of meat in minutes. The ribcage was pulled open as they worked together to dismember the beast, muscle torn away from bone by shearing teeth. When their bellies hung low, they paused in their ravenous feeding.

The hyena looked up and Blackthorn followed his gaze to see the vultures circling above. A lappet-faced vulture glided in to land close by, folding its great black wings. White backed vultures were close behind.

The wolf gave a nod, and they padded off as the scavengers swarmed over the ruined carcass, grey fur disappearing under a snarl of white and black feathers.

Blackthorn thought for a moment the hyena was smiling at him, teeth bared, and mouth hanging open releasing a streamer of drool.

"Clever chappie, you are." He shook his head free of a biting fly, large ears slapping his skull. "You must have a name of a sort." He canted his head to one side. "Though I am not sure what."

The hyena uttered a deep groaning sound, long and low, a sound that could only mean pleasure.

"*Kreun*, then. *Kreun*." Allowing himself a smile, he chuckled. "I suppose naming you for a groan works well enough." He turned to look back at the swirling pile of vultures, his brow raised. One of them hopped away from the carcass and turned toward the dark wolf. Blackthorn wondered if it was the same bird that meant to eviscerate him earlier.

"Every moment of life is stolen from my enemies."

Kreun gave a low whine.

"The bushveld still surprises me, even after all the seasons that have passed." Blackthorn regarded his companion. He closed his eyes to the sun and allowed the warmth to wash over him. "The path shall take us." His obsidian eyes opened again to see the hyena examining him. "As it takes us all."

They moved together into the thick growth of high grasses, the tall stalks folding in place behind them as the savanna swallowed them whole.

Two

A single blade of blue grass stood tall, coated in morning dew, twitching as a stick insect crawled up its length. The gleaming drops of water made the waxy surface of the blade slippery, and its progress was slow. Antennae waved as it neared the tattered crest of the grass. In the dim light of the dawn, the long slender brown body was indistinguishable from the stalk.

A shadow fell over the insect and the blade, and the antennae were stilled. Twin semicircular wings flashed wide, but the warning was ignored. Sharp incisors closed over the insect and the surrounding clump of grass and ripped free, crushed between powerful molars.

The eland took another step as its mouth ground down the tough grass. Its knees emitted loud clicks, informing all present that this was the dominant male. At its feet, the tussock of grass had been reduced to nothing, barely a remnant above the ground. Within days, new shoots of fresh, tender grass would grow to entice the next herd. A dozen eland filed past, males, females, and calves in a loose formation.

As another adult male strode forward to graze, the dominant raised his head in the direction of his rival. A steady glare was enough to convince the inferior to move away, giving a slow head-shake as he did so. The roles thus reaffirmed, the towering male continued his march across the grassland, stooping his nearly two meter frame to thrust his tightly spiraled horns into a pile of dead grass. Lifting his head again to survey the plain, the haystack remained perched on his horns, falling away gradually in clumps. The rest of the adults paced after him, females keeping their calves close by as they fed.

The lead male abruptly stopped, and the remaining grass pitched forward from his horns onto the ground. Hooves stamped heavily, and the male eland gave an imperious glare. Those who followed him did the same. Calves retreated behind the adults, who were prepared to fight to the death in their defense.

The wolf and hyena faced the imposing antelope that loomed over them. The dominant male dipped its head, not in deference, but lowering its pair of sharp spiraled horns so the carnivores could get a good look.

The hunters moved on, and the eland did the same in the search for the most tender shoots of grass while the wetlands of the Caprivi supported them.

"Do you hunt this?" Blackthorn nodded in the direction of the eland.

Kreun did not respond. The wolf uttered a gentle high pitched twitter, and repeated his question. Kreun cast his maroon eyes toward the eland, wrinkled his snout and ignored the antelope.

"There must be a manner of speaking between us." He twittered again, and indicated the antelope as they passed. "*Eland.*"

Kreun gave a slight giggle and loped ahead.

Blackthorn sighed to himself and dashed to keep up.

***

Every animal on the veld tensed at the sharp alarm whistle released by the reedbuck. They were close, but out of sight. Baboons bared long fangs with a *bogom - bogom* call, impala barked, and waterbirds took to the air. Grazers stood in the clearing, seeming to hold their breath. With a crash of branches, four reedbuck exploded from a clumping of *Combretum* shrubs, dashing into a shallow pool with a splattering of mud. A hyena and painted wolf were close behind, angling around the pool as they gained ground in their pursuit. As quickly as they appeared, reedbuck and hunters disappeared from view behind thick green foliage.

The rest of the animals relaxed slightly as the sound of the chase faded, and all returned to the business of feeding. Not a moment of foraging could be wasted with excessive vigilance.

"Flank him!" Blackthorn ordered with an agitated twittering chirp. "Bring him back to the chase!"

The hyena allowed the juvenile antelope to extend his lead and escape, instead focusing on another reedbuck. The swift adult bounded over the high grass, its long legs allowing it to soar over the thickets while the hunters crashed through the wet foliage. Again, the reedbuck pranced over the tufted red grass, its hind legs high in the air with the *pronk* meant to show its power and vitality to a hunt doomed to fail. With another crash through damp green, the wolf and hyena lost a moment looking for their quarry, only to see it vault above another, more distant thicket.

"*Bliksem.*"

The hyena panted, not understanding the word, but dipped his head in recognizing the anger behind it.

"The failure is mine." Blackthorn growled, his deep voice graveled with age. "Your kind simply cannot coordinate a hunt, Kreun." He reclined, scratching his ear with a hind leg to dislodge a tick.

Kreun sat as well, his short hindquarters squatting on a clump of grass.

"The closest your kind come to hunting as a pack is that *whooping* call you give at a kill."

Kreun looked up at the *whoop* sound, but relaxed again.

"And should you summon hyena to a kill, that is the last we will see of it. The females will dominate, and *voetsek* to us." He stretched out his forepaws. "There shall be a way. Your kind are clever *okes*. And I am no *domkop*." He laid down onto his side in the sun, the heat powering down upon them. Kreun did the same, feeling no need to work as the burning orb reached its apex in the sky.

A cape turtle dove called over the languorous wetland with a steady *Kuk-coorrrr-uk, Kuk-coorrrr-uk*.

***

Slender green stalks held aloft branches leading to pale blue edged flowers with central white blotches. The wild lobelia grew in a dense stand amid the herringbone grass, which sported less prominently colored flowers. The green reached high toward the sun, risking the clipping teeth of antelope.

Through the grasses the odd pair trudged, occasionally glancing at one another. Kreun strode forth, muscles twitching in his powerful shoulders. His mouth hung open, panting in the heat. Uniformly brown fur was marked with darker brown spots along his sides, shaggy tail nearly black. Roughly triangular ears twitched to ward off biting flies, one ear notched nearly in half from a battle.

Blackthorn's mostly black fur was a trait seen in wolves from further north. His mottled back and gold tail was curved up into the air, tipped in white. One of his ears was nicked as well, from a bullet that long ago failed to find its target. Black and gold flecked fur covered his crown, divided by a black stripe that extended from a charcoal muzzle to between his ears. His eyes were far darker than the usual hazel color of a painted wolf, and bored through whomever caught his gaze.

"It is growing late in the year to benefit from the dropped calves." Blackthorn nodded his head in the direction of a wildebeest herd, nearly two dozen strong. "They are young, but by now able to race alongside their parents."

The herd milled in a vast grass meadow positioned between hills topped with sparse acacia trees. Robust cows grazed at leisure. Their large heads with broad dark snouts were topped with upward curving horns. Their bodies were bluish grey in color, a dark dorsal mane of hair running down their spine. They moved about with ease, casting a look around to ensure their calves were close by. These had grown fast since they were born to the savanna, made strong with the rich milk from their mothers.

Oxpeckers hopped about on the high backs of the wildebeest cows, sifting through the fur for parasites. An attendant male surveyed the group, head held high, topped with curving horns more thickset than the females he guarded.

Blackthorn stopped, and crouched low in the grass. He watched Kreun, who came to a halt by his side, sniffing the air. He looked at Blackthorn hesitantly.

"I shall follow *your* lead." He dipped his head with the

slightest of gestures.

Kreun ambled forward, his mouth agape. He stood tall, taking no effort to hide in the grass.

"You know no subtlety, hyena." Blackthorn braced himself, ready to run if the herd bolted.

A few hundred meters away, the hyena slowed his pace from loping to a casual walk. Once again, his head lowered nearly to the ground, tail tucked low between his legs. This did not reduce his apparent size, and the male wildebeest had already spotted him.

Blackthorn waited in the grass, panting.

Closer the hyena walked, and his gait slowed, his body hunched over further. His gaze did not meet any of the wildebeest. His cowering form seemed ready to retreat into the ground he walked upon.

None of the wildebeest reacted, even as he closed the distance to a few meters. The large bull turned, regarded the hyena, and with a snuff continued to graze. Kreun walked right among them, amid the evenly spaced cows. The females began to snort, with one stamp, and then another. The cloud of flies buzzed angrily over them, harassing with bites and obscuring their sight. Kreun milled there, surrounded by the wildebeest and their offspring, causing no disturbance as he sniffed the ground.

One calf wandered a few meters from its mother.

Kreun abruptly stood straight and bolted in between the young and its parent, and chased the calf away from the herd. Finally, the rest of the wildebeest herd reacted with panic, but were unable to close ranks around the now sprinting calf.

Blackthorn's jaw hung open in stunned silence. As he watched, the hyena nipped at the flanks, guiding it first one way, then the other, away from the protection of the herd. When the chase was more than a kilometer away from the barrier of horns, the hyena lunged to grip the young wildebeest by its neck and lifted most of the body off the ground. He shook the calf vigorously, and the body went limp. Powerful jaws went to work, tearing open the belly and pulling the organs and viscera from the cavity. Kreun swallowed these whole, gulping down kilograms of meat and offal at a swallow. The shearing teeth ripped away the muscles from rib and hip, disappearing into a bottomless throat.

By the time Blackthorn was by his side, the bulk of the meat had been consumed. He took a small share, and left nothing more behind than hide and bone. Kreun panted, his eyes closed to the sun overhead.

"You *need* no subtlety." Blackthorn laid down, watching the hunter closely.

Three

Death pervaded the air.

Hanging heavily, it was an invisible fog, a substance coating every surface. Burning to the eyes, it dimmed the sun, pushed back against the breeze, weighed down all that was living.

The hunters had drifted from the wildebeest herd after their hunt, studying the land for other prey. Adjacent to the rich grasses of the wetlands was a tangle of brush, and Kreun led them inwards. Blackthorn expected it to end, and open back again into grasses or forest, but there was only more sedge. And then the thick pestilential scent enveloped them.

More than once, Blackthorn restrained himself from bolting in his unease. He could run, but had no destination. He could flee, but the stale murk seemed everywhere and nowhere.

Kreun trudged before him, head sunk low, his mouth wide open and running with slaver.

The impenetrable gorse of acacia thornbrush and *Combretum* shrub only added to the suffocating closeness. The leaves hung unstirred, and the air was devoid of bird or insect.

"Where do you hope to lead us, in this derelict *bos*?" The dark wolf wrinkled his snout, and snuffed his disapproval. The malodor intensified.

Kreun glanced back once, his red rimmed eye regarding him with satisfaction. His shoulders continued their machine rhythm as he pressed forward.

A dirge of droning flies and the inescapable fume of decay masked their senses. Apart from a rising buzz, he could hear nothing. The dark wolf looked around and behind them with disquiet. Kreun picked up his pace.

Thorns rattled against one another as the brush parted, and the hyena gave a mad giggle. He looked back with a wide gape that could only be a knowing grin.

Blackthorn froze, his slight paws rooted to the dry ground. Gasping in shock, he drew the viscous, fetid air into his lungs. A deafening noise consumed his ears as the carrion flies filled the sky.

Tangled in the bracken was the lithe, splendid form of a cheetah. The lean hind legs, seeming too long for the creature, were hung up in thorns. The long body was compressed against the narrow trunk of a squat sand camwood tree. The thin bones were shattered, ribs crushed. The fine head of the cheetah was nearly torn off, hanging by a strand of neck muscle from the shoulder. Dull, rusted iron formed the snare that abruptly halted the swift predator's last great pursuit, still wound about the camwood tree where the poacher had set the trap. Set, and then forgotten.

Blackthorn gaped in horror, but not at the cheetah. His gaze was drawn to the four withered bodies of the cheetah cubs that lay stiff next to the rotting body of their mother. They had huddled close, awaiting a comforting tongue and nourishment that would never come.

Kreun chortled and gripped one of the cubs within his great jaws, and with a slight toss swallowed it whole.

"Voetsek." He uttered this as a guttural hiss as a growl erupted within, and he stepped towards Kreun with a piercing shriek. *"Vuil bliksem."* His teeth bared, ears flat against his head, he put one paw before the other closer to the cowering hyena.

Kreun sharply dipped his head, nearly to the ground, his maroon eyes a storm of confusion. He stepped back, his hind end tucked under as though an attack were already underway.

Ragged breaths, emitted from the dark wolf from his tense, lowered frame, rumbled as though from a poorly oiled engine. Charcoal eyes poured forth hatred.

Kreun crouched in fear, and backed up, loud whines issued forth in appeal. His manner was as apologetic as it was uncomprehending.

As the spotted hyena backed out of the clearing, Blackthorn could not tear his glare from the iron wire that throttled the cheetah even in death. The bushveld around him disappeared, the scents, the sounds, and even the sun above faded. All vanished as his eyes narrowed to enraged slits, his world reduced to the iron snare.

His eyelids shut, every muscle tight as a bow strung for the hunt. His heartbeat bounding, the rhythm of another life ending.

A whimper swept aside his daze, and Blackthorn shivered as he noticed Kreun. The hyena whined again, seeking absolution from an offense he did not understand. His chin scraped the ground, eyes watching the dark wolf.

"Forgive me, Kreun." He glared again at the snare, for a moment his vision going black before he shook it off. He searched for words to explain, but the gulf between their communication was too great to bridge. He walked past the cheetah carcass on unsteady legs.

Three cheetah cubs lay motionless in their eternal vigil.

"Do as you must." His graveled voice was devoid of emotion. He padded on, hastening to leave the thicket before Kreun returned to his meal.

*****

When Kreun finally emerged from the thicket, Blackthorn was reclining in the shade of a corkwood tree. His mottled black fur with traces of white and gold melted into shadow, but his musk scent made him easy to find.

Kreun loped closer, and with some angst, laid near the base of the tree. He grunted his contentment, his abdomen distended.

Blackthorn closed his eyes and tried to clear his mind, but it returned unerringly to the snare. The rusted surface gave off no glint of sun, instead seeming to absorb the surrounding light. Twisting around the base of the tree, it tightened its grip on what remained of the cheetah's neck. The sockets of the skull were empty, but the cheetah was still regarding him.

Come with me. It is peaceful here.

Blackthorn shook again, giving off a sharp growl. Kreun raised his head in alarm, but lowered it again to rest when he saw his companion laying quietly on his side. With a full belly, he had no desire to hunt before nightfall.

*****

Whir-whirrr-whrwhrwhrwhrwhr!

A dark brown bird whipped over the grasses, past the cork-wood tree, and the fiery-necked nightjar vanished in the darkness.

Blackthorn aroused, raising his head from the grass where he lay. There was only the steady hiss of the wind stirring the tall grasses. The dim moonlight, interrupted by cloud, left the veld in inky blackness.

Kreun was walking past him before he knew the hyena was there. His narrow paws did not disturb the foliage, and he stopped to survey the clearing by the pool. Rounded ears strained to listen in the night, his brown snout twitching as he sniffed the air.

Blackthorn rolled onto his paws. He took a deep breath, taking in the subtle scents of animal and plant. Moisture foretold another rain in three days, the faint odor of elephants on the march. The news of the bushveld was told in a subtle language that shifted with the wind currents.

"What ails you, Kreun?" Another sniff of the air. "I can scent your anxiety." He peered at the moon, peeking between banks of billowing cloud.

His whines were muted, swallowed, though his bulging eyes made clear his disquiet. His black muzzle was in the air, mouth open to taste the signals that wafted by.

"If it is me you fear, then you need not worry." He prodded Kreun with his snout to reassure him. "It was not you that angered me so."

Still he panted, nose up, whining quietly as he smelled the air. He padded forward, sniffing the ground, then the air again.

Blackthorn felt a pang in his stomach as he considered what would cause such apprehension. He loped to Kreun's side.

"No lion has passed this way for days." He sniffed the air again to be sure.

Kreun glanced at him.

"You know the word for 'lion'."

The hyena's eyes narrowed.

"We are alone for now." Blackthorn surveyed the veld around them. "Though that will change as our kills gather attention."

Kreun seemed to calm at that and sat on his diminutive hindquarters. *"Ahh lone."* The groan yielded something that resembled phrases he could understand with difficulty.

"Ja." Blackthorn canted his head to the side, wondering to himself how much this creature understood of him. "It seems we do have a parlance in common."

Kreun sniffed Blackthorn, craning his long neck towards the wolf. His red eyes softened. *"Ahh lone."*

Blackthorn's face fell, slight but noticeable. He gave a reluctant nod. "I have been alone. Since the wet season was upon us." He met the hyena's stare. "But alone no longer."

Kreun lay down on his side, and the dark wolf reclined next to him in the dark.

***

Blackthorn was up with the sunrise, and padded away from the clearing where Kreun still slept. Sniffing the ground, he moved swiftly in broad semicircles away from the corkwood tree. The ground was damp, dewdrops clinging to the stalks of grass.

The mosquitoes waited for their wings to dry before taking flight while flies buzzed about. A deep droning sound pulsed by the water, echoed by more *kkk-ck, kkk-ck* calls resembling a steady knock. The guttural toad was gathered in numbers amid the grass lining the pool, warming themselves in the sun.

21

Lean legs resembling spring steel propelled the wolf forward quickly as he inspected the ground, his rounded ears bouncing just over the grass tips. He covered a square kilometer within the hour. Suddenly he stopped to examine the earth more closely.

"So here lies the source of your dread." A fading print was pressed into the sand, a central blot with four toes and light claw marks. "A clan of hyena." Far distant, the wildebeest carcass they had killed a few days previous attracted a soaring circle of vultures.

A giggle behind him alerted Blackthorn to Kreun's presence. His eyes bulged out once again as he watched the vultures, and then looked down to the hyena prints across the sandy soil.

Rather than rush to the carcass to feast on bone and hide, he gave an urgent cackle and bounded off through the grass.

Four

Westward the hunters moved, each led by different impulses.

Blackthorn scanned the ground, scenting the animals that had traversed the veld over the season, reading the tracks. Nowhere did he find the prints of an African wild dog. He paused every few minutes to spray a small amount of urine onto the grasses. These urine markings carried the smell of the wolf, and him in particular, hints of his identity and direction.

Kreun's behavior was more cryptic. He would pad forward, always with an eye on Blackthorn. When the wolf paused to mark, Kreun would pace about, then back into a stand of grass with his tail curled over his back. From an anal gland he secreted a white paste smelling of soap onto a few centimeters of grass stalk. He would do so with care, then lope away. He would look about and release his chuckling giggle, his eyes crazed with anxiety.

"You need not fear, Kreun." Blackthorn said, a tinge of sadness in his voice. "Your kind will find your mark, and soon after, you."

Kreun's eyes darted about, his tail tucked deep between his legs and head nearly on the ground. With another quiet giggle, he loped off.

"Apprehensive bugger." The dark wolf followed him at a distance, and before long the hyena slowed. He drew closer, studying the face of the creature before him. "You fear confronting your clan." He nodded. "You fear them, do you not?"

Kreun's eyes rolled wetly, and his throat swallowed his frightened giggle. From deep within, he gurgled. "*She.*" His head dipped. "*Angers.*"

"Your matriarch." He thought on this. "She may reject you should your paths cross."

"*She.*" His lope accelerated. "*Kills.*" He loped ahead again, the scent of terror pouring off his fur.

Westward, gradually. Days passed, and nothing more substantial than a scrub hare crossed their path. Stomachs began to curl into knots awaiting the next meal.

Blackthorn paused to urinate briefly, and Kreun stopped to paste the grass. Once again, he did so with great care, and then ran off, fretful.

***

Pensive whining rose above the rustling sounds as the wild dog and the hyena trotted through the herringbone grass. Insects fled from the stalks, and seed browsing sparrows took flight at their approach.

One sparrow swooped over them and was met by a darting arrow, a fluttering of black feathers on the collision. The lesser grey shrike gripped the kill in its talons, and flapped with effort to a nearby giraffe thorn acacia. Several thorns on a higher branch were festooned with impaled lizards and small rodents. The shrike landed with difficulty on the branch, glancing about. Its head and neck were covered with a grey hood of feathers, black wing tips and tail, with a black band across its eyes that gave it the appearance of a bandit. The dead sparrow was speared upon a vertical acacia thorn. The shrike hopped about on the branch, inspecting its larder. There could never be enough food stored for the dry season.

"Caution, my friend." Blackthorn intoned. His ears angled back, head held lower as he peered toward the veld ahead.

"*Furrnd.*" Kreun gave another whine, and followed Blackthorn's gaze. White backed vultures glided in circles, wheeling gradually down. As each raptor descended, their wings swept wider, individual feathers splayed out and feet forward to air brake as much as possible before setting down with a bound. Each vulture on landing joined a dense scrum fighting over a concealed form, a roil of dirty white plumage, razor sharp beaks and talons. Kreun took note of the surrounds, and seeing no other hyenas about, charged into the mass.

The vultures scattered, revealing the skeleton of what may have been a wildebeest, but there was no way to know. The rotting meat and hide was swarming with flies, a pool of liquefied entrails where the belly once was. Kreun sniffed about, and began to rip away what meat he could find under a flap of hide.

"*Vuil.*" Blackthorn wrinkled his sensitive snout at the over-whelming stench of corruption. He had scavenged on occasion before, but this corpse was far gone. Kreun picked over the putrefying flesh for a few minutes before the vultures surged back. Poking his vulnerable rump with their beaks, they chased him off. The moment Kreun retreated, the carcass again disappeared under the boil of feathers.

Kreun and Blackthorn shared a look before they turned to leave.

"It is just as well. You might run into other hyenas close to carrion."

Kreun lowered his head, and with a higher whine, loped off in a hurry.

***

With sunrise Blackthorn raised his head from the ground, dried leaf fragments hanging from the dark ruff of fur under his neck. Kreun snored lightly nearby where he lay on flattened grasses. He sensed the hyena stirring in the night, weaving through the nearby grass and shrub, but never going too far before returning to sleep. Whatever he was doing, he had not left to hunt.

The wolf lowered his head and foreshoulders toward the ground, arching his lower back in a satisfying stretch. Standing straight, his rounded ears swiveled to listen for activity. The savanna was quiet. Glancing at Kreun, he padded away to let him sleep.

Bounding through a field of tall grasses, his tireless lope carried him through stands of acacia trees and past dense thornbrush. With each bouncing step, his hind legs pushed him high enough so each stride afforded him a glimpse of his hunting grounds. Visibility was low, but he could scent prey distantly. After shuffling through a dense Combretum shrub barrier the scent became stronger, with the slightest hint of water.

Black ears folded back, his head lowered, his appearance coming to resemble a torpedo on slender legs. His bounce was gone, now swiftly threading between trees. He held his body slightly lower to the ground, smoothly making his way between thorned branches without disturbing them. Onyx eyes surveyed the lower veld as he left the heavier cover afforded by the acacia scrub.

A pool appeared before him, its edges stamped into a muddy wreck by a recent visit from an elephant herd. They had since moved on, leaving behind a small group of impala rams. The temperature was still cool, the sun low on the horizon, and they were grazing on the rich green grass and browsing upon acacia leaf from squat shrubs near the pool.

The rams sported upward curving ribbed horns, twisting into razor sharp points. Tails wagged and fawn colored rumps wriggled to dislodge biting flies. One male paused in his morning grazing to extend a hind leg toward his head, and scratched carefully just behind his eye with a hoof to scrape off particularly bothersome ticks. This took concentration, as the ticks had burrowed deep into his hide, and one was digging into his ear. He looked about briefly for the oxpecker birds that would normally service his herd, but they had followed larger antelope that moved through the area. The ram returned to carefully raking the side of his head with his hind hoof, and felt some ticks being pulled free from their meals. This was so gratifying, he failed to keep watch around his perimeter of the pool.

Blackthorn was bounding at top speed toward him by the time another impala gave a startling alarm cough. The ram turned to run, and sprang into a *pronk* to evade. It was too short, and the wolf had caught him at the bottom of the retreating leap, sinking his teeth into the impala's flank.

The ram bellowed, and pounded his hind legs into another

leap, wrenching free leaving a spraying hole and a flap of hide. His *pronk* was weak, and he was unable to run once he landed. Blackthorn quickly caught him, and there was no escape. This time his teeth gripped the flesh of the upper belly, and when he ripped away the muscle, the impala fell and did not rise again. It lay in shock, gasping, with time for only one more breath before the intestines were torn away and the blood loss ended his life. The only sensation was of slipping into warm water and the darkness underneath.

***

Blackthorn hurried back to the clearing and found Kreun awake, sitting up, sniffing the air. The blood that coated the dark wolf filled the air with scent, and the hyena was already drooling. He stood and padded over toward Blackthorn.

The wolf paused, his belly hanging very low. Kreun whined gently.

He is the only other member of my pack, such as it is.

Blackthorn leaned his head low to the ground and regurgitated half the meat from the kill. It sat steaming before them.

Kreun recoiled for a moment, gazing at his companion in disbelief. The moment passed and he devoured the entire pile.

"Come, my friend. There is more to be had."

The wolf and the hyena bounded quickly through the savanna toward the impala kill. Blackthorn noted he was light on his feet, bumping against him as he ran, much like a wolf would. He smiled to himself as they made their way to the pool.

Crashing through the thorned branches overlooking the low pool, they were greeted by a series of calls.

WHOOO-OOP! WHOOO-OOP! WHOOO-OOP!

"Steady on, Kreun."

They emerged to find three hyenas working over the impala carcass. It was in two pieces, and heads were buried in each. The third panted, looking about the pool. It turned and noticed Blackthorn.

"With me, Kreun." The dark wolf bolted down toward the pool, ears folded back, jaw agape, crossing the field in a few quick bounds. With a snarl, he closed in on the hyena that watched him, and it turned about with a coarse giggle. Tucking its hindparts low, it scooted away from Blackthorn.

The other two pulled their blood-soaked heads away from their meals.

Blackthorn rounded on them both, chasing one away from the lower half of the kill, then the other was on the run while the lifeless eyes of the impala watched. He pursued the female hyena away and she tucked her rump against the ground and bared her fangs.

Blackthorn sprinted after the other hyena, and she abandoned the kill to watch from the brush.

"Kreun, we will not have long to—Kreun?"

He suddenly realized he was on his own. Diving into the abdominal cavity of the impala, he was able to tear away some pelvic muscle before he sensed one of the female hyenas approaching. He pulled out, swallowed his take, and rounded on his enemy.

"Thought you had it easy?" He snapped his jaws in the face of the hyena. She withdrew, mouth hanging open, red eyes rolling with a chortle caught in her throat. *"Voetsek!"* He pursued her until she loped a respectful distance away.

Returning to the lower half of his kill, he noticed another hyena skulking in the brush, head barely visible before ducking low.

"Kreun, what are you on about?"

Kreun raised his head with an apologetic whimper. He gazed at the other three hyena, hovering at the periphery of the pool. Their lowing calls resumed. *WHOOO-OOP! WHOOO-OOP!* This was followed with a steady mooing dirge, and more distant whooping calls reached them.

"They are calling their clan, you dimwit. We haven't much time!" He choked down more meat, but noticed several more hyena approaching. He knew there would be no time to eat safely. Several hyena charged in with confidence, and Blackthorn was forced to yield.

"Do you fear the very land we walk upon as well?" He rejoined Kreun where he cowered, and gave the pool one more glance before setting off into the brush. They padded off together, one of them still whimpering.

Neither noticed the female hyena lurking after them.

***

Twilight.

The ground was still warm from the sun even in the descending darkness. The buzz from insects was a perpetual din, over which a freckled night jar called.

Cwow-wow Cwow-wow!

WHOOO-OOP!

Blackthorn was on his paws on the instant of the sounding call. His eyes pierced the dark, but he knew his vision was inferior to that of his enemies in the night.

"Kreun, awaken." He called in a warbling alarm bark. In the distance he could see movement, a flash of fur.

A giggle was uttered behind him, and he whirled about, recognizing Kreun in the gloom.

"Stand with me, as we may have a fight." The hyena shuffled next to him but held low to the ground, his head nearly resting on the grass.

"Bring your pestilential hides this way, and I will grant you a wound in return." He paced one way, then turned and paced back before the nearly prone body of Kreun.

"Coward." A voice whooped in the grasses. From that gelatinous curtain of dark emerged the forbidding presence of the alpha female. Her small slightly pointed ears were cocked forward, listening intently. Her tail was straight in the air, as though she needed an exclamation point. Her black mane was erect and her mouth was closed. All suggesting she was about to attack.

"Your clan will be in need of a new alpha." Blackthorn seethed, his voice redolent of a concrete slab dragged down a gravel road. "When I have opened your belly to the night."

"You stay away." She hissed at the hyena, seeming to ignore the wolf entirely. Another hyena female joined her, and they walked shoulder to shoulder, closer and closer. They glared at Kreun as he whined on the ground.

"I will not suffer you another moment." Blackthorn lashed out, prompting the alpha to withdraw. The other female drifted to the side, moving closer to him. She lunged toward Kreun to make a downward bite on his vulnerable neck.

Blackthorn charged back, snapping his jaws before her snout, and she dodged with a cackle.

"Black wolf yield."

Blackthorn sensed the alpha approaching him from behind. He whirled about, clamped his teeth on her ear, and ripped it free.

Her electric cry shattered the night, blood cascading down

the side of her head. She shrank back into the dark, and the rest of the clan withdrew several body lengths.

The wolf spit out the ear on the ground, slavering.

"There is no sleep, for rage is my respite. Anger, my beating heart." Crimson bubbled between his bared fangs as he gasped. Rich scents of fear and hate flooded the clearing, and the clan issued a steady lowing call. Each uttered a mooing hum, overlapping and penetrating. The grass and surrounding thornbrush resounded with the sinister drone.

Blackthorn did not make another sound, awaiting the attack to come. Minutes dragged on, and he remained alert, claws locked into the soil, malevolence boiling off his hide in waves. The clan could scent this as sharply as they could smell carrion, and the lowing call continued.

The standoff seemed to persist for hours. As the sonorous chant began to tail off from one individual, another carried the call, to one side, then the other, rustling behind them.

The alpha female, now with only one ear and a bloody scalp, emerged from the dim periphery of the clearing. A chuckle creaked from her lips, and she withdrew.

One by one, the hyena drifted off and the calls diminished, melting into the sounds of night.

Katydids resumed their chattering call, joined by the twittering nightjars.

Blackthorn remained standing long after the clan left, glaring at nothing, everything, resolute against the void.

Five

Yellow and brown chevron stripes covered the snake that lay coiled in the short grass. The stout body was wound in a circle, the triangular head resting atop. Basking in the sun was its habit in the wet season, always ready to move if need be, though it could rest for hours on end without the slightest motion.

The puff adder was dull in color, preparing to shed its skin soon. Blending in with the soil, it drew little attention from the hyena that moved toward it.

The wolf was chasing Kreun, close behind. He had been attempting to placate him all morning after a restless night. The hyena was distracted, not looking in the snake's direction. The puff adder missed nothing, its sharp eyesight alerting it to the danger. The head pulled back from the rest of the body, the neck curved in a question mark as it prepared to unleash the fastest strike of any viper alive.

The hyena yelped as Blackthorn nipped his shoulder, and he stopped his lope, bearing fangs of his own.

"Look before you, Kreun." Blackthorn indicated the venomous snake that lay nearby, at the ready.

The adder gave an aggravated *puff* towards the predators, but did not move.

"Your fear will be your end, *domkop*." Blackthorn ruff-barked.

The adder kept its head chambered and ready, poised until the wolf and the hyena backed off, then padded away in another direction. Resting again on its thick body, the snake continued to wait for the next victim to cross its path.

"Regardless of your worries, you must not abandon caution."

Kreun seemed to agree, and settled down.

"What has made you so skittish? Was that your clan?"

His mouth agape, he only uttered a moaning wheeze.

"She has banished you, has she not?" He stated this as a question, but as he read his companion's face, he knew it was true. "When a male is expelled, they are never to return." He shook his head. "Why chance this territory, then? Were you hoping for a way to rejoin them?"

"She angers. I run." Kreun became agitated again, stalking around the wolf in circles.

"We should be away, then." Blackthorn pushed against his body to reassure him, and to edge him further from the puff adder. "There is no reason to provoke an angry mob."

He glanced about at the savanna before him. Waterlogged ground was covered by dense greenery, thick grass interspersed with acacia and clumps of feverberry. A rivulet wound through the grassland, fed by the rains of the wet season, shaded by a dense stand of wild date palms. The leaves rustled in the wind above where a brown snake eagle rode the air currents, its keen eyesight searching for prey below.

Hok-hok-hok-hok!

Kreun glanced up at the eagle, its wings wide with white feathers edging its dark body.

"Our search must continue for hunting grounds of our own."

Six

Dim light, the dank odor of a subterranean earthen den. Even in the darkness he could sense small bodies writhing about. Slight forms with short tails, black and white fur, with ears too large for the diminutive heads, and pug mouths set in a permanent frown. The painted wolf pups had only just begun to open their eyes, though there was nothing to see in the den. They jostled one another against their mother's body, their muted whine quieted as each found a teat and began to feed in contentment.

The larger form had fur of black, white, and gold, reclined on her side. Her belly was engorged with milk. Her golden eyes met Blackthorn's.

"Do not disappoint me."

Hind legs kicked out against stalks of nile grass as Blackthorn jerked awake, sleep abruptly left behind. The smell of damp earth was still in his nostrils, but now replaced by the rich scent of flowers and rain. Compulsively, he sniffed around where he had slept, looking for the wolf prints that he knew would not be there.

The canopy of a giraffe thorn acacia hung over him, heavy with leaves. Drops of water pattered down from thorned branches above. Before dawn the sky seemed ashen, not yet suggesting a reluctant sunrise.

On the open bushveld before him, he could make out the busily moving form of a honey badger. The muscular body trundled through the grass, walking with a busy industrial pace. It stopped with a sniff. Abruptly, it dove into the wet soil, and a torrent of earth flew behind him. Claws attacked the ground as though a personal offense had been given, within seconds creating a deep hole. The small head stabbed into the yawning opening and a sharp squeal was heard. The honey badger lifted the field mouse from the hole, and holding down the small body with a muddy forepaw, he wrenched it in half, swallowing each half practically whole.

Blackthorn noticed Kreun watching him expectantly.

"So the hunt begins." The wolf was on his paws as the honey badger continued its machine like walk away across the veld. "It has been days since we found a substantial herd."

Kreun ran a pink tongue over his lips.

"We must stay ahead of it." He scratched his ear with a hind leg.

"A... *head.*" Kreun rasped. He looked about, more fidgety than usual.

"We must always move more swiftly than what chases us."

"*Chase...*" The hyena tucked his hindquarters down, instinctively protecting his vulnerable parts, casting glances over his shoulder.

"No, my friend." Blackthorn padded closer and brushed alongside the hyena's body. "I did not mean a physical threat." He resisted the urge to lap Kreun's muzzle - he had never seen hyenas do that to reassure each other. "Your kind... how do you..." Blackthorn stared at the ground and sighed.

Kreun dipped his head, red eyes wide with anticipation.

"When I run, Death is alongside me." His deep, graveled voice was hollow and far away. "It watches over me, ever waiting. Even as a pup, I sensed its shadow. Stalked the land for many seasons beyond counting, and there was Death, with me on every hunt." His brow furrowed. "And so I must move faster. Ever faster."

Kreun giggled faintly.

"As it has taken those who ran alongside me."

Kreun padded away, his hindquarters still held close to the ground. He spun about and ran back to Blackthorn, nudging him.

"Shall we chance a hunt today, Kreun?" He gave a thin smile, tips of white appearing as his lips parted. "Death must not be kept waiting."

***

The orange of the sunrise was searing through the horizon, and what seemed a bushfire would take to the sky. The leaning, bent bodies of giraffe thorn acacia were joined by the angled necks of giraffe, resembling trees until they moved to browse off the high leaves.

Kuck-coor-kuk Kuck coor-kuk purred a cape turtle dove. The katydids had silenced their interminable sawing as the night faded. As the moisture left the air, insects took flight, from grasshoppers that attacked the greenery to mosquitoes pursuing the necessary blood meal. One such mosquito was seized in midair by a blue emperor dragonfly, its brilliant green and blue armor glistening in the sunlight. It alighted on a stalk of nile grass, now in flower.

The wolf and the hyena crossed the veld at a steady pace in search for prey.

Blackthorn ran in a circle around the hyena, light on his paws, emitting a high pitched twitter like a bird. He brushed his body alongside Kreun, excited for the hunt.

The hyena only stared at him, a confused look upon his face.

Blackthorn stopped and shook his head. "Old habit, my friend." He calmed, and walked off, followed closely by the hulking form of the hyena.

"My *Volk*." He paused to smile for a moment at the word. "My kind would begin our hunts in such a fashion. Shortly after waking, each member of the pack would run about, and prod one another, barking in joy for the coming kill." A grin crossed his face for a moment. "Exultation for the hunt, and for the Pack."

Kreun stared at him, not seeming to understand.

"Did your clan have any such ritual?" Blackthorn sniffed him. "Hunting together?"

"*Alone*." He loped away, continuing the search, leaving the wolf behind.

Blackthorn snuffed at his departing hindquarters.

***

Hours had passed, and the sun was burning down with midday intensity. Nothing had crossed their path other than a single oribi which shot away from them before they could approach.

The ground was dry here, a higher elevation that would become desiccated in the winter. Little scent reached them as the breeze tousled their fur. Downwind, figures moved on the shimmering horizon.

"Eland... *sien jy?*"

Kreun did not seem to react. His mouth hung open as he panted lightly. They shared a glance and loped toward the eland.

They walked in a column, two dozen mixed male and female adults with several juveniles in tow. The adults loomed over the wolf and hyena, standing two meters at the shoulder, their bluish-grey sides resembling battleships cruising a grass sea. The nomadic herd wandered in and out of Namibia and Botswana at this border, crossing hundreds of kilometers as they followed the rains. Some of the adults had joined temporarily, seeking the protection of the larger herd with young calves, but they would flit in and out of one herd or another, always welcome and always on the move.

"Even the youngest would be difficult to tackle." Blackthorn took a step back as the column approached. "Unless you have a cunning plan in that strange head of yours."

Kreun took a bounding stroll closer. The dominant male eland broke away from the herd, leaping toward the hyena with shocking speed. He lowered his heavy head, dewlap nearly scraping the ground, straight spiraled horns leveled at the hyena.

Kreun bolted as the eland drew close, just avoiding being harpooned. He sprinted back to Blackthorn's side with all speed, and they retreated into the brush as the eland returned to formation and the convoy continued its grazing journey.

"Perhaps we should move our hunt south." Blackthorn closed his eyes to the burning globe above. He could see the blood through his eyelids as a steady red glow.

Kreun ran off with urgency, a wheeze punctuating the quiet.

"What do you smell?" Blackthorn was by his side as they

ran, their enduring lope covering kilometers with ease. Before long, Blackthorn could scent it as well.

"Wildebeest have been this way." The dark wolf broke his stride, and threaded through the grass tussocks. A dung midden caught his attention, fragrant and covered with flies. The flies scattered, revealing a fibrous mass that pulsated with life. Dung beetles worked within the droppings, cutting large balls from the pile, and rolling them away.

Kreun trotted up and sniffed the midden before taking a large bite.

"Are you mad?" Blackthorn wrinkled his snout. "Can you really eat that and not die?"

Kreun did not groan with pleasure as he did with meat, but managed to swallow his mouthful.

"Any method to beat the famine." He shook his head in wonder. "If you would prefer the source, however, we may not have far to go." The hoofprints were fresh in the ground.

***

The land was beginning to dry. Showers still crossed the savanna, but were becoming more sparse. Streams fed into a large pool, around which various antelope had gathered. Grey waterbuck milled by the water's edge, dipping their heads to pull mouthfuls of grass. Kudu strolled past to drink from the pool, spiraled horns of the males over a meter in length. Before reaching the water, two of the larger males bumped against each other, facing off. Horns were pointed, and with a clacking they locked, and one male pushed down against the other. The smaller combatant immediately withdrew, and with a last horn knock extricated himself from the dominant. Social roles thus set in place, the kudu continued to the pool to drink.

Oxpeckers patrolled the backs of the giant antelope, unconcerned about these displays. They sifted through the fur of the kudu, devouring ticks and other parasites. One bird found an engorged tick and gobbled this down, relishing the burst of blood as it crushed the tick body. With a flutter of its wings, the oxpecker hopped to the crown of the kudu's head and scraped its beak back and forth across a horn until it was clean.

Further from the water, steenbok grazed in a relaxed manner. Baboons harvested grass and flower, eating as they walked in a winding line headed and tailed by large males. All the herbivores present were at ease, with an army of lookouts ready to sound the alarm should predators approach.

In the grass fields beyond, however, wildebeest were on edge. Two males confronted each other with loud snorts. Each stood erect, showing off their full height and strength. One attempted to turn away, but the other angled his horns toward his rival, and rubbed his face against the other's rump. He gave an agitated nod, provoking a fight.

They faced one another head-on, tails swishing. They pressed horns together, the central bossing upon their skulls meeting with a thud. One twisted his horns and rammed hard, prompting the other to disengage. They resumed grazing, though under constant threat of a challenge. Through these skirmishes the dominant males would establish their sway over their lesser kind. Females watched at a distance, with anticipation.

"The rut has begun." Blackthorn observed. "The rains must be ending soon." He looked to the sky for a moment. "Those *okes* will be busy indeed. Too busy to see us approach, *verstaan jy?*"

Kreun seemed to understand, and flashed his teeth. The two made a large circle around the pool toward the more distant grass field where the wildebeest had established their territory. The air was alive with biting black flies in the sun. Shade areas were attacked by annoying clegs flies, all drawn by the feeding antelope.

"*Hunt.*" Kreun released this as a light groan, and took a step toward the herd.

"We wait." Blackthorn blocked his path.

The hyena blinked, his face blank with confusion.

Blackthorn lowered his head to the ground and sniffed. The two weaved between grass tussocks and found the source of the scent.

A lion print was pressed into the sand.

"Less than a day." He looked about. "No more than two."

Kreun nodded. They retired to the edge of a stand of mopane wood to survey the activity of the rut, ever watchful for the swish of lion tail.

Seven

id morning, the wildebeest herd loitered about the pool, fed by a stream now reduced to a trickle. The grouping consisted of adult cows, their calves, and a few yearlings. Two bulls loitered more distantly, their rivalry in the rut continued.

Near the grassy edge, there was a splash as a small form rolled in the black water. The slender head of a clawless otter poked above the surface. It looked about for danger, and seeing none, submerged itself again. A moment later, it crawled laboriously out of the water onto the mud bank. At first, it appeared to have been injured, but once on land it began to move off with a jaunting lope. One of its arms cradled a catfish like a rugby ball, a prize that weighed as much as the fisher who caught it.

"No disturbance in the night, it would seem." Blackthorn surveyed the herd from the periphery of the stand of miombo trees. "Lion visitors here may have been itinerate."

Kreun's head wavered, nostrils flaring. He crouched below the level of the grass and headed toward the pool.

Blackthorn remained back to watch his approach. As before, the hyena crept closer to the herd, shrinking almost from sight with a display suggesting utter passivity. Head down, tail tucked between his legs, forelegs bent that concealed the strength of his forequarters. The cows tensed slightly with his approach, grunting their ongoing conversation of *gnu... gnu... gnu...*

This time Kreun went up to the pool itself. He squatted, peering into the water. After several minutes, he dropped his head into the cool liquid with a splash. He rooted underwater for several seconds, pulling up a struggling fish.

"Your kind must never hunger, Kreun." He shook his head. "I, on the other hand, await a real hunt."

The wildebeest around the hyena relaxed once they saw him feed. They resumed grazing, heads down in the grass, seeming to disregard him.

Kreun crept away from the pool, leaving behind the half-eaten fish. He skulked toward one of the yearlings where it ripped away a mouthful of tender grass. The lack of alarm snorts from the adults had set it at ease. All the while, the hyena closed the distance.

Blackthorn broke cover and was sprinting toward Kreun before the hyena was upon his prey. They arrived together and as the wolf released his high pitched twitter, the yearling panicked, bolting away from the protection of the herd.

The hunters waited to close in after they left the herd behind. Blackthorn bit the flank, braking the powerful young wildebeest. For a moment it struggled on, its haunch wide open with a flap of hide and red flesh laid bare. Kreun bit the other side, and the yearling was brought to a dead stop before being pulled to the ground.

The dark wolf released his prey, and looked up to see a pair of yellow eyes locked onto his.

Blackthorn's heart froze. The lion was lying on the grass,

forepaws before him, but was no longer resting. His head was up, tawny face with great muzzle set in stern concentration. Black lips were parted, and opened to reveal long conical teeth.

"*Evade!*" Blackthorn gave his ruff-bark and shot away from the wildebeest, with Kreun close behind. Left in their wake was the flailing yearling, injured from the hunt.

He could hear the muffled footfalls of the lion, and glanced back. Its blond mane flowed as the lion sprinted, his powerful shoulders writhing with muscle. His eyes wavered, drifting from the wolf to the wildebeest, and he pounced on the young antelope. The yearling weighed nearly as much as the lion, but crumpled under the attack as though made of straw. Hooves flailed in the air as the heavy jaws clamped on the throat, holding tightly as the calf struggled.

Kreun cackled to himself, slowing to turn towards the lion.

Continuing to kick, the young wildebeest's body contorted, pulling its head away from the lion's jaws. The paws held their prey fast, and the lion adjusted its hold, clamping down again on the neck. The kicks and spasms gradually grew weaker.

His baleful yellow eyes did not leave Blackthorn.

"We must leave." The dark wolf panted.

Kreun giggled, taking a step toward the giant male. His notched ear flopped on his head.

"Are you *bosbefok*? He will leave you bloody when he is done."

The lion released the wildebeest, now dead with a froth of pink around its mouth. He strode forward past the body, back straight, tail curved up and forward, mane cascading over his upper back. He laid down, one of his lionesses strolling closer. Staring at the wolf and hyena, he did not close his eyes, remaining vigilant.

"Eat?"

"No." Blackthorn looked from the dead wildebeest to the reclining lion. "I venture they have eaten their fill recently, so there is no hunger in the pride. Should the lion have a chance to kill, the lion will take it." He nudged Kreun. "There will be no safety here."

Kreun took a few steps toward the kill anyway, his giggle taunting the large male.

The male lion launched onto his paws again, and released a roar.

"Do not doubt me." The lion spoke in a resonant growl. Two more lionesses appeared by his side. "Your blood will feed the grasses should you call this place home."

The wolf panted heavily, taking cautious steps back. His nostrils flared, and he glanced about him to see if another lion was stalking their flank. He had seen such a trap before, but sensed no other presence.

"*Gevaar* calls." The lion released a guttural roar, and the veld was silenced, bird and wildebeest alike. "And should you answer my call, *Gevaar* will have your throat."

Blackthorn grunted to his companion, and shrank back into the high grasses.

The hyena backed down, and joined the wolf as they fled the plain. Weaving through thornbush and savanna dotted with acacia trees, they placed kilometers between themselves and the lions they left behind.

"Perhaps to the west. There is always another hunting ground." He grunted to himself. "Strange, that."

Kreun whimpered, a sound Blackthorn had come to know as a question.

"That lion is one of the least aggressive I have encountered.

He issued a warning, and allowed us to leave." He panted.
"Your kind is not loved by lions, but for the wolf..."

Kreun whimpered again.

"They kill us on sight."

Eight

They moved swiftly, their pace steady and tireless. Stopping only to rest in the high heat of noon, they left the lion pride behind after three days of travel.

Blackthorn surveyed the ground before him, his black muzzle close to the dirt.

Kreun took a small mouthful of grass. His belly grumbled with hunger.

"The land is changing." He looked to the horizon. "The grazing has been heavy here, but I doubt by wildebeest." Padding over to a dung heap, he took a sniff. "Cattle."

The hyena took a sniff and snorted, backing away.

"Have you encountered them before?"

The hyena grunted, an answer in the negative.

"As my life has led me south, these cattle have become more widespread." He laid down to rest in the sun. "They clip the grass short, and mill about with none of the haste of antelope." He folded one forepaw over the other as Kreun joined him on the ground. "As they roam, the antelope disappear."

"*Kill beest?*" Kreun gave a halting giggle of anxiety.

"The wildebeest? No, Kreun." A subtle growl entered his voice. "It is not the cattle that destroys the animals of the wild."

***

Grey fur, invisible in shadow, crouched beneath the sickle bush. The cape ground squirrel was still as a stone, not budging even as the probing muzzle of the hyena drew near. Air was drawn deeply into its black snout, then rushed out, scattering dust in the squirrel's face. Another deep inhale. Silence, with no movement.

The muzzle turned slightly, now pointed directly at the small animal.

It bolted, fleeing the base of the sickle bush. For a second, it spotted escape beneath a tangle of sweet thorn acacia brush, before a paw slammed down on its back. The impact killed the squirrel instantly.

Blackthorn took the lower half of the squirrel in his jaw. Kreun clamped down on the other half, their noses touching.

What a strange season this has been.

Each ripped their half away. This small meal hardly sated the hunger of either predator, and their search continued.

Covering dozens of kilometers per day, the land transitioned from sand to loamy soil. The trees became more sparse, the ground more dry. The more palatable grasses were reduced to dried knots on the ground, and all that remained were stands of turpentine grass. The lush green was enticing, but the astringent flavor caused the cattle to turn up their noses. Ambling across the rolling plain, the bulls and cows mooed, ignoring the wild foliage. Two men walked beside them, dressed in tattered clothing. Each held a stick, and tapped lightly on the backs of the cattle if they strayed from a desired path. Their bare feet were heavily calloused from years of herding work and walking, thick as shoe soles.

One of them began to speak loudly, agitated, pointing toward the hyena and wild dog. They sprinted to the bulls at the head of the column, and waved them back. The sticks waved about with a whistle through the air, and on the bodies of the cows, *whap whap whap*. They bunched up together, the humans watching the nearby predators closely.

"*Kill them?*"

"The savor of the meat would never reach your tongue. Those sticks bring death with a *klap* of thunder." Blackthorn eyed the tools the men carried. He could not discern if they were indeed the fearsome weapons he had seen before, but was reluctant to test them.

***

The stomachs of both carnivores throbbed with gnawing spasms. They were again on their paws, sniffing for signs of prey, and found only the sledgehammer hoofprints of the cattle.

Wandering to the west, the ground became more sparsely vegetated, whatever grass present close cropped and of minimal nutrition. Gently rolling hills leveled out far from the river that flowed through the Caprivi region of Namibia. The wolf's snout hovered over the ground, seeking traces of the wild. With each step, scent glands on his paws marked the ground, leaving the rich musk of wolf behind him.

Kreun crept closer and nosed the wolf tracks. He whined softly.

"I seek my kind." Blackthorn saw the anxiety in his eyes. "As I must." He brushed alongside the brawn hyena, and he sensed reassurance. "You need not fear—I may never find another wolf, my *vriend*."

Kreun dipped his head again toward the dark wolf. "*Friend.*" He rasped.

"I am afflicted by that most insidious of parasites."

The hyena furrowed his brow, and sniffed Blackthorn again.

"Hope." He bared his teeth, the way wolves have of laughing. "Hope is forever pulling one apart, while holding one together." He reared onto his hind legs to box the hyena, batting lightly with forepaws.

Kreun recoiled for a moment. His face, initially drawn in distress, softened. He straightened his form as the wolf was back on all four paws. His heavy jaws parted and gripped the fur behind Blackthorn's neck high on his shoulders. Before the wolf knew it, he was pulled onto his side, legs kicking in the air.

He struggled as Kreun dragged him for a meter before the dark wolf freed himself and was on his paws again. He looked up to see Kreun with his head angled back, mouth hanging too wide to be anything but a laugh.

"Strong *bliksem*, you are." He shook the dust from his coat. "Too strong by half." He bumped into him as he ran past, and Kreun was fast behind him. He clicked his jaws on the wolf's flank, and found the wolf whirled around him and snapping at his tail. This play slowed as the hunger returned, and each predator found themselves surveying the horizon for prey.

"Have you noticed the biting flies?"

Kreun angled his head over to his companion, mouth hanging open, small ears perked.

"They do not seem to plague us here." He shook his body briskly, showering his companion with dirt.

The hyena uttered a slight groan, seeming to agree.

"I was born to a pack in the north, in a great wild area that was alive with antelope. All kinds, there seemed no limit to them. With this bounty, however, came hordes of biting flies. They were everywhere, and no escape." He closed his eyes to the sun above. "As my journeys have taken me south, I find those flies to be rarely encountered." He opened them to the empty veld. "And with them went the antelope." As thought upon it, more than one winter had passed since he had the painful experience of a bite from a tsetse fly.

In the distance, cresting a hill was another group of cattle, accompanied by men with sticks.

"Perhaps that is why these cattle are so common here."

The men carried the sticks aloft, on occasion bringing them down upon the bulls with faint slapping sounds. Their mouths were moving, their indistinct jabber meaningless to the wolf.

"I once wished death upon those flies." He nodded to Kreun, also eyeing the distant herd. "I now wonder if one should wish for their return."

The wind rattled the branches in the trees above. A dried leaf drifted to the ground beside them.

"One plague has left us." Blackthorn eyed the men. "Replaced by another."

Kreun sniffed the air, his snout wrinkled.

"Despite the danger, we must see. These humans are everywhere. Little else is left for us."

They padded off toward the line of cattle, and a stand of mopane wood between them.

***

Soft calls of *moo - moo* were given by the cattle as they ambled across the rolling grasses. Two herders were with them, sticks in hand. Horns jutted from broad heads straight out before curving upwards. Ears flicked away annoying insects as they walked. None of them looked about for enemies, docile and ignorant.

Blackthorn laughed to himself, a guttural cough.

Kreun looked at him warily, unaccustomed to a wild dog laugh.

"Musing to myself whether these things *pronk*." He imagined these hefty bovines leaping gracefully into the air and snickered. "Those things do not move much." He indicated the two men with his snout. "Nor do they need to."

The column of bulls were led over the hill, the animals wandering about. Trudging across ground dry as chalk, they threaded through deciduous trees with yellowed leaves. Crossing a dirt road, the hooves stomped through twin worn ruts that faded into the distance. A sign next to the road stood on twin steel posts. Upon the sign was a drawing of an antelope under a tree, the paint faded. "CONSERVANCY" was inscribed on it, marking the wild area where the men led their cattle to graze.

"They cannot pay attention to all of them." Blackthorn peered at the column as it wound through the sparse trees. "The cover is scant, but we may yet take a straggler."

"*Strag?*" Kreun's tongue lolled out in the heat.

"Follow me closely." They padded out of the brush, giving the men a wide berth. Their bodies were low, and they kept to thicker portions of the scrub. Blackthorn's ears were folded back, head held low as he moved toward the furthest extent of the cattle herd. He led the hyena into the brush around a yellow hornbill as it browsed on an aloe plant. The two were silent in their approach.

"There. That is where our hunt begins." Blackthorn indicated a smaller bull, its horns less impressive than others in the herd, bringing up the rear. "We run straight at it, and when it runs, we take it down."

Kreun giggled nervously, but quietly.

"*Now.*" Blackthorn twittered to Kreun, his birdlike chirping pealing through the bushveld. His body sleek, loping, each claw dug into ground, propelling him forward faster than the acceleration of any car. The hyena was close behind, and the bull noticed them immediately.

The bull let go of the grass in his mouth and mooed loudly. He turned, took a few steps, and then turned back. Staring at the predators, he moaned.

"What is he doing?" Blackthorn asked, knowing there would be no answer.

The bull continued to stare, and snorted.

"*Run, you domkop!*" Blackthorn charged closer, body tensed for an attack by those horns.

None came, and the bull continued to moo.

Blackthorn circled the bull, unsure of what to do next. Wolves generally chase their prey down over long distances, pulling them down at high speed. He was not used to prey standing still.

Kreun did not brood over this unusual problem. He shirked around the bull, drifting out of its sightline. With a subtle grunt, he darted between the tall hind legs and with iron jaws ripped away the bull's testicles.

The large bull shuddered, and moaned its pain. It began to trot away from the attack, but was too late. Kreun took hold of the soft belly and pulled away. The entrails fell from underneath the bull like rain, and the large animal keeled over and fell onto his side.

Blackthorn gasped for a moment, wondering why the bull went down without a fight, but did not wonder for long. He dove into the belly and ripped free the liver, and kept digging with his razor teeth deeper in the pelvis, muscle and organ vanishing down a bottomless throat. Despite the hearty meal, he paused, suddenly feeling a subtle electric twinge down his spine.

He pulled his blood soaked head free.

The men were running straight at them.

Blackthorn growled deeply, and Kreun withdrew his head from the bull's chest cavity. His entire body was slicked with blood, unrecognizable as a hyena.

The men waved sticks over their heads as they shouted. Their clothing was torn, feet clad in plastic sandals.

"Run, Kreun." He bolted, fleeing toward the mopane wood. He turned to see the gore-coated hyena close behind, appearing as though the internal organs of the bull had fled their body.

The air split with a deafening *crack*. A wasp buzzed past his ear. Another.

"*Faster, Kreun!*" Blackthorn ran flat out, every muscle straining for the tangled wood ahead. Another bold *clap* split the air.

The hyena yelped, but did not slow his pace. The blasts from the rifle no longer echoed, but Blackthorn did not stop running. A tree flashed past them. Another and another. Soon they were lost in the gnarled trunks of acacia and mopane, and the hunters slowed. The blood had dried on their fur, now matted in a tangle.

Kreun was limping. He favored one of his hind legs. Black-thorn licked the blood and matter from the hyena's wounded leg, and soon found a furrow dug into the fur.

"*Bug.*"

"That was no wasp, my friend." The wound was deep, and bled steadily. "That was the weapon of the human. And we are fortunate to be alive."

Kreun attempted to bear weight with the leg, but quickly slumped onto his rear and rolled. His wounded leg splayed into the air, and the interior part of his leg had a corresponding hole.

"Across the veld, beyond the reach of any being, and still they pierced your leg." Blackthorn's graveled voice was nearly inaudible. "Never again will I go near the animals that humans keep." He sounded far away. "Never again."

Kreun whined as he rested his throbbing leg.

"Ever more land that is beyond our reach." He growled. "They take what they do not need." Blackthorn laid down, his head resting on his forepaws. Resting, but not relaxed, his ears swiveled about listening for the approach of human feet.

Nine

Morning came with an abrupt squawk, and Kreun lurched to his feet as a beetle cut into his skin. A cloud of flies took flight from him, fur still matted with a layer of gore.

Blackthorn padded over to the hyena, who promptly collapsed back to the ground, rolling onto his uninjured side. Though it was difficult to tell for certain, the wound did not appear to be bleeding.

"Can you hunt, my friend?"

Kreun's eyes were wide and pleading, poking out from the clotted blood that still covered his face. He whined softly, punctuated with chuckles. He shook his head, spraying bits of matter about him, his notched ear flopping uselessly. He struggled to put weight on the leg with the gunshot wound, winced, and eased back onto his side.

"Right." He reassured the hyena with a close brush, and padded off into the bushveld.

***

His gait bounced, moving swiftly with an easy lope. The thornbrush thicket opened into nile grasses, with no antelope in view. The scent of cattle was everywhere, with occasional piles of manure writhing with dung beetles. One kilometer after the next unfolded before him, with little in sight. He moved in a large circle across the veld, and spotted some activity as he was returning to where the hyena rested.

A white backed vulture cruised in for a landing, brown and off-white wings scooping out as it alighted on grey feet sporting black talons. It stepped gingerly toward a grey mountain that rose three meters in the air, now covered with a dozen other vultures. The only sign that it was an elephant were four voluminous cylinder legs jutting from the base. The head of the elephant was gone, and the hole where the saw had removed the trophy was occupied by the probing heads of vultures.

Marabou storks milled close to the carcass, each standing stiffly on long legs stained white by their droppings. Wide black wings were closed, with a pendulous throat pouch hanging low. Naked red heads terminated with elongated sharp bills. The storks widened tears in the elephant's skin and stabbed deep to rip away flesh.

In the abdominal area a cavity had been rent open, and a clan of spotted hyenas took turns at the feast. None of the scavengers took notice of the wolf, and stayed focused. Blackthorn could see any attempt to salvage here would be a painful one, every bird and beast armed with sharp teeth or bills to ensure they could compete with his kind. The search continued.

***

The crested francolin stood still, its brown plumage with subtle

59

white stripes allowing it to melt into the dried grasses. When the wolf passed, it resumed browsing for seeds, though with caution in case the hunter returned.

Blackthorn had ventured in the edge of this wild place, but found no herds. A distant gunshot echoed across the veld.

Perhaps the herds scattered for that reason. He mused to himself, pausing to scratch behind his ear. *Or they retreated further into the wild.*

There was a high dirge produced by crickets in the grass, and no other sounds reaching his sensitive ears.

They encroach. The wild retreats.

Remote metallic sounds, an engine far away. A martial eagle soared high overhead.

Will there always be a sanctuary? Or will this, too, fall?

Only the whispers in the grass spoke to him.

* * *

The sun sank in the sky, nearly obscured by the flat arbor of a giraffe thorn acacia. A drying stream trickled down a hill into a shallow pool, thickening into mud as the season grew steadily drier.

A baboon spider crept across the higher dry ground of the hill, its mottled tan and brown coloration blending seamlessly with the sand and grass. Leaving its silk-lined burrow for the evening to hunt for insect or invertebrate prey, it moved swiftly down the hill toward a knot of nile grass to prowl. Eight black eyes peered down over the stream and pool. Hairs covering its robust legs sensed any nearby movement in air currents suggesting the approach of a predator. They failed to sense, however, a motionless killer waiting in ambush.

A cavernous mouth snapped open and a flat pink tongue splayed out to strike the baboon spider with a smack. The sticky surface held on, and the heavy spider was yanked as easily as a mosquito into the yawning maw of a giant African bullfrog. Crushed by powerful oral muscles, the spider was turned to paste.

The bullfrog was grey on olive green skin, still moist and glistening in the sunset. He hopped his way with confidence down toward the pool where he surveyed a small patch of water boiling with his tadpoles. Hundreds of dark blobs with tails wriggled against one another, seeming anxious in their cramped home. Digging with clawed forefeet and powerful hind feet, the bullfrog hollowed out a trench from the tadpole sanctuary to the nearby larger pool, freeing them to occupy a larger space. There was little for them to fear, as their parent had eaten everything in the pool.

Blackthorn padded past the bullfrog as it gave a deep groaning *woooop*. He paused to sniff, but quickly moved on as it seemed more trouble than it was worth.

Leaping into the pool, he splashed about until his black and gold coat was soaked. Another leap and his forepaws found a deeper hole and he was immersed. Pushing out onto the muddy edge of the pool, Blackthorn shook his body, ears slapping the sides of head until he was somewhat dry. He sighed, remembering the last time he played in a stream with a pack.

His pack. Slender bodies leaping about, crashing into water, onto each other. Whirling black and gold, flashes of teeth. The high twitter of wolves at play. For a moment he watched them, but this vision faded into wetlands empty save for him.

He moved on, loping through the bushveld, and uttered a dry cough.

At this, a head poked up from the grass, just a few meters from Blackthorn.

A male impala, his curved horns perched high on his narrow head, stared at the wolf. He stood frozen, his black marble eyes filled with hope that standing still would save him.

Blackthorn's ears folded back, his head down, powerful hind legs pushing off toward his quarry.

The impala bucked, and with a single *pronk* was swiftly away from him.

Blackthorn charged, his bounding strides quickly catching up to the antelope. Across uneven ground, the impala pounded with hooves through grass toward thorn thickets.

The wolf shot across that ground, carefully looking out for warthog holes or other obstacles. Claws upon rocks, he powered through thorned branches that snapped and were left spinning in the air as he whistled past.

Grunting and snorting from the impala before him.

Rustling and breathing behind him.

Blackthorn slowed, and turned about, sensing the presence of another. His dark eyes studied the veld, and saw no swish of lion tail, no spotted hide of cheetah or leopard.

The brown mane of a hyena vanished behind thick brush.

"I will not hunt on your behalf, *vuil bliksem*." He uttered this, and broke off the hunt. The impala's slender body bucked into the air once more and disappeared into the fading light. The dark wolf snuffed his disappointment toward his escaped prey.

Blackthorn trotted the long way back to where he left Kreun. Looking behind him from time to time, he did not see anyone trailing him. Nonetheless, he sensed someone following. An errant twig snap, an unexplained rustling of foliage. Blackthorn spun about to find no one. It was after nightfall when he returned to his injured pack-mate.

The hyena regarded him with a petulant whine, and sniffed for meat.

"I have not provided for you. Not this time." He lay next to Kreun. "We have once again drifted into the land of a hyena clan."

Kreun sighed.

"Whether we have encountered them before, I know not." He closed his eyes, his dish-like ears still listening, straining to hear over the rising noise of nightjars and crickets.

Ten

They did not awaken until well into the morning. Kreun sat up, licking the flies from his bullet wound.

Blackthorn roused, his exhaustion pushing him back to the dirt. He looked about to see the sun well above the treetops, a martial eagle gliding on the wind. A cape turtle dove perched in a nearby feverberry tree. *Kuk-coor-kuk. Kuk-coor-kuk.*

Further from where they slept, chalk white dung middens sat amid the grasses.

"That leaves little doubt." Blackthorn was on his paws, his fatigue forgotten. He grunted his disgust. "I knew a hyena was tailing me. Sadly, he was more skilled at remaining concealed than I was at eluding him." He shook bits of grass from his coat. "On your feet, Kreun."

The hyena seemed to nod, and stood uneasily on his wounded leg. Tottering for a moment, he moved forward with an awkward hop favoring his good leg.

The hunters moved further south.

***

Blackthorn's pace was slow, a gradual lope, stopping to wait for Kreun to hobble next to him. One hind leg was held off the ground. His head was bowed, face locked in a macabre grimace.

"There must be prey." The dark wolf's head shook. "Before we reach the end of the earth."

"*They follow.*" The hyena choked on his words.

"Are you certain?" Blackthorn looked about, reared on hind legs for a moment with a half turn and he was down again on all four paws.

"*Follow.*"

"Then any hunt we chance upon will be taken."

"*Taken.*"

"Following us. If they were after our hunt, they should have given up by now." He muttered, almost to himself. "This is your clan, is it not?"

Kreun chortled nervously.

"They are after you." Blackthorn growled. "*Vervloeks.*"

For hours they trundled into the bush, and Blackthorn turned over in his mind what to do. As they milled in the grass, a figure paced nearby. Over a meter and a half in height, the secretary bird stalked through the tussocks. It walked steadily, head darting forward with each footfall, until it spotted a field mouse. A clawed foot shot out and smashed the rodent, and the kill was hefted in the sharp beak.

The towering bird noticed the approaching hunters, and gave them an imperious glare. After pausing to swallow its catch whole, it took to labored flight, landing further away from danger.

"I have *you.*" Blackthorn pounced on a grass tussock, looked about, and spotted the scrub hare enshrouding itself in the taller blue grass. Another pounce, and he broke its back.

Kreun hobbled to his side to take a share of the meat.

Blackthorn looked up to see a hyena observing them from afar. "Digest that on the move, Kreun."

***

Dusk approached, and with it Blackthorn could sense the veld weighing upon him. The air felt close and heavy.

"Down."

Kreun did as he was ordered, crouching in the sweet thorn acacia brush. He glanced along the wolf's snout, and noticed the impala feeding on the grass.

"If I prevail in this hunt, the kill may provide us with some time to escape from that hyena clan." He peered down at Kreun. "I will take the far station – you start in."

Kreun stared at the wolf for a moment before he gave a slight grin.

"There is the hunter I need." Blackthorn crept off as the sun began to set behind the distant line of mopane trees. After several minutes, Kreun began to whimper. The hair of his mane was standing on end. Lunging forth, he limped toward the antelope.

The impala straightened, gave a harsh alarm bark sounding like a congested cough, and darted away. The lithe body arced gracefully through the air, only to find the dark wolf bounding from the thornbrush toward him. The impala panicked. It planted hooves, turning to *pronk* in the opposite direction, and Blackthorn gripped its flank. The powerful impala kicked, but was held fast.

The hyena limped to the side of the impala and took hold with his jaws. Each took a half and pulled. Kreun was unable to anchor himself to the ground. Blackthorn released his hold and took the impala by the throat and ripped it open. Vessels of the neck released arterial jets that quickly lost pressure, and the antelope sank to the ground, lifeless.

WHOOO-OOP!

Blackthorn turned and glared at Kreun, who looked at him sheepishly with downcast eyes.

"Why the bloody hell did you call out?" His dark eyes darted about, and soon picked out the loping body of another hyena. It paused to give its own call into the twilight. *Whooo-oop!*

"Your instincts have betrayed you." He crouched down, but knew he was already seen.

The hyena was soon joined by another, and both ambled past the offered impala kill. They glanced at the fallen antelope for a moment, and their gaze returned to the dark wolf and the cowering hyena.

"*Bliksem.*" His stomach gurgled. "Here it is, Kreun." Blackthorn faced the approaching clan. At first he could not see the others through the thick foliage, but could hear them drawing close. The tips of the blue grass stems wavered, pushed about by larger bodies below. They finally parted, and the alpha female emerged from the brush.

She wore a rictus of anger, her scalp raw and bloody where the ear had been torn.

"Stand fast with me." Blackthorn clawed the ground. "This will be a fight to the very last."

The lowing call erupted again from the blue grass, waving in the failing light. The malevolent dirge intensified, punctuated by a whoop from the hulking alpha female who stalked the dimly lit meadow.

Blackthorn suddenly gave a yelp, jumped in the air and turned around. His flank oozed red with a ring of teeth marks.

Kreun stood behind him, his injured leg planted solidly on the ground, blood dripping from his fangs. He gave a high giggle.

Blackthorn backed away from Kreun, his heart pounding. The mooing rose around him, the veld alive with hollow cackling from the hyena clan. He looked all around as the alpha closed the distance step by step.

She paused by the impala carcass, nostrils flaring at the rich scent of fresh blood. The dominant female gave a groan toward Kreun, who moaned with pleasure at her acceptance. Behind the two, over a dozen other hyenas loped toward the impala kill.

"*Meat.*" The alpha hissed.

Kreun chortled, his massive canines exposed.

"*Meat of wolf.*"

Blackthorn bolted from the clearing, leaving the impala behind. Hyena snapped at one side, the other, the air all around him filled with a floridly rank scent. His tail was nipped. Another set of teeth gashed his flank, and he slowed. Several hunters surrounded him, blocking his escape. Every direction he turned, he faced cackling hyenas. The vast savanna was gone, time collapsed, the entire world reduced to the gaping jaws that ringed the dark wolf.

He darted at first one hyena, then another, snapping his teeth and keeping each on the defensive. He reeled about as he snapped, driving back each individual before any could take hold of him.

Striking towards him was Kreun, full weight on his hind legs as he lunged.

Blackthorn rolled aside from the attack and plunged into one of the smaller male hyenas.

Bowled over into a ball of tawny gold fur with black spots, he giggled madly, tucking down his hindparts against the blow.

Free of the circle, Blackthorn bounded away, every claw stabbed into ground, every muscle straining for salvation. The ache set in, but he did not slow, racing through the bushveld with hyena close around him. He dove into and through the thornbrush, ignoring the spears that tore his skin and nearly ripped out an eye.

Clattering in the bushes before him, he sensed a group of hyenas attempting to close in. In the dim light, shadows of brawny forms positioned themselves across a grass path between thickets to wall off his departure. He angled off to the side, tearing through the sedge, leaving them behind. A click of hyena jaws behind him, just missing the white tip of his tail. His narrow form held low to the ground, driving onward.

Onward, and onward, he refused to allow the veld to claim him.

His large ears strained for sounds, only capturing the thwack of branches, the skittering of thorns on hide, the incessant giggles behind him.

Crashing of brush, the heaving as he gulped air in desperation. The pounding pulse in his head.

As one cackling, scraping body after another dropped away, the wolf could hear the chase coming to a close. Gradually, the rustle of the thickets came from his body alone, and he slowed his pace. Heaving, panting, he stood still, the wall of black absolute. His wounds bled rivulets, the pain wracked his aging body, ribcage searing, his muscles afire from the desperate flight. Blackthorn grinned, savoring the agony.

I drink deeply this torment, for it means life. Eagerly I await your next cruelty. Should you consume me, Night, I make this covenant: you will strangle upon my corpse.

Eleven

Sandy soil undulated across the dry riverbed as though the waves of water had petrified. A stand of sweetgrass had grown up to the edge of this, taking advantage when it was a time of plenty. Now that grass was browned, soon to wither, having withdrawn its nutrient into a vast root system to await the next rains. Autumn was upon the savanna.

A lumbering form dragged itself out of a hole that yawned from the ground above the riverbed. Dark eyes peered from a tawny, leathered head that protruded from a shell. The high carapace of the leopard tortoise was of speckled shielding, withstanding the most curious of claws. It was a heavy burden that four stout legs resembling knobbed stone hefted slowly along the ground. The serrated beak slowly took a mouthful of a succulent leaf. He paid little mind to the taller carnivore that walked past him. The scent of wolf musk told him not to expect harassment, at least not unless pups were around.

Blackthorn sniffed the tortoise, and moved on. He lifted his snout and drew in the air, scanned the ground with obsidian eyes, tasted the smells with his wrinkled pink tongue.

Expecting nothing, and receiving nothing.

He padded onward, mindful only of the path ahead.

A cloud obscured the sun, drifting on as it dissolved gradually into the endless blue.

How long had it been since he had last eaten a substantial meal? Days upon days. Since parting ways with Kreun, weeks had passed. He did not care, his stomach withered and reduced, sustained on the odd ground squirrel or lizard that he could entrap. He vaguely recalled eating from the dead body of an impala calf, perhaps a yearling. The remains were mangled beyond recognition, the rich smell of decay tinged by the musk of black-backed jackal. He suspected the jackal had watched from the shadows, waiting for him to pass.

Walk, eat what one can, sleep if the night is too dark to see. Onward.

***

Blackthorn's black and gold paw pressed down on the winding body of a rufous-beaked snake. The nearly two meter long form was covered with a latticework pattern of pale blond and brown. The pointed head had been severed. His sharp canines chewed through the scales. He stared at the exposed pale white vertebrae poking from the wound he had made.

Are you the last of your kind?

The lifeless snake could provide no answer. He continued to gnaw through the skin, nipping away what meat he could expose. He suspected there were more to be found in the bushveld.

What creature will I feed when my body fails?

As he pulled away more of the scaly skin, he found the meat could be separated more easily in long ropes. Easier to swallow, though mixed with sand.

Will Blackthorn be the last wolf to see this world?

As the wind stirred dried leaves on its currents, his body wavered on lean legs. His mind swam, wandering far from here. Though his stomach was mostly empty, it did not call for him to continue eating.

"To what end." As he uttered this, he was unsure if it were a thought or spoken aloud.

When one is alone, does anything matter?

He stepped away from the half-eaten snake and laid down. The straw stalks grew tall around him, and he looked up to the sky, an infinite pale blue above.

As the hours passed, and dusk approached, Blackthorn had not moved. As though pulled by an unseen force, he stood on his paws, returned to the brown-scaled creature and continued eating.

Twelve

imble feet curled around the branch of the sickle bush. Each foot was made up of partially fused opposing toes that closed into a claw. The green scaled body was flushed emerald green, and pulled itself slightly along the branch back, then forth, resembling a fluttering leaf. The turret-like eyes swung up, down, and around, each moving independently in a survey for danger. Seeing none, the flap-neck chameleon locked both eyes forward on their target. Another grasp of the hooked foreclaws brought it closer. The mouth gaped open, and a bulbous tongue jutted out. In a flash, the pink missile shot an entire body length from the mouth, striking the head of a grasshopper and quickly wrapped it in a sticky trap.

The insect was pulled in as the tongue reset for another attack, and the jaws clamped down on the prize. Clawed feet continued their climb along the bush.

A shadow fell upon the chameleon, and the green body flushed black, eyes swiveling about to understand the nature of the threat it faced.

Blackthorn peered at the chameleon, his nose centimeters from the small hunter. He snuffed, and the black coloration warped into blotches of brown and green. He continued his march, ignoring the bewildered reptile as it gradually regained the green color of relaxation.

Decay is in the air.

His dark snout was held high, as it had been day after day on his meander. Padding down into a dried stream, he followed the lingering scent. Around a boulder and under a pod-mahogany tree he searched. In the shade of the broad arbor he looked about, the dish ears angling about listening for a threat. Above the wolf the gnarled branches creaked, stretching improbably far from the central trunk to embrace the sky.

The scent faded, disappearing as the winds picked up, and stirred the dirt of the rocks. Blackthorn snorted his disappointment. Nails clattered against the sandstone as he returned to the ground near the riverbed. A dark line along the ground drew his attention. The line flickered with thousands of waving antennae and legs - a battle column of ants.

Sniffing the ground, he followed the line, careful not to get too close to the stinging soldiers that guarded the ranks. Around a squat thornbush he found what mobilized them.

A severed paw.

It was small and blond, nearly white in color. Rounded in shape, it was smaller still than his own narrow paw. The black spots could only mean that it belonged to a leopard cub.

The ants swarmed over it, the workers cutting away meat for their army.

He stared at the paw. As he watched, the fur began to move, disturbed by activity beneath the surface.

Blackthorn lurched away, and resumed his steadfast gait.

***

Cattle wandered even here, sometimes with accompanying herders, sometimes alone. They grazed on the remaining desiccated grasses, leaving their dung in large piles behind them. Heavy hoofbeats clattered on hard ground and rock. Blackthorn looked up to the distance as the bull wandered through the savanna. Despite the buried urge within, he knew better than to consider hunting it. His attention returned to the corpse before him.

The scrub hare had been torn apart, killed instantly with his practiced bite. Holding the carcass in place with one paw, he ripped away what meat he could from the hare's hind legs and pelvis.

Nearby, perched on the thick succulent green leaf of a tall aloe, a go-away bird watched. The harsh, nasal *kwaaaayyyyy* startled Blackthorn for a moment, and he met the stare of the pale grey bird. Its head tipped to one side, the tall pointed feather crest fluttering in the breeze.

Kwaaaayyyyy!

He returned to his meal, but something in the air caused him to lose interest. A vague power tugged at him, and his pulse quickened.

Blackthorn straightened, his ears swiveling to capture some faint signal.

Nostrils flared, snout pointed to the sky, waiting. Nothing. Something.

He stood on his paws, again sniffing the air. There it was again - faint but unmistakable. Overlying this scent was smoke and gas, the cigar-like stench of human industry. Underneath, however, he found certainty.

Kwaaaayyyyy!

Pulling away what meat could be easily stripped, Blackthorn

took off in the direction of the scent, padding with a renewed vigor in his pace.

***

HAWWNNGG

The heavy truck thundered down the black ribbon, from wherever to whatever, the horn blaring at a child who crossed the road with seconds to spare. People ambled along the dirt edge of the highway, younger men clad in worn T-shirts, older men wearing grey suits, women in colored dresses. The air above the asphalt boiled in the heat.

Noise filled the area, of moving vehicles, trucks laden with cargo, cars darting onto the road or cruising to a stop on the side gravel. Minibuses sagged under the weight of passengers, their shocks strained and tires groaning their displeasure. Stray dogs stayed just out of kicking distance of the people on the roadside, fur worn through with mange and neglect. They sniffed at garbage off the road, or in ditches, some piles of refuse smoldering with columns of ash rising into the autumn air.

There were smells to entice or offend human noses, between the trash or puddles of beer residue, and the rich flavors of fried dough wafting on the breeze. The dogs and cattle milling about picked up more subtle odors from grasses, foliage, birds and beasts from the fields nearby.

One such dog trotted into a field, his dirty white fur matted with burs and mud. He sniffed the ground, unsure of what to make of the strange musk on the ground. A small print, central blot with four toes and corresponding claws, with a pungent oily scent emanating from the center. The tracks led far from the road, across an abandoned field behind the ENGEN petrol station off the main highway.

He had smelled this musk before, present for the past year, isolated to a nearby farm. There, the aroma was thick, all lingering behind a tall fence where four predators slept.

The white dog followed the trail of prints behind the petrol station, straining to ignore the penetrating stink of gasoline. The prints were subtle and disappeared on firmer ground where the grass retained a foothold, and reappeared where the earth was more soft.

Anxiety set in. The dog crept more slowly, sniffing each print, realizing as he reached the end of the trail, that he stood before the farm. He looked up.

Four figures regarded him from within an enclosure, lean and powerful forms of black, white, and gold with large dish like ears.

The prints led around and up to the fence. His heart pounded as he realized the tracks were made by one of the creatures before him—the dreaded painted wolf.

The dog looked about, wondering how one of these strange hunters came to be outside of the impassable chain link barrier, and he was consumed by an implacable terror. Images welled up from an ancient memory buried in the instinct of generations past. Once, there were vast armies in grey patrolling lands of forest and snow, and the feared gold and black assassins of the African savanna, felling the greatest of beasts. Wolves that resembled dogs in a way, but possessed of a savage nature that knew no pain, and feared no darkness. The wild that crept to the edge of the town now seemed to surround it, and penetrate the very shadows.

He fled with a high whine, disappearing without a trace in

the grasses.

Thirteen

"We were watched. And the eyes upon us were those of a wolf."

"You suppose too much, Visarend." The male African wild dog stretched, hind end in the air, head low, forepaws straight out, followed by lowering his bottom with a grunt. "Feeding time is soon."

"Ignore instinct at your peril, Blouvalk." Visarend was on her paws, and padded back and forth along the length of their enclosure. "We are ignorant of a great many things."

"Such as?" He yawned, showing off sharp white fangs and black gums.

"Knowing the answer would be a paradox, would it not?" Her coat was light in color, splashes of white across her breast and sides, with black-ringed blotches of gold resembling drips of paint. "Mysteries abound. The humans who come to the fence. They come from and return to somewhere."

"They leave to fetch more food." Blouvalk was of light coloration as well, with a strip of white along his back. He paused, looking into the sky at nothing. "Are the humans the same ones each time?" He smacked his lips. "Or do replacements bring us food?"

"I could not see the wolf in the dark." She ignored his musing.

"He was there nonetheless." She sat for a moment, but was unable to remain still, and continued pacing the chain link fence.

"Has there been a wolf, other than us?"

Visarend did not answer.

"I suppose one must ask whether—"

"—there is anything else beyond the fence." Visarend reversed her pace. "You ask it, and do so often."

Two other male wolves sprinted around the twisted trunk of an apple leaf tree, at first racing side by side, then chasing one another by the tail. As they whirled around the tree, their coats were a blur of black, white, and gold.

She reared onto her hind legs and boxed one of the wolves as it raced by, knocking him over, tumbling in the dust. He rolled onto his feet and pounced, his jaw lightly gripping her snout.

"Foul creature." She batted him away.

"*Yoh!* Dare to *klap* me?" He leapt on her back and they rolled into a heap.

"Swartwou, you are a big *oke*, but dim as one of their dogs." A swift kick with her hind leg, and the larger male was pushed away.

"Visarend – they come!" The other wolf stopped his chase and pressed his snout against the chain link fence.

"What have they, Kleinsperwer?" She padded to his side.

"A large thing this time." His tail whisked back and forth, nostrils flaring in search of a clue about what the men carried.

The men were dressed in faded khakis, one of their faces obscured by a wide brimmed hat. Boots clomped on the hard dirt ground. They hefted a giant parcel between them.

The wolves stood attentive, eyes not leaving the bundle of black plastic. Tails swished, paws twitched, at the ready.

"Are they feeding us other humans?" Kleinsperwer's golden tail swished.

"Interesting thought." Blouvalk sidled up to him. "See, I thought they fought one another, competing for the chance to feed us."

"Unlikely. The humans lead around those big things with horns." Visarend chuckled at their theory. "They probably eat them and feed the remains to us."

They came closer, heavy boots stirring up dust.

"Maybe the things with horns lead the humans around?" Kleinsperwer said, a touch of wonder in his voice.

The men trudged up to the chain link fence, setting down the load. One fiddled with a ring of keys, jingling.

The wolves began to salivate.

Working the key into a lock, it opened with a pop, and the gate swung wide. The men picked up the object wrapped in a tarp, and carried it inside the gate. This was a small staging area where the outer chain link fence met an inner fence, each a rectangle with a meter space between them. This separated the captive African wild dogs from the diseased local domesticated dogs. The door swung shut with a clink as the latch caught. Keys jingled again as one of the men worked to open a lock on a second door on the inner fence. The rusted iron creaked as the door swung open, and the men unwrapped the black plastic tarp. Inside was the remains of a side of beef, the best cuts of meat already carved away by a butcher.

The men carried in the carcass, and the wolves began to scamper, one way, then the next, until the two men were in the center of the enclosure next to the trunk of the apple leaf tree. Four wolves sprinted in circles around them.

The moment the carcass was dropped, the wolves darted

in, serrated teeth shearing meat and tendon from bone. They ate in near silence, punctuated only by a slight whine between bites and swallows.

Creaking of iron as the door swung open again, shut, and there was the click of a lock. Heavy boots stomped away from the enclosure, past a stunted sickle bush shrub against the outer fence. The sickle bush grew in an unruly fashion from a central stump, branches looping over and drooping onto the ground. Green leaves covered the thorn-laden branches, and a tangle of grass covered the base of the shrub in shadow.

Within that shadow lay a freshly dug hole.

***

The trill of katydids and the whistles of nightjars blended with a deep, snoring pulse from guttural toads through the night. The noise was a pervasive din that rendered the sounds of digging undetectable.

A light spray of gravel and dirt came from the sickle bush, followed by more. Blackthorn stopped, looked about, his ears the only shape that could be seen against the tangle of branch and grass. There was a light clink as his claws hit the chain link.

"I knew we were not alone."

Blackthorn froze. He looked up from his work. His eyes met those of another wolf, standing on the other side of the fence.

"The night previous. I sensed that we were being observed by another."

"I have been watching for far longer than that." Blackthorn's guttural rasp did not rise above the clamor of katydids and toads.

"You are cautious."

"I do not wish to be kept on the other side of this fence." Blackthorn looked again toward the nearest building, and saw no lights or signs of human activity. "How long have you been imprisoned here?"

The female stared at him, blinking.

"A long time, I would venture." Blackthorn clawed at the ground, releasing more dirt behind him in a spray.

"What does it mean—'imprison'?"

"Held against one's will." He glanced up at the high barrier, topped with loops of razor wire. "How many seasons have passed since your capture?"

"Seasons?"

"Change in the weather, from warm to cool." Blackthorn continued to hack away at the dirt.

"It has gone from quite warm to cool, once and again."

He stopped digging, mulling this over. He guessed she was born two years ago.

"Long ago, there was a dark place, smelling of earth, and of us. I knew mother." She examined the ground before her, scratching at rocks. "And then she was gone. Loud cracks filled the air with sound, and... we were alone."

"And they took you."

"Another dark place, moving, creaking. A cavernous animal that stored us in its belly, and yet did not eat us." She looked around again, and laid down on her side. "And this."

Blackthorn stopped for a moment before continuing to dig.

"I am Visarend."

"Your mother named you for a fish eagle?"

"No - we fashioned our own names here." She looked to the dark sky, the crystalline stars twinkling. "For the birds that could soar as though fences did not exist. And you?"

"Blackthorn." The scratching resumed.

"For what reason did you come?"

"To dig this hole." He frowned at her.

"They bring meat for us each day." She scratched at her ear with a forepaw. "I suspect they will bring more for you."

He stopped again. "Curiosity compels me to ask." He stood straight. "What reason do you suppose I have for digging into your enclosure?"

"You are hoping for a mate." Her voice was flat. "In that I can disappoint you now. Despite my best efforts, I have had no pups during my time here."

"That has occurred to me." He thought for a moment. "However, what makes you think I want to live in such a tiny place?"

"Why would you not?" She stood again. "The food comes, and we are safe."

"This is no wild." He struggled to find the words. "You cannot live a free life here."

"Our days are quite free. We eat, and then sleep, and laze, watching the sky..."

"And is that all you want?"

Visarend looked his way, and for the first time realized he was angry.

"Is it?" His eyes were a darkness mired in confusion and annoyance.

"We want for nothing in this place you regard with contempt." Her voice was soft in its rebuke.

"You *okes* may as well be the dogs that eat rubbish in the town."

"Town?"

He sighed, and clawed the fence. "Hopeless." He extricated himself from the sickle bush.

"Will you return on the morrow to complete the hole?"

"A waste of my time. *Voetsek*, the lot of you."

A clink of iron. He turned to see her forepaw drop from the fence.

"What is the wild?" Her voice had risen, and she looked longingly toward the hole.

He studied the dirt before him. "Why do you ask?"

Visarend padded along the fence. "I have long wondered what lies beyond, finding a way through the gate the humans open, if only to run for a day, and return for the meals they provide."

"Return?" The sound of his chuckle resembled a crumbling breeze block. "Should you leave this sad place, you will never tire of the wonders outside it."

"What is the world like outside our home?" She spoke in a faint whine.

"Filled with menace. Every shadow conceals jaws that would have our throat, every step only just keeps us beyond the reach of death. Each day is a brutal endeavor to escape starvation."

Visarend's jaw was slack.

His obsidian eyes softened. "Among your *Volk* you would endure this struggle. Witness with me the beauty of a world vast beyond comprehension. An adventure each day renewed with the promise of the wild."

She gave a long, slow exhale, her lips curling over bared fangs.

Fourteen

The following night, the two men who provided the leftover carcasses stayed outside. They laughed easily between themselves, rolling speech punctuated with loud guffaws that bounced off the buildings. Each held a brown glass bottle, spilling some of the fluid as they spoke. One gripped the barrel of a hunting rifle, the stock resting on the dirt by his boot.

Blackthorn's eyes never left the rifle. He crouched in the sickle bush, thorns pulling at his fur as the wind teased the branches.

"Is he out there?" Blouvalk twittered.

"Silence, *domkop*." They could not see him, but could hear Blackthorn's growl in the night.

"I do not see the point of this." Blouvalk muttered more quietly. "We have attempted to dig before."

"He is digging deeper still, it would seem. Perhaps there is an end to the fence." Visarend whispered.

The men turned their attention to the enclosure. All four of the wolves within were standing by the fence, and their nervousness was palpable.

"He is coming." Visarend hissed. The other wolves froze.

Boots plodded on the ground, the sound of cracking gravel

underneath. He gripped the rifle with one hand on the bolt, the other swinging by his side. He stopped, his boot crunching down next to the sickle bush.

Blackthorn breathed gently, stirring dust onto the man's black boot.

Nobody moved. The man tapped the butt of the rifle lightly on the ground. He looked over the wolves within the enclosure, and they stared back at him. He muttered something unintelligible. The other man yelled something to him, laughing.

The man with the rifle waved a hand, muttering again.

Blackthorn eyed a worn path across a field leading to the remote *miombo* wood. Perhaps half that distance would be covered before he was cut down. Bounding, his pulsing heart drowned out any ambient sounds.

He startled as something hit the ground beside him in the sickle bush. The empty bottle bounced off lower branches without shattering, and came to a rest against his side. A stream of water splashed on the ground, drops pattering off the thorns and leaves of the brush. His sensitive nose registered immediately that it was urine. It pooled away from the shrub as the man grunted with relief.

Eventually the stream stopped, and the man took a step from the bush. The black boot took a half turn, and thumped away, back toward the structure where the other man stood. There was more muttering, and rising laughter again.

His claws began scratching again at the bottom of the hole, careful to avoid scraping the chain link. The dirt moved was in small amounts, the most he could move quietly.

The two men ambled away from the structure, and a door banged shut as they went inside.

Torrents of dirt now flew from the base of the sickle bush,

creating widening piles beyond. Between the fences, the ground shifted, then gave way. A narrow head with dish like ears rose from the hole and shook off the dirt. Blackthorn leapt out and pressed his snout against the inner fence.

"Has it occurred to any of you to start digging a hole of your own?"

The three male wolves exchanged glances. Visarend began furiously attacking the soil on her side of the inner barrier, clawing free clods of dirt. Blackthorn dug on his side, watching their progress. The loud clamor of night bird calls and katydids obscured their noises, and clouds above rendered them invisible in the dark. Within a few hours the hole was deep enough under the inner fence for a wolf to climb through.

Blackthorn went back through the hole under the outer fence, climbed out of the sickle bush and looked back.

The four wolves stared at him. The males cast their eyes about as though lost.

"Where are we to go?" Kleinsperwer whispered.

"Will we return for the daily meal?" Swartwou paced the fence.

Visarend dove into the earthen hole they had dug, and after a cursory look back into the enclosure, she went through the hole under the outer fence, and was at Blackthorn's side.

"Follow us quickly, or remain where you are until your last days." Her voice was a hiss in the night.

The other three wolves haltingly made their way under the fences, catching up with Blackthorn and Visarend loping across the field. They vanished into the line of *miombo* trees, leaving behind the rank smell of petrol and smoke coming from the ENGEN station. In less than an hour the town was left behind.

"When do we rest?" Blouvalk panted.

"Not until we are out of range of those humans." Blackthorn rasped. "I suspect they will pursue you. And they will be none too fond of me."

Blouvalk stopped and laid down.

"Back on your paws." The dark wolf stood over Blouvalk, a shadow in night untouched by moonlight.

"*Hang aan 'n tak.*" Blouvalk laid his head on the ground. "I need to rest."

"You can 'hang onto a branch' when we are in safety."

Visarend prodded the prone wolf with her snout. "We have not had a run like this in our lives." She shrugged. "They are all exhausted."

"We have been on the run for less time than it took to dig that final hole." He shook his head in frustration. "Those humans could catch up to us at a leisurely walk."

Visarend reclined as well, though she cast an anxious eye back in the direction of the town.

"We are resting in the open, a perilous choice even in the daytime."

The others did not respond, other than Blouvalk, who snored gently.

"This was a grave error, and the wild does not suffer recklessness." Blackthorn lay down, but did not rest. "Would it have been better to languish in that place, than chance the free world?"

He soon realized he was talking to himself.

Peering into the darkness, he saw nothing beyond the tangle of thornbrush distantly. His ears angled one way, then another, listening intently. So many enemies in the night possessed sight superior to his own.

A branch cracked, not far away, towards the village. His heart pounded as he waited.

No humans approached.

All around was the rising clatter of katydids and calls of night birds that might obscure the approach of danger.

He settled down onto the ground, but did not dare sleep. He remained awake, holding vigil over the sleeping wolves.

Fifteen

Paws crept through the grasses, each footfall hushed by the owner. The angular head, narrow ears, and slim muzzle was held just above the wavering sweet grass tips. Black and silver fur cascaded down from the neck to the bushy tail. The jackal closely watched the sleeping wolves, sniffing the air for any food left over from a kill. With wolves, there would always be a kill, and leftover meat. Unless there were pups in a den, in which case there would be not even a scrap of hide to gnaw.

The quiet was disturbed by the distant sound of a truck engine, the revving sound waxing and waning as the vehicle bumped over rough ground far from any road. The harsh *chaa-chaa chek-chek* of a spurfowl made the jackal crouch for a moment before continuing its large circle around the wolves. His triangular ears were directed forward, then swept back. He sensed there were others, but could see none. He raised his head to survey for signs of carrion.

"You will have no good fortune here."

The jackal leapt in the air, jarred by the deep voice, and spun about, realizing it came from behind.

"These *okes* have nothing to eat now." Blackthorn looked over the jackal's shoulder. "Perhaps not ever."

Crouched low, prepared to run, the jackal backed away, his silver and black back melting into the tall grass.

Blackthorn ignored him, and padded to the sleeping wolves. He bayed to them, and they lethargically aroused.

"On your feet!" He probed one, then the next, batting Blouvalk's head with playful forepaws. "The prey will not kill itself!"

Kleinsperwer rolled back over to sleep.

"Shall we hasten their demise?" He nosed Visarend until her eyes blinked open with effort.

"What could you possibly be suggesting?"

"The hunt is on."

Visarend was on her paws, and helped him wake the others. "Come, Kleinsperwer."

"I am a tree, sister. Can you not see my roots?" Kleinsperwer's jaw hung open, pink and black tongue lolled out the side as he rolled over.

"A tree, brother?" Swartwou bounded to his side and planted forepaws onto him.

"*Ag*, Swartwou!" Kleinsperwer whined as he rolled onto his feet.

"Uprooted this one!" He knocked the smaller wolf over, laughing.

"You silly *bliksems* are of the same litter?" Blackthorn rumbled. His unusually dark eyes regarded them as they climbed over one another, gnawing on a paw or tail with light biting jaws.

"All but Blouvalk there." Kleinsperwer indicated the wolf with the white stripe down his back. "Our mother joined his group."

"Right." Blackthorn twittered loudly to them all, and their

playing stopped. "Morning has come, as has the time to hunt." He gestured to a distant stand of corkwood trees. "And the prey is to the east."

"What, then, is a hunt?" Visarend looked to him expectantly.

Blackthorn stared at her, uncomprehending.

"Is it food?"

"Yes, it involves food." His voice was flat in tone.

"We can return home for that." Visarend's head was turned to one side, as though working through a riddle.

"And now I fail to understand." Blackthorn glared. "What is 'home'?"

"The place where we have stayed." She looked about. "All our lives."

"The wolf knows no home." Blackthorn rasped. "The wolf needs no home." He stepped around her, and the others. "Home is where the enemy finds you, and traps you. We are never so stupid as to wait for our enemies."

"Are we to look for food at another enclosure?"

"No." He stopped his stalking. "We are well able to kill our own."

The four exchanged glances, and watched him, waiting.

"You have no idea what I mean by 'kill'." Blackthorn's jaw hung open.

"Does that mean 'claim', or 'drag'?"

Blackthorn closed his eyes, long enough for Visarend to poke him with her snout.

"I am not sleeping." He shook his head. "Only I wish to be so." He loped away. Calling over his shoulder, he bayed to the others. "Stay, follow... not sure which is worse for me." He grumbled as he sprinted off across the field.

What have I stumbled into?

***

The blood pooled under the impala, and the dry ground took it up eagerly. The belly was laid open, bowels spilled out, torn free. Blackthorn stepped away from the kill, lowered his muzzle and hoo-called into the ground. *HROOO - HROOO - HROOO.* The low-pitched call resonated, sounding as though echoing through a concrete tunnel. The vaguely metallic signal could be heard for kilometers.

Setting aside the entrails, he began pulling away the rich meat of the liver and heart. Gulping these down a bottomless throat, it was several minutes before he noticed there was no return hoo-call.

Pausing again, he called into the ground. An eye was cast to the periphery of the field, a line of acacia and mopane wood. He did not think there were hyena about to steal this kill, but a wolf must be wary. Eating was a dangerous activity in the wild.

HROOO - HROOO - HROOO.

He continued to gulp down mouthfuls of meat from hip and shoulder, scissoring the muscles away from bone.

"Vervloeks. Where the bloody hell are they?" He looked in the direction of where the rest of the wolves were left behind, and glanced for a moment at the carcass. Loathe to leave behind good meat, he loped off, cursing to himself.

Within the hour, he found them, still resting in the high of the day, in the middle of the field where they had slept.

"Did you not hear my call?" Blackthorn was fuming. "Are you not hungry enough to follow?"

"Apologies, Blackthorn." Visarend padded to him. She began to lap his muzzle.

The dark wolf began to drool at this, and felt the need to

regurgitate his kill. He recoiled from this.

"You need not beg meat from me—you are not pups, and you are not bloody helpless."

She looked down.

"Now follow me, all of you, if you have any interest in eating today." He turned and sprinted off to return to the dead impala. His path took him through a grass plain, dotted with giraffe thorn acacia trees and the occasional broad arbor of a sycamore fig. He could sense the presence of the wolves somewhere behind him, rustling through grass, stumbling on warthog holes. He did not look back.

Few animals moved about in the heat of midday. The occasional buttonquail hummed as it pecked for seeds, and a black-bellied bustard strutted through grass tussocks. The tall bird craned his long thin neck over the delicate flowers festooning the grass tips, watching the wolf bounding past.

Blackthorn allowed a growl to rise in his throat as he reached the impala, finding the black-backed jackal tugging at the meat in the open belly.

"Keep your distance, *bliksem*."

The jackal pulled its blood spattered head from the impala and trotted a respectful distance away. He hovered on the periphery of the kill, watching for an opportunity to snatch a scrap, however small.

Blackthorn continued eating. He would raise his head and give a subdued ruff-bark to the jackal when it drifted close, but otherwise kept to eating his fill.

Eventually, the other wolves found him, following his scent. The jackal gave greater distance at their approach, but sensed a lack of danger from them.

The four edged closer to the impala kill, unsure what to

expect of the dark wolf. They eased into taking bites from the carcass, ripping away what organs remained, stripping the flesh from the bones, and pulling away the hide in sheets. When they were finished, all that was left behind was the glistening skeleton, hooves, a carpet of entrails, and the decapitated head. The wolves left the kill behind. Gradually, the jackal returned to inspect it for what nutrient was left.

Blackthorn padded underneath the glow of a nearby fever tree, and laid down next to the gnarled root. The bark was almost phosphorescent, brilliant in the intense light. His rested his head on forepaws.

Kleinsperwer groaned where he lay.

"What ails you?" Blouvalk prodded him with his snout.

"A gnawing inside, as though the impala is trying to escape my belly."

"Take a mouthful of grass." Blackthorn grumbled indifferently. "It helps with indigestion. You *okes* are not accustomed to wild meat, and so much at a sitting." He rested his head.

Visarend laid down next to him, and struggled in vain to make eye contact.

"Blackthorn. I am grateful for what you have provided."

He did not open his eyes.

"And for freeing us to the wild."

"Gratitude is not what I perceive from you all."

"Have I displeased you?"

"Not only must I kill for your daily meat." He raised his head, onyx eyes glittering with anger. "I must drag you to the feast. Were you not listening for my call?"

"What call do you mean?"

He sprung onto his paws, and she shrank back. He brought his jaw toward the ground. *HROOO!* The sound echoed across the veld.

"That was you?"

Blackthorn collapsed into a heap and shut his eyes.

"I have never heard that call before." Visarend lapped his muzzle. "We did not know."

"And what do you know? How to wait for your meals, seated patiently like dogs of the village, awaiting the decay of time across the seasons?"

"I am coming to understand the difficult task you now find before you." Visarend sat close, her forepaws touching his. "We know nothing. We have seen nothing of the wild, and can only say that we have been fed on time for as long as I can remember."

"Your ignorance is of a lethal depth. I am of a mind to leave you altogether and search anew for my kind." He sighed, leaning against the fever tree. "I cannot provide you the lessons of youth." He glanced up at the other three males who lazed on the ground nearby. "And they appear to have no desire to learn."

"I am willing." Her golden eyes stared into his, and she touched noses with him.

"I do wonder if I have doomed you." His dark eyes softened. "Would you have lived full lives within the fence?"

"Survival, perhaps. But in less than a day my world has become another entirely." Her eyes flashed. "I have run free, through field and forest, the greatest distance I have moved in my life. I found an antelope—'killed', as you say—by your design. Birds and beasts, the names of which I have yet to discover." She smiled, teeth flecked in blood. "So many things I did not know could be discovered. I welcome death if it is the price."

He sighed. "We shall see, Visarend." He only looked down at the dirt, as a train of industrious ants crossed in front of him.

"One moment, if you please." She padded away.

Blackthorn looked up as she left, and wondered for a moment if he had been too harsh. *After all, they know less than you did even as a pup, looking out of the den for the first time, at a light from the free world above.*

Visarend had trotted over to the other wolves. They were out of earshot, but they suddenly snapped to attention and their ears were erect. She continued muttering something to them. One was on his paws, then sat, then abruptly stood again. He heard a high whine from one of them, likely Swartwou. Then the three males stood, and were pacing fretfully, looking over toward him.

All four then padded over to Blackthorn, and the heads of the males were angled low over the ground.

"Forgive us, dark teacher." Swartwou bowed. "I am at your command." He sat attentive, head still held below the level of Blackthorn's.

"Show us the way of the wolf, Blackthorn. I shall become a killing shadow." Kleinsperwer sat, also bowing low, scraping himself closer with his foreclaws.

Blouvalk at first did not speak, sitting a short distance away, until Visarend whispered in his ear. He edged closer, and was bowing lower than the others.

The dark wolf surveyed the four wolves sitting before him. Their eyes were fixed upon his. They did not appear to be breathing, except with caution.

"Is there a point in teaching you how to survive?" He glared at them. "In this place?"

"Yes..." Kleinsperwer whispered.

"I am all too familiar with instruction. And aware that no one is listening to it. Whether due to pride or foolishness, one's guidance is wasted."

"It will not be wasted on me." Kleinsperwer said.

"Nor me." Swartwou wagged his tail in spite of himself.

"Very well, then." Blackthorn sighed. "Rest today, for on the morrow I shall run you *bliksems* into the very ground."

Swartwou grinned for a moment, but this vanished with the dark wolf's growl.

"We shall hunt, and you shall follow my command. There is meat to be had on this veld, but it is bought with great pain." He paced before them. "You lazy *dikgat* wolves will shed blood, just as you take the blood of your prey. None shall feed you now. There is only the Pack."

They looked at one another, brows furrowed.

"I shall teach you to be the fearsome wolf to which you were born. And some of you will die if you are not up to the task." He paused. They were rapt. "In the wild, nothing is 'left' for you." A growl resounded in his throat. "On the morrow. You shall hunt, or the vultures shall dine heartily on your corpses."

He padded back to the foot of the fever tree. Visarend joined him.

"What did you say to them, Visarend?"

"That they would either be apt pupils, or I would kill them in their sleep."

He looked at her quizzically, and she only gave an enigmatic smile.

Blackthorn lay his head on his forepaws and closed his eyes to rest.

And should I fail as a teacher, we shall all die together.

Sixteen

With dawn came the chorus.

Rk-k-k-k Rk-k-k-k, the rattling snore call of the guttural toad.

Kuk-coorrrr-uk Kuk-coorrrr-uk, the rolling voice of the cape turtle dove.

HA-DA! HA-DA!, the morning blast from the hadeda ibis.

The wolves did not have a morning call. Blackthorn was awake first, and padded in a broad curve around where they had slept at the base of the fever tree. He saw no spoor of lion nor prints of hyena, and closed his circle on the rest of the wolves.

"*On your feet.*"

At first they roused, and continued to laze on the ground. Blackthorn had none of that, planting his forepaws on Swart-wou's ribcage. The larger male groaned, and looked up into the black marble eyes of the old wolf. He stood at attention on the instant.

"Awaken, my *kinders*." He went to each, nipping flanks, and probing with his eager snout.

"Am I a child, now?" Blouvalk groused.

"A *kind* indeed, and a young one at that." He prodded Blouvalk until he was on his feet, and boxed him about his head with forepaws. "And a child you shall remain until you spill blood from a hunt of your own."

He raced about them, and lapped Visarend's muzzle. She lapped his, and raced about with equal excitement.

She went to Kleinsperwer, and licked his muzzle with enthusiasm. As though some long dormant sensation had surfaced, he did the same, and they were racing about the base of the fever tree.

"Feel the rising wolf within." Blackthorn raced from one wolf to the next, and his energy was infectious. "Your heart races, and the veld compels you." He was on hind legs, and batted Visarend with his forepaws.

She was on her hind legs as well, meeting his playful attack. They were back on all fours, racing, greeting each wolf, and they shared exhilaration. Leaping, dashing, turning about, breaking into a dead run to nowhere, returning to the fervor of the Pack. The traditional hunting rally of the painted wolf was underway.

"In whose name will death visit the savanna?" Blackthorn's rasp brought them all to a frenzy.

"The impala tremble!" Swartwou twittered in a high pitch, nearly running headlong into the trunk of the fever tree.

"The sparrowhawk shall fly!" Kleinsperwer stood for a moment on hind legs, lost his balance, and fell onto Swartwou.

Visarend yittered happily, colliding with Blouvalk.

"ENOUGH!"

The wolves were stilled. Their joy at beginning the hunt melted away as they watched the dark wolf, who with a flash of teeth shifted from a jubilant pack mate into an assassin.

"And now we bring the blood river." Blackthorn turned and bolted away from them.

The rest of the wolves shared a glance, and took off in close pursuit, exulting in the great open wild before them.

***

They moved in a column, weaving through medium sized acacia and spiny corkwood trees and shrubs. The four captive wolves moved with some hesitation, constantly looking around themselves. Blackthorn would orbit them in tight circles, watching them, with an eye on the ground and horizon for threats.

"The earth before you, observe every patch you cross." His voice rumbled quietly. "Your prey leaves signs you use for the hunt." He twittered, and the wolves followed the direction his snout indicated. "A dung midden - here." He padded toward it. "Dung in balls the size of large seeds - the impala has come this way."

"Just now?" Kleinsperwer's tail swished.

"This is old - a few days have passed, the dung dried out." He sniffed. "Fresher dung middens can give one direction." He sniffed along the ground. "No tracks, so the periodic rains have washed some of that spoor away. We move on."

"Is this an impala track?" Swartwou paced around a small depression in the soil. Narrow paw prints, a central blot with four toes, slight indentations marked the dirt just above each toe.

"No - the jackal has been this way. Claws are a mark of a carnivore." He padded on. "Those are the most important tracks of all to register. For our kind will often fall to the strike of another hunter."

The five wolves padded onward, the dark wolf's paws spring-

103

ing on the ground with each step in a steadfast advance. The other four panted behind him.

The bushveld was thick here, consisting of stands of various acacia trees with medium height nile grass and clumps of wooly caperbush that spread over the savanna in scrambling shrubs. The hooked spines of the caperbush pulled at the fur of the wolves as they padded through, greyish green leaves teased by their passage.

The halt was so abrupt, the four nearly bumbled into Blackthorn's rear. Swartvou would have pushed him over if the older wolf were not a wall anchored to the ground.

"What is it?" Swartvou stepped to his side.

Blackthorn stared at the ground, his breathing a steady grinding sound, deep and racing. His ears were flat against his skull, and his body seemed to crouch lower, as though ready to run or hide.

"What—" Swartvou's eyes drifted down to the dirt before Blackthorn, and the largest print he had ever seen.

"Lion." Blackthorn's voice was hushed, but no less alarming, his tone sending a chill through their spines. He glanced up, to the sides, through the dense foliage around them.

"What is a lion?" Blouvalk's whining chirp was met with a growl from Blackthorn, and he did not speak further.

The dark wolf padded forth, and a glare behind him bid them silence without saying a word. He pushed his way into the sedge and disappeared.

"What are we to do right now?" Swartvou wondered to the others. They eyed one another uneasily.

"He is afraid." Kleinsperwer intoned. "You can scent it on him."

"The obvious need not be spoken." Visarend hushed him.

She herded them closer around the print. A broad central pad with four toes, pushed deep into dried soil.

"There are no claws." Blouvalk canted his head to the side.

"That is because they save their claws for *you*." Blackthorn rasped, his sudden reappearance startling this others. "Lion and leopard sheathe them when on the move." His onyx eyes flashed, still darting around, peering into the brush around them.

"What, then, is a lion?" Blouvalk pressed.

Blackthorn glared at him, and at the print. His breathing remained rapid. "I see no other tracks. This one is older, somehow enduring." He looked up. "Hardened in the sun." He huffed, and padded off quickly.

"Are we likely to see one?" Visarend spoke at a whisper.

"I do not suspect we are in their territory." His ears were still flat, fangs bared. "Be vigilant nonetheless."

"Is he trying to frighten us?" Blouvalk murmured.

None of the others responded, and Blackthorn did not speak again for hours. As the sun crept across the sky, he hurried his pack through the savanna.

***

The light rustling of green leaves and wind blown grass was all that could be heard in the afternoon. Impala milled about in the field, while a troop of vervet monkeys browsed in an acacia tree. Wary eyes were peering in all directions.

In shadows, Blackthorn paced before his pack.

"This shall be your first hunt." He turned from the view of the field ahead, speaking to the pack within the *miombo* wood where they hid. "And your part shall fail."

"Why would it fail?" Blouvalk managed to sound indignant.

"It takes great skill to fell prey as swift as an impala. You lack these skills, but with time, you may develop them."

Blackthorn passed before the female. "Visarend – you have taken the name of a Fish Eagle."

She nodded.

"A masterful predator, able to soar through the sky, and with precision spear a fish from the river and take flight with its bounty." He sighed. "It will be some time before you can compare to such a hunter."

He passed by the larger male.

"Swartwou – the Black Kite. A swifter hunter you will never meet, one which has nothing in common with your oafish demeanor."

Swartwou appeared crestfallen, his black brow furrowed.

"Kleinsperwer – the sparrowhawk. Skillful enough to chase down and slaughter prey quick as lightning, birds on the wing." He leaned close. "A trifle too ambitious with that chosen name, would you not say?"

The male stared at the ground.

"And Blouvalk. A rat catching kite." He chuckled. "Your name suits you."

Blouvalk grunted. "And you were named for a thornbush. Your mother expected lesser still of your agility."

The male was sent reeling, rolled over the dust before he knew he was hit. Blackthorn placed a paw on either side of Blouvalk's head on the ground. His breathing was an engine exhaust, rolling and pulsing, muzzle parted to reveal white knives against black gingiva.

"Do we have an understanding, rat-chaser?"

Blouvalk did not utter a sound.

"Wisest words you have spoken thus far." Blackthorn left him, and padded back to the others.

He prodded Kleinsperwer with his snout. "The trees. The silvered monkeys there – their eyes are sharp, and give a warning bark understood by all with our approach."

"I see them. Can we kill them?"

"Hardly." Blackthorn bit down on his laugh. "They move ever so quickly."

"We may run down an impala yet." Visarend stood on hind legs for a moment before thumping back down. "There are so many of them."

"So many, and when they bolt, their numbers will seem greater still as they leap about in a display that deceives the eye. When they do, be not confused – continue to drive into them."

"Relentless, we shall cut them down." Swartwou batted Blouvalk's sour expression with a paw.

"Be cautious, however." Blackthorn indicated the male impala with his snout. "They can fight back as they flee. Get horned in the body, or a hoof to your jaw, and you will surely die."

Swartwou took a step back, considering this.

The dark wolf trotted off.

"What shall we do, then?" Swartwou whined.

"Wait here, ready to run straight into the herd. When the vervet monkeys in the acacia trees give their first alarm bark – charge."

Visarend watched him go. "He will watch our hunt. And gauge our ability and daring." She leapt on Swartwou, leaning on his golden back with her forepaws. "Perhaps we shall surprise him."

"In position, then." Kleinsperwer walked toward the open field, staying just inside the fringe of trees. The others were by his side, muscles tensed, waiting.

"Why do we not just run?" Blouvalk grumbled. "Surely—"

"We wait." Visarend was curt, and her chirping call silenced the rest.

The wolves crept closer, holding their bodies low. Each looked to the other, uncertain how to approach prey.

"Look - to the sky!" Kleinsperwer grinned.

A small bird, its white plumage with brown speckles almost invisible against the clouds, flapped overhead, alighting on one of the acacia trees in the field before them. Wings were folded shut as the little sparrowhawk gripped the slender branch in its talons, its dorsal grey colors striking against the green leaves.

"Fortune favors us." Kleinsperwer whispered. "The wind is speaking - can you hear it?" His hazel eyes sparkled. "The wild is ours, and we are one with the wild."

"You are one of the monkeys." Blouvalk muttered, and the others twittered their laughter with him.

A loud cough broke the calm. One of the vervet monkeys, facing away from the wolves, gave a gruff bark. His silvered fur appeared to stand on end, tail hanging low.

The wolves advanced, and they noticed the impala beginning to move their way.

"Straight into them!" Visarend called her order in a high twitter that sounded like a squeaking bird call. The four rapidly advanced to maximum speed, pairs of rounded ears bouncing above the grass tips as the wolves bounded into the field.

The impala herd hammered the ground, alerted by monkey's call. Some began leaping into the soaring *pronk* that carried them several body lengths over the ground.

"They are coming toward us!" Kleinsperwer chirped with joy.

As they noticed the four wolves closing in, the herd stopped, turned about, frantically recalibrating their evasion against this attack. They began sprinting away, each in separate directions, and the wolves split apart chasing after them all.

Several resumed their great leaps over bush and tussock, lean and splendid bodies demonstrating for all in view their power and viability - there were no sick or old animals to prey upon here.

The rest of the herd turned and headed back swiftly to where they stood before the alarm, and the four hunters scattered.

None of the wolves could decide on a target. They each chased their own impala, and when another antelope crossed their path, they broke off to chase another, and then back to the first. The distance between predator and prey increased.

Further distant, a 'squark' was uttered, followed by a heavy thud to the ground. The impala herd continued to fragment, each extending their lead over the hunters chasing them, and finding gaps in the wolves' phalanx. The herd escaped.

The wolves looked about in confusion before they noticed Blackthorn wrestling an impala male to the ground. Gripping the shoulder with his jaws, he wrenched the male over, collapsing him into a heap before the sharp horns could swing about.

"Quickly now!" Blackthorn twittered this and with his jaws gripped the impala again before it could gain its feet.

The other wolves moved in, and surrounded the impala.

"Take hold, and pull."

They heaved, and as they pulled on the limbs, Blackthorn seized the hide of the belly and ripped it open, unrooting the intestines. The impala bled to death in seconds, and the body went slack.

Visarend strained, and with a pop, the forelimb was torn loose.

"Good – keep pulling against one another."

Blouvalk yanked against Kleinsperwer's grip and the hind leg uncoupled from the pelvis.

"We must dismember the carcass quickly."

The wolves relaxed and began to pick at the sections they had freed.

No – no, wrong, you *okes* are not at leisure here." He batted Visarend and Kleinsperwer where they reclined. "Eat as though you had moments to consume your kill." He looked over his shoulder, seeing only the scattered herd reforming further away.

"What is the urgency? Is the hunt not finished?" Blouvalk gnawed the hide of the hind leg.

"This is where the wolf is destroyed – the kill is a danger as it draws more formidable jaws than ours." He buried his head in the abdominal cavity to pull away organs and meat. After a minute, he was out and surveying the area.

The other wolves eyed one another, resisting the urge to ask what creature he had in mind. They hurried, stripping hide and exposing what meat they could, ripping away and swallowing great hunks as swiftly as their throats could manage.

In minutes there was only bone, hoof, and head left. The spine had been pulled into pieces, the ribcage adorned with slivers of meat. Already a black-backed jackal was skulking on the periphery of the field.

"Is there reason to be fearful with that one?" Kleinsperwer wondered.

"No – jackals move only in pairs. Clever *okes*, to be sure, but they lack the numbers and the brawn to attack us."

"And this other hunter." Visarend glanced at the others, then at Blackthorn. "Lion."

Blackthorn crouched slightly at the word.

"They have the necessary brawn?"

He peered around again, to the horizon, through the sedge, at the ground, for some time before answering.

"They do."

Visarend lapped his muzzle, covered in impala blood.

Blackthorn inspected the field and the carcass. "There is nothing left of the kill." Vultures circled overhead. "And we must leave this place at once."

The pack moved off, further to the east across the hills, the ground growing moist under their paws as they progressed.

"Why further east?"

"With time, we will encounter lions."

Visarend and the others stopped. "You *want* to cross their path?"

"It is unavoidable. Lions rule the savanna, and have absolute hold over the darkness. None of you will truly understand the hazard, no matter what words I utter." His black eyes glittered. "Experience is the supreme teacher."

"Will we learn to track them?" Kleinsperwer twittered with excitement.

Blackthorn nodded. "Discern how they are a threat, and you learn how to evade their hunt." He brushed past the young wolf. "As you learn hunting skills of your own."

***

111

Darkness was near complete, with only a faint glow from the moon above the horizon. The breeze teased the blades of grass while katydids razzed the night.

"You learned tonight, but far less than you think."

"A kill was made, Blackthorn. We can do so again." Blouvalk mused, while rolling onto his back to scratch it against rocks.

"Today was merely to introduce you to how antelope move. Their bodies are finely built to avoid the hunters of the savanna, and avoid they did."

"How did we eat so well, then?"

"I pulled it down. You merely provided the distraction." He was on his paws, pacing before the wolves. "And there are many different antelope out there. You shall learn, as we encounter them. Exercise caution, as the horns so carried can skewer a wolf, dead before you realize the cause."

"What did we do well?" Visarend yawned.

"You did as I asked. With the dawn, you must do so again, and continue to without fail. The season ahead will be a lean one, with more days devoid of food than with it. All one can demand is to learn quickly. As all pups must." He paused as the whistle of a nightjar startled him. "Tomorrow we press that herd again, in a straightforward hunt. We run them down, all of you following my lead. We can stand to starve for a day or two hence."

"Can we hunt the night?" Kleinsperwer sniffed the ground.

"Only if the moon is bold in the sky and illuminating the fields. Unlike our enemies, we cannot see well in the dark." He lay on his side.

The trill of katydid intensified. The razzing lowered as the wind picked up, and distant calls of nightjar resounded through the savanna.

Blouvalk hesitated a moment before asking. "Tell me of a lion."

Blackthorn took a breath. "Hulking in size, strength far greater than ours." His ears folded flat again, white knives unsheathed from beneath his lips as he spoke. "Tawny in color, with fangs able to punch through a skull."

Blouvalk looked at the others, and opened his mouth to ask a question, but Blackthorn continued, not noticing him.

"They hunt us down. Kill without hesitation." His teeth glittered in the dark. "They cut down entire packs. Right down to the pups. Generations cleansed from the earth in the space of day." He seethed as he spoke, voice barely above the trill of insects. "And they do not eat. The massacred are abandoned to rot."

Kleinsperwer and Swartwou reclined in a heap by a corkwood tree, but they did not appear to be resting. Each whicker of a bird in the night drew their startled glance, and the rustling of branches in the breeze tensed their muscles. Blouvalk joined them, trotting over, making a turn in the grass and lying down. None of them lay their heads down, anxiously glaring about. As the time passed, their heads were pulled down by fatigue. Fighting sleep, they eventually lost the battle and their snoring joined the cacophony of noise from the night.

Visarend nudged Blackthorn's snout, taking his attention away from the sinister darkness.

"You survived for some time before finding us. Do wolves normally live alone?" Visarend spoke in a near whisper as she looked about anxiously in the dark.

"There is only the Pack for us." He allowed his head to rest on the ground. "The Pack, or solitude with the gradual erosion of mind and body, like mud along the shores of a mighty river."

"The reason you freed us."

"That is so." He scratched behind his ear, chasing away a mosquito.

"And to have a litter of pups." She revealed her teeth in the dim light.

He raised his head from the ground and peered at her. "We shall see."

"Did you live in a pack before finding us?"

He did not answer for a long time. As she opened her muzzle to ask again, he answered.

"Yes."

"Close by?"

"Far from here." His voice ground like stones on a riverbed.

"What happened to them?"

He gave a long exhale before speaking. "Rest while you are able. Dawn, or ambush by enemies in the night, will be upon you before you are ready for them."

Seventeen

The dew was still clinging to grass in the morning as the pack departed for the hunt. The rally started with Blackthorn, and as he whipped them into an energetic froth, Blouvalk moved to take the lead.

"The herd is this way." Blackthorn indicated a southerly direction.

"They were this way the evening previous." Blouvalk continued his jog.

"And they moved in the night. Scent them upon the air, it can save considerable time." The dark wolf trotted off into the bush without a look back. Visarend followed him, and the rest did the same, one after the other. Blouvalk joined them with reluctance.

Blackthorn glanced back at Blouvalk, white stripe shuddering as he kept pace, head down, but mouth ever moving, teeth exposed in a grimace.

He led them through acacia trees and brush, interspersed with stands of krinkhout. These wild violet trees, clad in pale grey bark that resembled bone bleached in the sun, had long since shed purple flowers from their sparse crowns and winged fruit that sailed upon the wind.

Blackthorn's head was low, ears folded back, nose in the air.

With a gesture he indicated the jackal shadowing them.

Blouvalk moved to chase it away.

"Stay on task." Blackthorn twittered, and the wolf rejoined their formation. "Spread out, and probe the edges of the herd.

"I can smell them – just ahead of the next rise." Kleinsperwer nearly yelped with excitement.

"Choose your prey and stay consistent in your pursuit. Even if another comes close, focus on your selected target. Distraction is their most effective defense, far more crucial than the use of a sharp horn."

"And if we maintain a chase?" Visarend panted in the rising heat.

"Signal the rest with your calls – those with unlikely prospects shall join you. If you have no likely quarry, join another wolf on their signal."

"There they are." Swartwou twitched with anticipation. The herd grazed in the sweet grass field below the rise crested by the wolf pack.

"And stay alert for other hunters."

With this, Blackthorn shot forth down from the rise into the herd. The impala spotted them immediately and turned to run with coughing alarm barks.

All five wolves fanned out, engaging the herd. The strongest of the impala began high *pronk* leaps above bush and grass, springing into another titanic jump as soon as they hit the ground.

Swartwou powered ahead and closed the distance with one older impala, but was distracted by the close approach of another antelope. He broke off one chase to another, and the loss of momentum allowed both to escape him.

Kleinsperwer selected an impala, attempting to rake its flank with a snap of his jaws, but missed, and his prey continued its *pronk* until the pursuing wolf was outdistanced.

Visarend managed to nip the flank of her chosen target, but could not hold on. The impala sprang away, and she continued the chase as they left the herd and the rest of the pack behind. Beyond the field, she chased the antelope into a gully, stumbling on the loose rocks. As this opened into a wider waterlogged field, she was outdistanced, and the impala fled into a large pool of water.

Instinctively, she halted at the edge of the pool. Her brown eyes scanned the surface, a placid mirror. Unable to see into the depth, she backed away.

Just off the muddy edge of the water, a log seemingly surfaced, floating gently. As she watched, the rough surface of the log shifted, floating, but not drifting. A pair of eyes opened, and Visarend stared. Perched atop a long, broad head, the green of the eyes resembled algae, the vertical pupil a stiletto that stared at her, and through her. The wolf retreated back into the gully. The crocodile slid back under the surface.

Hoo-calls resounded across the land, and this time each wolf answered with a hoo-call of their own. *HROOO! HROOO!*

The pack converged on the field where the hunt had begun. Each regarded the other, and the lack of blood upon any of their coats gave the only answer necessary about the hunt.

"We hunt like—" Swartwou thumped to the ground, a frown on his face. "Wolves fed in a cage. Most disappointing."

Blackthorn allowed himself a smile. "On the contrary. Some of you came close. So early in your learning, that is all one can hope for." He padded to Swartwou and boxed him with a forepaw. "Stay focused on your prey. You will not spill blood on the savanna every time. Or even every day, especially for a

Pack as small as we."

He prodded Visarend with his snout. "And you must call for help. You were so very close to your impala, as you left our sight."

"I thought I was able to chase him to the very horizon." She sounded dejected.

"You need not do it alone. Together, the Pack shall close the chase. Rest for now."

The wolves lazed in the rising sun, with the exception of Swartwou, who chased a butterfly across the meadow. Leaping into the air, he managed to nearly snag it with a snap of his jaw before disappearing into a tussock of grass with a thud.

***

The wolf sniffed the ground, walking as he went. Weaving through the brush, the gold and black form went in and out of sight, the white stripe along his back the only clear way to identify him.

"What do you presume you are doing?" Blackthorn's guttural voice shocked Blouvalk out of his search.

"You startled me." Blouvalk stammered.

"Return to the rest of the Pack. I have no time to shepherd you together as though you were pups." Blackthorn rasped.

"I am looking for lion prints." He stood taller. "In case we are approached."

"You will be instructed in time how to find them."

Blouvalk grunted. "Instructed? You look down as you walk."

Blackthorn closed his eyes. "Very well. On your way." He padded off into the scrub.

Blouvalk watched him go, his eyes narrowed. Snout toward

the ground, he continued ambling through the brush, lowering his head to duck under acacia thorns. The ground was littered with leaves discarded from the sparse crowns of violet trees and the yellowed oval leaves of kuduberry. Ants crisscrossed his path along with the shadows of the branches that wavered above him. Scents wafted before his sensitive nose, though so many were alien to him. All he could identify was that of straw from the fields of grass all around them.

He stopped. On the ground before him, a paw print. A broad central blot with four toe impressions over the top of it. Each toe had a corresponding claw mark. His heart froze, pounding in his chest, as he remembered the warning of the dark wolf.

Claws are the mark of a carnivore.

Several more prints in the dirt. Claws upon each. He suddenly noticed them everywhere, and they were larger than the prints he made.

The massacred are abandoned to rot.

His bowels felt hot and loose. He took a deep breath to calm himself, and after a few minutes his heart was no longer pounding. Calm enveloped him and he took a deep breath.

Struck from the side, he was knocked to the ground before he realized he was under attack. His heart exploded with a machine gun thump.Panic set in as he rolled to a heap in dust. Scrabbling back to his feet, his claws clicked on the ground and gravel as he stood to face his enemy.

Blackthorn glared at him, a dark form that resembled a hole cut into the daytime.

"You never even heard me approach."

Blouvalk growled.

"Mewl at me all you wish. You tremble with fear, but creatures concealed in the veld should inspire greater fear still from you."

Blouvalk looked around in spite of himself.

"You are observant and clever. Do not waste your ability with your need to appear overconfident." He turned to leave, and spoke over his shoulder. "Those are cheetah tracks. They do not bother us." Blackthorn trotted away without another word.

As he padded his way back to the rest of the pack, he could sense Blouvalk behind him. Closer, then further, the scent of anger pouring off his fur.

Parting the tall grasses, he sighted the rest of the wolves resting under a plane tree. The round green crown shaded the wolves below, the white bark peeling like so many narrow sheets of paper from the broad trunk. Approaching Visarend, he opened his mouth to greet her, but was stopped by a hiss.

"*Never again.*" Blouvalk stalked past them and laid down elsewhere in the thick brush.

"The *bliksem* cannot even threaten properly." Blackthorn snorted after the wolf left them.

Visarend chuckled. "His rankling is understandable."

"How so?" He scoffed.

"Have you ever lost a position of leadership?"

"He was *your* leader?" Blackthorn was aghast. "That fool?"

"Well, he is the eldest of us, a member of the pack my mother joined. The rest of us were pups when we were all captured."

"Age does not imply wisdom."

"No, but being outside the family meant he would be the only mating partner possible."

Blackthorn looked into the bush where Blouvalk had disappeared.

"So now you see."

"I see he was as skilled at mating as he is at tracking."

Visarend batted his face with her paw, and he returned the playful gesture.

"Be patient with him as well. We must all work together to survive." Visarend purred. "There is only the Pack."

***

The afternoon came and went without a successful hunt. The wolves grumbled about their failure.

"Hunting skills take many seasons to master, and you have lost untold amounts of time behind the fences." Blackthorn rested on his side, panting. "The abilities will come."

"I hunger." Kleinsperwer rolled over, his legs in the air. "Or another animal has burrowed into my stomach."

"And you must become accustomed to these lean times. They are a part of living in the wild." He surveyed their field, and glanced toward the orange sun as it began to set on a burning horizon. "Nothing is promised. Each day is owned by none who traverse the bushveld."

Blouvalk sulked in the shade of a corkwood tree. He stared at a dung beetle that wrestled a ball of perfectly round elephant dung across the ground before him.

Blackthorn made his way over to the prone wolf, though he had no idea what to tell him.

Blouvalk looked up.

The dark wolf stared down at him for a moment before he grunted. "Well done today." He gave the wolf a nod, and returned to the rest of the pack where they rested in the sun.

A yellow-throated sandgrouse browsed for seeds in the grass, taking to wing with a deep *aw-AW!* It flew off toward the

121

nearest body of water. Crickets sawed as dusk overtook the land.

"Have you ever taken to marking your territory?" Blackthorn sat next to Visarend as she gave a wide yawn.

"From time to time along the fence line. There seemed to be little point." She smiled. "Strange, it seems so long ago. Another lifetime entirely."

"You should resume that habit. It can serve as a warning for hyenas that may otherwise stumble upon us in the dark."

"What other purpose would it serve?"

"Establishing a perimeter around a den. The threat implied can prevent conflict with other predators."

"A den." She sounded far away, her voice hollow and stumbling. "How could I possibly consider?"

"You may grow used to the notion in time." Blackthorn stretched, back arched, his hind end in the air.

"I know nothing of being a mother." Visarend shook her head.

"No mother does." He chuckled to himself. "Until they become one, and wonder why they did so. My mother never seemed to have enough of sleep, plagued as she was by a horde of pups that stampeded around the den."

"If only my mother was given time to teach me." She shook her head. "The way forward is obscured to me."

"You shall learn, in your own time. Curiosity, not instinct, is what makes our kind clever enough to survive. Ever seeking new tactics to employ against hunter or prey." He raked the ground with a foreclaw. "I have watched you. Thus far, you have been quite keen. Never are your eyes taken off a subject of interest, and all the same mindful of your own movements. Your speed is poor, due to your imprisonment.

And yet earlier today you nearly chased down a full grown impala." He prodded her with a forepaw. "Not from running fast, but running smart, adjusting your approach, and cutting into their movements, allowing your quarry to waste ground. Your only error was not to call for us to follow you."

"Why did you not come to help, then?"

"You did not bid me to do so." Blackthorn stared at the dirt.

"That is not my place."

"Quite the opposite, Visarend." He met her gaze. "You are the alpha female. And as such, the Pack is under your absolute charge. As am I."

"The alpha?" She furrowed her brow. "I could not possibly—"

"You must, and will." He laid his head on his forepaws. "You set the pace for the Pack, and hold the discipline. The first teacher of the young, and their last desperate defense. You decide where we explore for food, and come time to establish a den, your judgment will be the final one." Raising his head for a moment, he regarded Visarend. "It is the place of the female to command."

"As of now, my only desire is to vomit."

Blackthorn rolled to his side. "Then you will do fine. I have served many alphas, and the greatest among them shared the quality of considerable self-doubt."

"Self doubt and absolute power." Visarend slumped to the ground. "An odd combination."

"Utter conviction is for cretins and the cretins following them. With an uncertain but curious wolf as leader, against the Pack there will be no victor."

Visarend sighed, and stood. She walked around the others, and lightly sprayed urine on tufts of grass around them.

Rejoining Blackthorn, she laid down, and drifted into an uneasy sleep.

Eighteen

laws hit the ground lightly, without sound other than errant crunch of gravel. Each wolf held their heads low, ears flat, tails down in an unbroken silence. Dirt paths crossed their trail in an area that once had human habitation in the Caprivi strip of Namibia.

A metallic ding broke the quiet, and Blackthorn looked toward the source. Swartwou scraped a paw across the ground, revealing a rusted spent bullet casing. There were several along the path. Hidden in the grass were the ruined remains of an AK-47 rifle, wooden stock rotten, trigger guard gone, sliding bolt now fused in place over the decades it decayed there.

Fresh tire tracks were encountered on the dirt path, crossing over from one spot to the next, into the grasses. Through a line of trees the wolves could see a smallholding, a farm where a family grew subsistence crops. A boy muttered toward a group of goats and two cattle, tapping them gently with a stick.

"Give them a wide berth. They have no claws, but they do not need them."

The pack made a broad circle around the farm, across a field of beans and maize. As they skulked through the field, Blackthorn issued a sharp, short chirp.

A small paw mark, the size of a coin. Claws tipped the toe

pads over a central blot.

Visarend canted her head to the side, unsure what to think of the track. She looked up to see several small bodies rustling through the partially harvested crops. Dark brown to black stripes of fur rippled as the shapes ran, resembling a blanket dragged over rough ground. The troop of banded mongoose moved with purpose, systematically harvesting insects, rodents, anything on offer in the field. Individuals stopped to scratch at the ground, digging, moving on when nothing was found.

Blouvalk and Swartwou bounded off in the direction of the mongoose family. Kleinsperwer was close behind, and they twittered quietly to one another and split up.

Blackthorn stood next to Visarend and leaned close. "Watch and enjoy."

She glanced at him, his dark features softening into something like a smile.

The troop of banded mongoose halted, and one of the larger adults turned and issued a sharp squeaking whistle. The three painted wolves emerged from the maize stalks, encircling the troop.

At first, several of the banded mongoose attempted to flee, then retreated back to where the rest sat in a tight group. As the wolves edged closer, the small hunters formed a grey and black ball. Roiling with a constant machine like trill, they bunched so close together they would barely cover a dinner plate.

The wolves edged closer, step after step. Each sniffed this strange new discovery.

"They get too close, and you are in for a laugh." Blackthorn rumbled, his voice descending into a chuckle.

Swartwou brought his snout within a paw length to the furry

ball and he withdrew with a yelp. His snout was flecked with red.

A pointed grey nose poked out of the fur ball, mouth snarled wide with needle teeth displayed. With a hiss the head drew back into the ball. As one, then another wolf got too near, several other heads protruded towards the threat, sharp fangs deployed.

"A single beast, with so many mouths." He mused to himself. "Great hunters. This way, they can repel even a curious lion."

Visarend issued a sharp twitter in their direction, and the wolves left the purring ball of teeth and claws alone.

As they padded away, the grey ball suddenly stopped writhing, and separated into a dozen mongoose, bounding quickly from the wolf pack. The grey blanket fluttered across the field until the last bushy dark tail vanished in the grass.

Blackthorn gestured with his head to move away from the maize, casting about a wary eye. He visibly relaxed as the ordered rows of stalks were left behind, and replaced by the comforting randomness of grass and thicket. A scent lingered in the air, however, that put him on edge. The smell intensified as they walked, and he tensed, ears folded back, head held low.

The pack encountered an angry cloud of black flies. The buzzing intensified as they approached, as did the rich, sticky smell of decay.

"Stay back. Hyena and lion can be seen around carrion." Blackthorn crept closer to investigate.

A goat carcass had been slit open, intestines black and liquefied, and most of the meat had been cut away. He peered at the abdomen and flank. The skin, though drying and pulled tight, was not chewed open – the line was straight from neck to pelvis. He looked over through the thick veil of flies to see a dead lappet-faced vulture, lying on its side. The black plumage on its wings were undisturbed, and he could see no wounds.

"We leave this place."

"It could be food - this is how they would feed us." Blouvalk stepped closer.

"This meal would be your last." Blackthorn's twitter was sharp and final.

The wolves filed away from the poisoned goat carcass, and continued east.

The land opened into plains with fewer trees. Smallholding farms were rarely present, limited affairs with no machinery. These tiny plots seemed to barely exist, on the verge of reclamation by the wild.

***

The wolves rested at night under a stand of kuduberry, the broad arbor of wide branches hanging close to the ground. Blackthorn regarded the others laying in the shadows. His large black ears, rounded apart from the notch in one, swiveled to listen for distant threats. His dark muzzle wrinkled as he sniffed the scents carried on the breeze.

Visarend padded over to lay next to him, and they surveyed the field below the stand of kuduberry trees, a lawn of green broken by thornbrush and rocks.

"So many sights." Visarend spoke in a soft whisper. "They never seem to end." She raised her head from her forepaws, meeting Blackthorn's eyes. "Is the entire world this way?"

"The adventures are boundless, no matter one's familiarity with the veld." Blackthorn scratched behind his ear with a hind leg, and sat in the near darkness. He looked over to see the others resting in the shade. "To the world each day we are a stranger. Introduced anew, we rediscover its wonder."

"What is the oddest thing you have encountered?" She leaned closer.

"Four wolves in a cage, named for birds of prey."

Visarend leapt at him, knocking the old wolf over into a dusted heap. He rolled onto his back.

Her jaws were fixed on his forepaw, hazel eyes looking into his.

His obsidian eyes gazed back, his lips pulled back to reveal his fangs. He brought them gently to close upon her forepaw, and gripped it. It was enough to cause pain, but she did not recoil.

Her jaws closed tighter still on his paw. Enough to draw blood, but he did not pull away.

Night took the savanna, hunter and prey alike, enfolding all in darkness.

Nineteen

"The herd is breaking up," Blackthorn rasped. "This will be the last attack on this group."

"Would they disperse if hunted too vigorously?" Visarend paced. She looked down from the hill on the scattered pale brown shapes on the field below.

"They may." He walked forward from the crest of the hill, and the wolves filed behind him. "If you bleed a herd too often, it may move off."

"And other hunters may scent the blood river." Kleinsperwer chirped happily.

Blackthorn nodded. "Remember this place, and we may return another season to find our prey waiting for us."

As they padded through the brush, their pace quickened. Pulses pounded, and each began to salivate as the scent of impala permeated the air. Rustling filled their ears with sound as their bodies were brushed by sweet grass blades or scratched with acacia thorns.

A cough. A moment of restless quiet, and the field was awash with noise of alarm barks, hooves on hard ground, and the clattering of branches as the impala fled.

Fixed upon the hindquarters of an impala buck were hazel eyes, grim with determination. Below the eyes the face and muzzle were black, down to a brown ruff of fur around her throat. Her ears were folded back, head held low. Slender legs powered her forth, claws upon the grass covered soil.

"Patience, Visarend." The graveled voice trailed behind her, but she could hear it easily.

"So close - I can overtake him before we reach the thorn-brush." Her chest heaved with the effort.

"Wolves are not hares - we are coursers, not sprinters." He accelerated to her side, but seemed relaxed despite the fast pace. The grass field was dotted with broadleaf and acacia trees, but a line of dense knobthorn acacia lay ahead. This was cut by a dirt road far to their side, ruts stretching off to the horizon.

"He shall escape us." She watched the impala close the distance with the sedge, curved antlers bobbing as his strides carried him away.

"Perhaps. Charge straight through thicket." He rasped. "Thorns bloody me, but I have forgotten such trivial wounds."

Visarend suddenly broke away, running parallel to the line of brush, no longer following the antelope.

"Get back to—"

"Follow me." Her high pitched twitter cut off his protest as she ran at top speed. Her course curved away from the track of her prey, around a clump of short green spikethorn trees, and straight into the dirt road. The well worn track was a stripe of unruly grass bordered by parallel flats of mud and dirt. The deep indentations created by tires had not seen vehicles for some time.

Blackthorn pursued her quietly, his ears up and listening. Their paws struck the hard ground, scattering gravel as they powered swiftly down the road. The path twisted slightly as it swerved around larger silver clusterleaf trees, flat crowns providing shade. Unencumbered by thornbrush, they sped along the track.

"Listen." The wolves slowed. To one side they could hear crashing of branches. A thud and another snap, and the impala rocketed out of the sedge nearby. Sighting the predators, the impala continued its sprint down the road, followed closely by the hunters.

A kilometer passed as the hunt continued, the road opening up into a broad field. The wolves slowly closed the distance, and they could detect the labored breathing of their prey.

"Hyena!" Blackthorn growled.

On their flanks, two spotted hyena held station, keeping up with a tireless lope.

"Abandon the chase." He spat his words out, saliva dry with dust.

"I have him." Visarend practically sang this as she powered forward and clamped down on the impala's haunch.

Instinctively, Blackthorn did the same, but after biting deeply, he let the antelope go.

Visarend pulled, and the exhausted impala flopped to the ground. She dug into the belly to the rising sounds of *Whooo-oop!*

"Let it go." Blackthorn ruff-barked to her.

She did not answer, pulling open the abdomen and spilling the intestines on the earth.

A whooping hyena trotted close, and Visarend whirled about to snap her teeth in its face. The female hyena turned and ran, her hind end dragging close to the ground.

Visarend turned again to the impala, but scarcely was able to nibble on the liver before another hyena nipped her tail. Once again, she chased it away.

Blackthorn pursued another female, but saw more hyena coming, several answering the whooping call. The circle of hulking beasts drew closer, and ever smaller around them.

Before she tried to dive into the belly again, Blackthorn gripped her foreleg with his jaws.

"Enough – we yield this kill." They loped off and the hyena clan closed around the carcass, tearing it to pieces. A hoof went flying as fights began anew over the bounty.

"A fine chase, Visarend." He lapped her muzzle. "Your use of the road was clever in anticipating where it would go."

"All for nothing." She fumed, her teeth glittering. *"Nothing!"* The hyenas paused at her growl, but resumed devouring their meal.

"So much we do is for naught. A day, several, a season lost to no benefit. Grow accustomed to loss, for it is our life to the very end."

"You are *kak* at encouragement, Blackthorn."

"That our *Volk* draw breath upon the veld, one day after the next, ever threatening to bring litter after litter of pups to our world—to endure is our triumph." Another lap on her muzzle, and he relished her taste. "And you survived another day, becoming that much more formidable a hunter."

She gave another forlorn look to the hyenas before turning back the way they had come.

"Learning comes with time, Visarend." He looked toward the kill and saw a familiar face.

A hyena watched him from afar. The male stood with hunched shoulders, tail tucked low between hindquarters as he looked toward the feast with anxiety. One of his ears was notched from a long ago battle. Kreun and the wolf shared a moment of recognition, before he bounded off around the kill, searching in vain for an unguarded scrap.

"Learning comes for us all."

***

A medley of chattering noise came from the giraffe thorn acacia above, where a black bird with an orange bill surveyed the wolf pack below. The male buffalo weaver stood amid a large untidy mass of thorny sticks, roughly woven together into what was barely recognizable as a nest. Though it appeared a mess, the sticks were carefully chosen to provide a chaotic barrier of thorns, set to impale snakes or other intruders. A female prepared an inner chamber of softer straw.

"The hunting will be precarious in the season to come." Blackthorn rested in the shade beneath the acacia tree, and watched a beetle trundle past his paws. "We are in lands controlled by hyena."

"What of it?" Kleinsperwer rolled onto his back.

"Hyena shadow our movements, and steal our kills. As they have today."

"We may have chased them off." Visarend groused.

"It is important to know when to quit a hunt. By felling that impala, you took the risk of injury only to feed their numbers. And one must know when to flee." His throat rumbled. "Hyena are unavoidable, and are quite cunning. And there may be worse coming for us."

"What would that be?" Swartwou paced over some fallen seed pods.

"Lion may soon follow."

"And you will instruct us in how to run away?" Blouvalk lay

134

with head resting on forepaws, his stomach growling.

"You may mock the notion, but that is precisely what I will teach."

"I did not realize we needed lessons to set one paw before the other." Blouvalk stood and trotted away from the tree, off into the brush.

Blackthorn sighed, and closed his eyes.

"Hunger makes him coarse, Blackthorn." Visarend prodded him with her snout.

"Coarser." Swartwou padded past them. "He was always this." He sniffed about the grass, finding nothing more than flies.

Blackthorn lay with his eyes closed for a while, listening to the quiet of the evening. The squeaking *kwaraa - kwaraa* call of a purple roller reached his ears from a nearby tree. He opened his eyes to see Visarend staring at him.

"Still here. Despite your wishes." She managed a smile, exposing her fangs.

"What would that mean?"

"At times such as these you miss the safety of solitude."

"Isolation is hardly safe." He rolled to his side and closed his eyes again.

"Perhaps safety is not the right word. The comfort." She nodded. "The comfort of not needing to see to another's well being."

"This has been an adventure. I have become another creature entirely." Kleinsperwer crawled closer to them. "Even if we are no better fed."

"A painted wolf is never *fed*." Blackthorn opened his dark eyes again. "A painted wolf *kills*."

"That was what I intended to say." Kleinsperwer lowered

his head.

"We would all do well when you cease *intending* to be a wolf." His eyes were shut again.

Kleinsperwer grunted, and was on his feet, padding off into the brush. Swartwou joined him.

"You advised patience, Blackthorn. You must be patient with all of us." Visarend intoned. He could hear her footpads on the ground.

"I was never much of a teacher. Perhaps I—" He opened his eyes to see she had vanished. Standing up, he worked to ignore the aches in his joints that had set in the previous year. He had long since stopped waiting for them to resolve.

Laying down again, he sighed, his exhale giving rise to a puff of dust on the ground.

His thoughts drifted, far from where he lay, to a land of the distant north. Images swam into his head.

Broad open fields of green. Far beyond the horizon, a forest of teak wood. Further to the east scattered *miombo* woodland of *Brachystegia* trees. The edge of this was marked with scattered *Mnondo* trees, reaching high with branches giving off more branches that terminated in globular green crowns that seemed to buttress the sky. The season was dry, but the plains were a vibrant green from water delivered by a *dambo* river. Termite mounds, thousands of them, covered the limitless plain.

The images drifted across Blackthorn's mind, eyes still closed, as he sighed.

Toward the edge of the plain where it transitioned to *miombo* forest, an ancient termite mound hundreds of years old supported the growth of a jackalberry tree. The grey trunk held up a round canopy of elliptical leaves, bunched with green fruits turning yellow as they ripened. Browsers, baboons, and even jackals coveted these sweet berries, but none dared approach.

Near the base of the tree was a hole, dug years ago by an aardvark. That architect was no longer present, but the hole had been repurposed by another. Hunters clad in gold and black lounged in the shade of the tree. Two adult wolves were in a den below the ground. The only sound was a plaintive whisper.

Do not disappoint me.

Blackthorn opened his eyes to see the dark—he had fallen asleep without realizing it. There was a crashing sound coming through the brush. Multiple bodies were incoming.

He stood, head down, ears flat, pulling his lips back with a flash of white.

Wind wafted a scent toward him, and he relaxed. The rich musk of painted wolf, at once reassuring to him, preceded the pack as they exited the undergrowth. Four bounded toward him, ecstatic, smiling in that way only wolves can smile.

Swartwou nearly ran headlong into him, muttering something though his mouth was full.

"Success!" He bellowed, releasing his prize.

A hare dropped onto Blackthorn's head. Its mangled body slid to the ground before him.

"Blouvalk killed it." Visarend spoke with pride, and was on her hind legs boxing the other male.

"The stalking was none too easy in the dusk." He lay down next to Blackthorn, one forepaw folded over the other. "Eat well."

Blackthorn regarded the hare.

"Are you not hungry?" Kleinsperwer twittered, his hind end

gyrating with excitement. "This hunt was for you."

He exhaled heavily, eventually giving a nod. "I thank you."

The other wolves shared glances before padding off some-where in the dark to rest. Once he was alone, Blackthorn began to pull at the hide of the rabbit. In the pit of his stomach, a painful knot burned. Despite the nutrition and the savor of the meat, that knot continued to burn throughout the night.

Twenty

Calm in the meadow at daybreak, the water suspended in the air was just beginning to alight on stalks of grass. The dew sparkled with the first rays of sun, casting innumerable rainbows over the ground. After the scattered rains of the night, clumps of mushrooms had arisen from the fertile earth. Flat, scaly white umbrellas stood between clumps of grass, the white parasol mushrooms filled with spores that would rise off the caps like smoke throughout the day. They would take advantage of these, the last sparse rains of late autumn.

Katydid calls receded with the dawn, and mosquitoes roused from their night torpor. Antelope were already up and about, the business of crunching grass into a somewhat more digestible paste never truly finished.

A yellow billed kite shook its body with a rapid shiver, throwing off moisture. Painstaking effort was put into examining every individual feather for stability, combing out excess dust or parasites, and each feather set into place to form a perfect aerodynamic surface. This would be crucial to flight, and they must be ready. After all, there were wolves about.

Blackthorn was the first awake, as usual, and set to awakening the rest.

"On your feet!" He prodded each of the sleeping forms. "The hunt awaits, and we shall not keep it waiting."

Each blinked away the sleep, and were quickly on their paws. Kleinsperwer wavered a moment, angled his head down, and shook his body back and forth. Dust filled the air and showered to the ground as his large ears slapped against his skull. Blouvalk did the same. As though a switch had been tripped, they burst into excited twittering, one greeting another with rolled tongues and enthusiastic lapping of muzzles and faces. Blackthorn went from one to the next with greetings. Visarend did the same, pausing to think of whom had yet to accept her exuberant tongue. Bounding about in circles, colliding with bodies, each wolf of the pack counted as they greeted a pack mate.

One... two... three... four... five.

In their excitement, the wolves defecated and urinated all over the clearing where they had slept, a rich odor that would declare their presence to friend and enemy alike. Visarend urinated on a bald patch of ground. After she finished, Blackthorn sidled up to her, and took care to urinate on the same spot. She gave him a subtle smile, a flash of white fangs that he answered in kind.

Blackthorn bolted away with a steady lope, followed by the others.

"The rains are becoming more sporadic. Autumn is lumbering toward winter."

"What are those things?" Visarend indicated a herd ahead of them on the vast open plain.

The field was full of them. Stark black and white stripes, vertical on the robust bodies, down to the white of lower leg that ended in heavy hooves. Up the broad necks, the stripes continued into a stout brush of a mane that stood on end, up to handsome faces that regarded the wolves with mild curiosity. The zebra milled as they munched down on the sweet grass, ripping bunches at a time, grinding it down with powerful molars.

Females, with slightly smaller bodies and less pronounced muscle continued their grazing. As the wolf pack drew the notice of the zebra herd, the females began to snort loudly. From the harem a tall stallion emerged, glaring at the wolf pack. He planted a hoof on the ground, the reverberation reaching the small paws of the wolves half a kilometer away. The impact resounded in their frame, and four of the wolves looked at one another with alarm.

"We will not attack *that*?" Visarend yittered.

"No, we will not." Blackthorn snuffed. "It takes a special touch to bring down a zebra. The foreteeth of those creatures go through bone like water."

"They do not seem to fear us." Blouvalk coughed.

"My father hunted them." Blackthorn mused. "My mother spoke of it with pride. He was able to charge them, where they stood proud, and would seize them by the upper lip with his jaws."

"He *what*?" Swartwou sounded aghast.

"With his fangs dug into the nose and lip, even a powerful stallion bowed low, and fell to the killing bites of the hunters under his command." He gestured with his head, and the wolves padded with care around the herd. "Stories passed from one generation to the next told of wolf packs that numbered as great as this herd. They cut down buffalo and wildebeest, and kept lions at bay. Dozens of wolves, ranging to the very horizon. And we could find signs of wolves that held territories beyond even that. Our world *was* the world entire."

"What is our world? I once thought it ended at a fence." Visarend lapped his muzzle.

"It still does. More distant fences than yours, perhaps." He glared at the ground before him. "There are times I wonder if one should forsake these stories." Blackthorn rasped, seeming to swallow his words. "Do they still have a purpose?"

"Indeed. The words will strengthen the wolves to come with the knowledge of hunters long since dead. And for your pups yet to greet the veld."

Blackthorn stopped and glanced her way.

Another smile, and she raced ahead. The pack trotted forth as the hunt commenced.

***

"This is closer to our abilities." Blackthorn regarded a small herd of impala through an opening between knobthorn acacia trees. Nearby, a white bellied sunbird called with a rapid series of trills, flashing its iridescent green back before taking flight.

"Would we not learn more from hunting a different antelope?" Blouvalk scratched his ear with a hind leg.

"Yes, though impala can be a source of learning throughout life. No two hunts are the same, and they will not allow you to forget this." The dark wolf padded through the trees, head low, ears flat. He twittered his instructions to the others.

The four spread out to one side, and Blackthorn slowed his pace. The others ranged further out, curving around the herd in a large C, threading between smaller trees as they drew close. They took note of each other's positions, together a single weapon. Visarend was the very tip of the whip, while

Blackthorn crouched at the handle.

The wolves, apart from Blackthorn, raced into the herd.

Several barking coughs erupted, and the herd took action at once. The healthiest among them leapt into the high *pronk*, others stayed on the ground and hammered with hooves to gain distance.

Visarend curved into the group, and twittered her commands. The other wolves turned toward the impala, forming a rapidly moving wall.

Bold impala leapt into a *pronk* straight at them, one shooting past Blouvalk's head. These were disregarded.

The herd was driven in Blackthorn's general direction, to a point in front of him. The dark wolf then broke cover and headed toward that point.

As he powered forward, he noticed a part of the group moving more slowly. One impala ran with the others, but was losing ground with every step of a hind leg. That leg carried an open wound, deeply scarred and naked of fur.

Blackthorn released a sharp peal of chirping, and the other four bore down on his location. He accelerated to maximum speed, fell in behind the injured antelope, and swiftly closed the distance. A grip on the flank slowed the impala. A release, and Blackthorn felt the presence of the others around him. He slowed and watched as the other four wolves each gripped the antelope, struggling to maintain hold. The buck pulled away each time, another bleeding wound on his haunches each time he evaded. Finally, Blouvalk took hold of a hind leg, and closed his jaws with a wet snap. With the limb broken, the impala flailed, and collapsed.

As Blackthorn observed, the wolves that so recently had escaped from a life in a cage pulled the impala in two, spilling the intestines and killing it in less than a minute.

"Well done, all of you." Blackthorn lapped each of their muzzles with affection. "Your skill is growing each day."

None of them answered, busy as they were ripping away hide and burying themselves in the abdomen and chest to gulp down organs and muscle. After several mouthfuls, Blouvalk pulled away and laid down next to the carcass. Swartwou did the same, his entire upper half coated in blood and gore. Kleinsperwer trotted off and managed to climb atop a felled tree, balanced carefully on the horizontal trunk.

"Keep eating, all of you." Blackthorn grumbled.

"This impala, if you have noticed, will not be going any-where." Blouvalk muttered, his eyes already closed.

Swartwou laughed, his mouth wide as he rolled onto his back.

Before Blouvalk realized it, Blackthorn had latched his jaws onto his shoulder. His body was jerked roughly onto its feet, and he bared his jaws toward the older wolf.

"Are you hoping for a fight?" Blouvalk hissed.

"Get back to eating, and you will not find out."

"I am not under your bidding, jackal." The younger wolf bared his fangs.

"No. You are under *mine*."

Blouvalk turned about to see Visarend, fangs dripping crimson, creeping toward him.

"Return to the feast, *domkop*, or I will dine upon *you*." Visarend opened her jaws wider, prepared to deliver on her threat.

Blouvalk glanced from her to Blackthorn, and grudgingly resumed eating. The others went back to devouring meat, with only Blouvalk pausing to check his hindquarters from time to time.

The only sound, once the kill had been made, was the occasional twitter and whine from one of the wolves, and the tearing of flesh from bone, smacking, and swallowing. The impala herd had moved away, but not far as their enemies would not be hungry for some time.

Yellow billed kites swooped in, one after the next, their dull brown plumage present as a flutter. Moments after one would land, its yellow skinned feet dug in with black talons, a gold beak would rend a piece of exposed muscle away, and it would take to wing, the theft taking less than a second.

Kleinsperwer stopped eating to ruff-bark, and leapt at one of the kites. His teeth clicked on empty air. Two other kites did the same, and after failing to stop them, he gave up the pursuit.

The snap of a branch was heard as Visarend dragged one half of the impala while tearing away the heart.

The kites fluttered off and did not return.

Quiet again, punctuated only by ripping and tearing of meat.

"*RUN WITH ME!*" Blackthorn ruff-barked, the edge of panic in his voice. The abrupt call brought a spasm of fear within them all.

The other four scattered from the carcass, glancing about.

Visarend felt Blackthorn brush past her, a twitter rising in his throat. She looked over her shoulder at him to see a bounding figure, golden, muscular, powerful forelegs powering forward on silent footpads. A tufted tail swished behind the brutal figure that bore down on them. Dilated pupils in dark yellowed eyes were fixed upon her, jaws slightly agape, exposing conical fangs.

"*LION!*" Blackthorn howled, an alien sound to their ears. The wolves bolted, close on his hindquarters, and only then did they hear the crunching of grass underfoot from the lion pursuing them.

Sounds. Breaking branches, paws no longer hiding, thumping on the ground.

More lion than one, now grunting sounds on the verge of a guttural roar.

"Faster - we outpace them!" Blackthorn rasped, his chest heaving as they sprinted at maximal speed. Rather than leap over brush, they dove straight through walls of thorns, ignoring the spears that tore at their fur and skin.

The grunting grew more distant, the branches breaking further from them. As suddenly as it began, the sounds of pursuit stopped altogether.

Blackthorn whirled about, and the pack stopped running as they saw his body relax. His nostrils flared, chest pumping, ears erect and swiveling about in search of sounds.

"They have given up." His graveled voice ended in a snarl. He exhaled with some relief, but he remained tensed. Padding for a short distance, he leapt onto a dirt rise that was once a termite mound. He saw four lions pulling at what remained of the impala carcass.

Returning to the wolves, he could see them sharing fearful glances with one another.

"That," Blackthorn rumbled, as he passed Blouvalk, "Is why we kill quickly, tear the body into pieces, and eat in great haste. Wait here."

He crept back toward the kill, his gaze not leaving the pride. Casting a look around him, he did not detect the presence of any other lions in the vicinity. He felt the breeze tousling his dark fur, blowing steadily into his face. He emerged from the thornbrush, watching from the shade where the lions fed.

Only grunting and the sounds of ripping flesh reached his ears. The lionesses sat close, waiting patiently for the approval of the male before eating. He continued to devour the remains of the impala, a rattling purr his only commentary.

Suddenly, the breeze shifted, blowing from the wolf's tail toward his head, in the direction of the pride. At once, the male looked up from the kill. His blond mane rustled in the breeze.

Blackthorn tensed as the male stood, and took a few steps away from the impala. Pale yellow eyes locked on his.

"*Gevaar.*" The lion purred, his name reverberating in the wild dog's ears. The lionesses glanced from the wolf to Gevaar, and quickly began to gnaw meat from the carcass.

The male returned his glare to the impala and growled, prompting the females to yield, retreating a few meters away. He resumed eating, ignoring Blackthorn.

He made his way back to the pack.

"Are we in danger?" Kleinsperwer twittered.

"No. Oddly enough, we are not." He glanced back toward the carcass, the lionesses still waiting their turn. "As far as lions go, not that aggressive. I have seen that *oke* before. Normally I would still be running, lions in pursuit." He grunted. "No matter. You have learned from this encounter?"

"Indeed we have." Blouvalk grinned. "And we have learned well."

Twenty-One

A trilling *prrrr* was issued by a small male black and white bushshrike, gripping the branch of a giraffe thorn acacia. The answer *eeeuu* came from the female next to him. They traded these calls in the morning, as the slight chill of night passed.

"Stamina, Swartwou. You must push yourself." Visarend prodded his golden back with her snout.

"Wait on it. I will be stronger tomorrow." He turned over, his hind legs splayed in the air.

"Your promise yesterday. Apathetic oaf." She licked his muzzle to stimulate him awake, practically shoving her nose into his open mouth, but he turned over and would not move.

"We must press on. No doubt we are still in that pride's territory." Blackthorn padded into the clearing where the others lazed. "I see no lion prints, but when those appear, it is often too late."

"Any impala herd is far off." Blouvalk stood, nose in the air. The strip of white fur along his back was obscured by dirt. "A hunt does not appear to be the order of the day."

"Even so, one must patrol." Blackthorn prodded Kleinsperwer to his feet.

The pack roused in spite of themselves, and padded off after the dark wolf. Their path carried them back to the west.

"I am still acquainting myself with directions, having had no need for them." Blouvalk jogged alongside Blackthorn. "But are we going back the way we came?"

"Yes." He shook his head. "This is the challenge we have."

"Going in a circle?"

"Finding one's place." His lean legs drove forth tirelessly, claws clicking on rocks. "We were drawing nearer to permanent water."

Blouvalk furrowed his brow.

"Right. You do not know water sources." Blackthorn cleared his throat, suppressing his annoyance. "We are entering the dry winter, when the rains slow or cease. So pools of water recede or dry entirely. Permanent water can be found by rivers or lakes, and we were nearing a river catchment area." He waited until Blouvalk nodded his understanding. "Where there is water in abundance, you will find prey in abundance. And the predators follow them. Lions will seize the best lands—always."

"Can we not fight?" Blouvalk sneezed as he walked.

"Not with our numbers." He furrowed his brow. "That male lion was a strangely forgiving one, however."

"Something to consider." Blouvalk grunted. "So we need only move outside their territory?"

"We must also worry of hyena pressure." Blackthorn glowered. "They are ever searching, ranging wide for the good of their clan. Hunting on their own, but more than pleased to take your hard-earned kill. Or kill *you*."

"They would eat us?"

"Without hesitation. And hyenas are always hungry. The males are not as aggressive as the females. They are, however, eager to please their matriarch." He practically spat this out with contempt, remembering Kreun.

"And so we must keep running." Blouvalk grumped.

"Until we encounter humans, with their fences, farms, and disease." His twitter became more agitated. "They are ever waiting to cut us down for their amusement."

"You sound as though weary of this life."

Blackthorn turned to meet his gaze, anger rising within. He grunted before padding ahead of the rest, grateful for the quiet.

***

"These lands are marginal." Visarend surveyed the bushveld below them from a ridge of porous rock. "We have travelled for days without encountering a herd of any kind."

"The land is meager – as is the season." Blouvalk raised his head, surveying the land below a furrowed brow.

Further from rivers, they found the veld increasingly dry. The rains had failed earlier than usual, and the days grew hotter as another drought worked its way across southern Africa. The sweet grass by now was more desiccated, no longer with fresh growth as the nearing of winter brought on a state closer to suspended animation. Smaller river tributaries dried out. The wolf pack filed down from the ridge into the thornbrush, and through a stand of trees.

The *miombo* wood was absent of sound. Leaves had begun to fall, cushioning the forest floor. Though the branches were still heavy with greenery, the deep of the dry season would bring the shedding of leaves to reduce water loss. Once entirely denuded, the *Brachystegia* trees would endure the hard times. The winds blow, and the worn wood creaked, and the trees would stand in infinite patience. In the leaf litter below, beetles and tree cockroaches would forage for what nutrient remained, unless fire raged through the dry undergrowth. The arid winter would be still and quiet, but for the occasional foray of an antelope or the buzz of carrion flies.

A month before the return of the rains, on unknown signal the *Brachystegia* trees would burst into a riot of coppers, reds, and pinks. The young leaves would appear as if a fire was consuming the *miombo* woodland, resembling death in the forest's rebirth. The patter of rain upon leaf in spring would reveal the lie, as the forest yielded to fresh green, and the crowns of each tree would cover the returning grazing animals in cool shade.

For now, however, the forest was in the grip of the dry season, and only those built to weather the change would endure.

Several younger trees had been pushed over, the cracked trunks exposing sharp splinters and drying vascular wood pointed in accusing spires to the sky. The bent and broken crowns were crushed on the ground, and all foliage within reach was eaten. Round shapes had been pressed into the dust, hundreds of them, stamped in a broad swath toward the nearby forest.

"Elephants were here." He examined the ground as they emerged on the other side of the stand of trees. "I am only finding larger prey that is beyond our grasp. Migration is underway."

"Migration to what?" Visarend wondered.

A sudden groan jolted the wolves, and they padded away from the source. From the edge of the *miombo* forest the groan continued, a steady thrum released from a titanic grey body that strode out of the trees. With the sheer size of the matriarch elephant, one would expect a raucous noise. Once her groan stopped, however, she moved in near silence. Each step of her four meter frame was cushioned by broad feet on dusty ground. The tail, ending in a tuft of grey hair, extended away from the body, ears fanned out as she sighted the wolves. The heavy head shook back and forth, ears flapped against the skull like burlap against stone. Her gait resembled an enraged boxer, head canting back and forth, ivory tusks chipped and worn, copper eyes flashed in anger at the presence of a challenger.

Behind the matriarch three other female elephants strode from the wood along with an adolescent bull. Two smaller calves followed them with awkward confidence, stumbling against one of the younger females. A mature cow brought up the rear, just younger than the matriarch, ever watchful of the young.

"Be on your guard." Blackthorn intoned.

"Your warning is hardly necessary." Kleinsperwer gasped. "The size of those things—the very hills have grown legs." He gawped, his jaw hanging open as he panted in the heat.

"They remind me of buildings that humans built in the town." Visarend chirped, her tongue lolled out.

"They do not move like buildings." Blackthorn's twitter was more excited than agitated, and he spun about as he took in the position of the pack and the elephant. "Nothing, however, is as swift as the *wolf*."

As the four of them watched, Blackthorn raced off toward the mother elephant.

"Has he gone mad?" Visarend cried.

The towering elephant lowered her great head and charged, and the distance between elephant and wild dog shrank to nothing. The trunk whipped aside, and she struck toward the dark wolf with a tremendous sweep designed to crush his rib cage in an instant.

Blackthorn banked to the side and rounded the giant, twittering as he loped.

The elephant blasted a trumpet call, advancing on the wolf, but Blackthorn was already scampering away, as light on his feet as the butterflies that fluttered about the clearing. The other female elephants watched from a distance, guarding the two calves.

Blackthorn tensed, hunched down, then took off running from the matriarch as she charged again, and took a wide circle around his adversary. He seemed to float through the air as he bounded up to the wolf pack.

"You seek death with this nonsense?" Blouvalk ruff-barked.

Blackthorn's jaw was wide, tongue lolled out, teeth on display. *"There is more to the wild than death, my friends."* His eyes flashed, and his brow furrowed, but his grin widened. "Run with me, Kleinsperwer!" He dashed away as she neared them, and Kleinsperwer lunged forward, both tearing across the clearing.

As the gold, black, and white hunters powered through the grasses, another female elephant trumpeted her anger and charged toward them. The two stayed wide of her trunk, making a great loop around the elephant herd. As they moved further away, a high peal erupted above all the noise. It could only have come from Blackthorn as he howled his joy to the wolves, to the day, and to the wild itself.

Visarend sprinted off, followed closely by Swartwou, and finally Blouvalk, joining the dark wolf as they ran circles around the angry mother elephant.

Another trumpeting blast was released as the matriarch of

the herd chased Visarend, and she quickly raced away from the threat. Dust rose around the heavy cylindrical grey legs of the elephant as she glowered at the small hunters around her. Ears larger than the wolves themselves flapped forward in warning.

The rest of the cows and the adolescent bulls resisted joining the fray, staying close to the pair of calves, sensing a lack of danger from the pack. Visarend looked back, took a turn, and ran back toward the herd, squatting low on the ground, ears high, white tip of her tail high in the air, limbs poised at the ready.

The matriarch hesitated, lurching one way, then another, now knowing there was no threat other than to her pride. She swung her trunk again, missing Kleinsperwer by a body length.

"The sparrowhawk flies!" Kleinsperwer chirped, leaping and spinning about in a full circle before coming down on his springing paws.

The wolves danced on the veld, ignoring all else around them. A martial eagle gripped a nearby half-dead acacia tree by a naked branch, watching the commotion. Red-crested korhaan birds kept their distance, browsing for seeds in the grasses further away. Their nondescript mottled brown and white plumage blended in with the dried grasses.

Kleinsperwer collided with Blackthorn as he spun about to face the mother elephant again.

"I am of a mind to keep this one." Kleinsperwer panted, jaw gaping.

"Keep this giant *oke*?" Blackthorn chuckled.

"As we were kept. Would that we all could play with an elephant." He raced away, to the very foot of the matriarch as she charged forth to skewer him. The charge was in vain as Kleinsperwer deftly leapt aside.

One of the calves gave a high-pitched blast from his trunk as he noticed Swartwou jogging toward him. The calf started to trot out toward the wolf, but was stopped with a resolute low pitched rumble from his mother. The calf turned back toward his mother, and reluctantly left the wolf behind.

The great matriarch issued a long groan of her own, and glared at Blackthorn. She turned around, and lumbered back toward the rest of the herd, now forming a column.

The wolves padded away from the departing elephants to watch.

The grey giants continued their march from the forest. The matriarch took the lead and they filed away across the grass plain, moving mostly in quiet apart from an errant high-pitched trumpet blast from a calf.

With graceful speed, the elephants kept in a disciplined line. Mothers hurried their offspring along, as the young ones occasionally drifted from the herd to examine some new discovery. The young were flanked by slightly younger adults, ever cautious and scanning the horizon. One by one they disappeared through a cut of acacia trees, leaving the clearing in silence.

The dark wolf padded back to the rest of the pack, mouth open in a pant.

"Elephants are always good for a *jol.*"

"*Yoh!* That big *oke* might have run you through, Kleinsper-wer." Swartwou lapped his muzzle.

"They were not even close to the sparrowhawk." He shook his head, deterring the biting flies.

Blackthorn sighed. "Our frolic is over, and the search continues."

***

Stout hind legs stepped over rocks amid the sparse weed undergrowth. They carried a figure clad entirely in a cascade of brown and blond shields. The small pointed head held two small black eyes and a sensitive nose. Flat shield plates started just behind the head, growing larger across the elongated back and broad flat tail. The plates were a derivative of hair, but were strong and deflected even the sharpest of claws. The pangolin walked on hind legs alone, smaller forelegs held up as it trundled along the ground. It paused at the base of a termite mound and sniffed. He did not pause for long, as the ancient mound had died out hundreds of years ago, the three meter bulbous monolith pointing to the sky in mute commemoration of its long dead creators.

The pangolin hurried along into denser arid shrub as its nose detected the pungent smell of wolf, though it was not concerned. Simply rolling into a ball would deter any hungry predator.

"We may rest here." Blackthorn laid down next to the empty termite mound, sniffing it closely first to ensure no other animals had taken up residence. He looked to the sky, now bruised with an angry purple as dusk approached.

"Have we made another circle today?" Blouvalk eased himself to the ground, muscles aching from their now constant movement.

"Yes." Visarend twittered.

"Would not migration be quicker in a straight line, Blackthorn?"

"The idea is to swing around a large area, and try to catch the scent of something within that circle." He ran his tongue

156

over a wound on his flank, the deep bite of an acacia thorn still healing. "Should we detect a signal, we close the circle."

"We are getting closer to a human settlement." Kleinsperwer's snout was in the air. "Ash. There it is again."

"Your nose is a sharp one, sparrowhawk." Blackthorn rasped. "Humans are always burning something."

"One could say we have gotten to know them well over the seasons that passed." Kleinsperwer's tail whapped against a rock where he lay.

Swartwou thumped down on top of Kleinsperwer, who groaned under the weight.

"Should we go further in a line to a new area, Blackthorn?" Visarend yawned.

"Perhaps, but if we go much further, we will reach farms."

"Farms?" Kleinsperwer shrugged off Swartwou's weight. "And people?"

"Always people near the farms. They do not abandon their lands."

"Maybe there is food to find." His white tipped tail swished. "Wrapped hulks of meat waiting to be taken. Is that what farms do – make giant pieces of meat?"

"No. Maybe." Blackthorn shook his head. "What does it matter?"

"Lined up pieces of meat in a building." He licked his chops. "They make them for wolves, and for their dogs. Do they get the meat from animals? The big things with horns on the farms we passed?"

"Perhaps, sparrowhawk." Blackthorn yawned wide, lips pulled back showing serrated teeth, pink tongue rolled out. "They kill things all day, and each day for their meat." He closed his jaws with a click. "Things like cattle—the big *okes* with the horns—like goats. Like us."

Their subdued twittering quieted.

"Some of the farms we saw were small." Kleinsperwer offered. "Not many people about."

"They need only one to summon more." Blackthorn swiveled his ears, listening to the sounds of the dusk. "Communication is their great weapon."

"We can outrun elephants and lions, and perhaps humans as well." Kleinsperwer was on his paws. "We are a song upon wind, Blackthorn."

"A what?"

"Swiftly we hunt, weaving through the trees like the whispering wind. We leave behind the blood river as we *trek*, and none knew we were there. Only the wind marks our passage with a rattle of thorns in the branches."

"Trees speaking?" The dark wolf chuckled. "The others are liable to think you have the Sickness, speaking that way."

"He has always been eccentric." Visarend chirped. "The wolves are birds, to fly from their cage, the trees and rocks move, and the wind speaks to us all." She smiled despite the growling of her stomach. "Perhaps the boredom of where we lived since we were pups got the better of him. The mind occupies itself somehow."

"In other ways, that place got the better of us all." Blouvalk mused.

"Indeed." Blackthorn grimaced as the gnawing in his belly grew more intense. "And you plan to raid this farm for its vast supply of meat?"

"Or stay there and keep the farm for myself." Kleinsperwer straightened his posture, head high.

The other wolves twittered their high pitched laughter at

this. Even Blackthorn chortled in spite of himself.

"A better hunt has not been on offer." Kleinsperwer whined.

"I cannot argue with that, sparrowhawk." Blackthorn shook his head. "You underestimate humans, however. They occupy the world with an insatiable hunger, and regard the wild with malevolence."

"They hunt us, same as we hunt, I suspect." Blouvalk mused.

"There is more that moves them, which I do not understand." Blackthorn rumbled. "Their greed is legion. There is only them... and the rest of the world is in their way."

"We saw no cruelty from them while in our cage." Swartwou laid down.

"I caution against considering this. There is little good that will come from challenging humans." He angled his head to Visarend, his dark eyes regarding her. "Only your matriarch can decide."

The other three wolves looked to her anxiously. The breeze tousled their fur, a touch of cool in the air as a dried leaf blew past them. A gurgle in Blouvalk's stomach was the only other sound.

"We raid the farm."

Twenty-Two

A goat perched atop a squat termite mound. All four of its narrow hooves were close together, covering an area as small as a teapot. Its brown ears drooped over a dirty white neck, sharp incisors gnawing upon a sprout of grass from an opening in the mound. The teeth ripped free a shock of green, slowly pulled into the mouth as the molars ground it into a paste. Small horns curved to the rear, white as chalk. The body was marked with splotches of brown and white fur, with streaks of mud.

"Should be no problem, that." Blouvalk muttered, straining to repress the desire to strike. "Is there a weapon hidden from our sight in this adversary?"

"Our true adversaries will soon reveal themselves." Blackthorn gave a lowing growl, almost ultrasonic. He peered beyond the goat toward a hut far distant. The hut was of mud walls, as high as a human at the shoulder, with grass thatching for a roof in the shape of a cone. Some of the thatch had been blown away by winds, revealing a jagged hole and the supporting poles underneath. No smoke rose from the roof, and no humans, big or small, were present in the clearing before the hut. A small bundle of straw tied to a short stick with twine rested against the mud wall by an opening covered with a blanket. The area in front of the doorway was swept clean of leaves or litter. A single pink plastic washbasin lay next to the doorway.

"None are present." Blackthorn sniffed the air. "So many strange smells linger." His nostrils flared, his nose sensitive for even the faintest of odors. "Dominating the air is the scent of flowers, but... so strange. The flowers are all wrong."

"Soap." Kleinsperwer wagged his tail with a swish. "It is a thing they use."

"They use flowers?" Blackthorn's brow arched again. He was unsure how much to believe of this.

"It smells like flowers, but I suspect it is something they make to resemble flowers. Their clothes get soaked in it."

"So they reek less?" Blackthorn mused. "The few times I have come close they stink of fear and, well, other things." Odors of burned meat, sweat, cigarettes and the astringent of beer came to mind, though he had no name for them.

"No, they smell just as badly. They only want their clothes to smell like flowers."

"Nonsense, all of it." Blackthorn growled. "Stay here." He padded off away from the hut, disappearing into the brush, leaving the four alone.

"They like to mimic the things of the wild." Kleinsperwer stood taller as he peered at the mud structure, one paw held in the air as though to take a step. "Their home is like a termite mound. They smell of flowers, they create fields near their dwellings of plants they manipulate. Even the sounds of our world they remake somehow. Do you remember the men who walked the length of our cage?"

Blouvalk thought for a moment and nodded.

"They carried a small box that howled and barked. It sounded like something between a human and an animal." He looked back at the others, wondering how else to describe a radio.

"And what was our cage meant to be?" Visarend twittered.

"They were making a wild place for us."

"A small one, compared to how far we have travelled." Visarend scratched behind her ear with a hind leg. Her lightly colored coat of white and gold seemed to glow in the sun, broken only by splotches of black.

"Perhaps it would have been bigger over time. Why else would we have been kept?" Kleinsperwer padded away, toward the hut.

"Should you be moving closer, before Blackthorn returns?" Visarend looked about.

"Why not investigate?" Blouvalk followed the younger wolf. The four spread out, moving closer to the odd structure. Noses close to ground, their paws left prints in the dust.

A rectangular fence ringed with chicken wire was near the hut, but contained no garden. Only lonely dried stalks of maize stood from the arid ground. Scatterings of corn were on the dirt. There was little grass covering the dusty earth around the hut. A ball of clear tape sat under a tree. It had a core of grass, with layers of tape wrapped over and around until it was nearly the size of a football. Footprints, small in size, were all around the ball. Other prints were on the ground, human as well, but larger than the footprints under the tree. These marks were made moving away from the hut into the grass field beyond the dotting of acacia trees around the house.

Blouvalk nosed the blanket aside, and his hazel eyes peered into the gloom within. As his eyes adjusted to the low light, he could make out a rude table and a scattering of blankets on the ground. From a string hung from two high points on the wall inside was a selection of clothing. Some of these were drab khaki or black, others brightly colored.

Swartwou prodded the pink basin. It was full of water, but smelled of flowers with a chemical odor that made his snout wrinkle. Bubbles covered most of the surface, and slowly small bubbles popped, one, then another. He looked up to a line strung between the roof of the hut and a nearby acacia tree. Clothing was slung over the line. Water still dripped from them onto the ground.

"AH!"

The wolves jerked, all at once crouched closer to the ground, muscles locked, ears erect. They turned their heads as one in the direction of the exclamation.

A woman clad in a red and purple wrap stood in the grass field far from the hut, but there was no doubt she saw them. One hand held a small child, naked and barefoot. Another stood behind her, wearing black pants but no shirt. Her other hand held in place a towering stack of thatch grass balanced on her head.

None moved for a moment.

"HAH!" She shouted, face contorted with anger, still holding the thatch and the child.

The four wolves departed, padding back the way they came into the brush. Their pace was unhurried, and Blouvalk turned to see the woman hastening back to the hut with her children in tow. The thatch was left on the ground in front of the door, and the blanket was batted aside as the people disappeared into the dark interior.

"Wait—they have gone." Blouvalk twittered to the others, and licked his chops. "Into their termite mound."

"The human seemed disturbed. Do they all react that way to

our kind?" Swartwou looked to the older wolf.

"Maybe. If we are not enclosed by fence." He saw a face glare from the shadows behind the blanket. "They fear us." Blouvalk trotted closer, and the face vanished.

He gestured to the others, who left cover to stand next to him.

"This changes things considerably."

"What are you *domkoppe* doing out here?" Blackthorn rasped, before the others knew he was there.

"Regarding one of these humans you fear so greatly." Blouvalk turned toward the hut, urinating on the ground.

"Make for cover - the sedge just there beyond the sweet thorn acacia trees will prevent them from following us." Blackthorn loped off, but quickly realized none were following him. He trotted back. "Are you hoping to be killed?"

"Killed? With what?" Swartwou spoke, his voice playful as ever.

"I have seen their weapons strike down a wolf from across a plain, further even than a cheetah can dash." His dark fur seemed to stand on end, his onyx eyes consumed by an even darker storm. "And they can hunt in packs, same as we."

"Is this a weapon then?" Swartwou chirped.

The woman now stood before the door of the hut. Her children were behind her in shadows.

She brandished a long stick of wood, one end held by a stiffened hand. Her teeth were glaring white.

"RUN!"

Blackthorn raced away, and this time he detected pawfalls behind him, crunching on dried leaves and grass, light thumping on ground. Less than a minute later, they had just entered dense thornbrush, and he sensed the human was far behind him. He knew what vehicles were, and the way they intensified the speed with which humans moved. For some reason, this human had no such vehicle.

"I heard no thunder." Blackthorn panted, slowing to a halt, and looked back at his pack.

There were only three others with him.

"Where is Blouvalk?" Blackthorn growled.

The wolves padded back to the edge of the brush, and saw him.

A slender wolf, thin but powerful legs pumping, ears flat, and head low, powering through the distant trees. He was far away, but the stripe of white along his back was unmistakable. Further behind him was the woman, stick in the air. Her shouts just reached them, but the words made no sense.

"It is too late." Blackthorn's guttural voice was resigned. The three wolves around him gasped.

He waited for the ear–splitting thunder to emanate from the end of the terrible stick.

There was no sound, however, save the light thudding of paws on earth.

And hooves.

The woman was quickly left behind, and the stick was silent. As Blouvalk drew closer to the pack, it became apparent that he was actually chasing something.

The dirty white goat ran, darting one way, then the other, releasing a call of *Nyeeaaah!* As it quickly shifted course, Blouvalk stumbled, then corrected his chase. Another feint, and Blouvalk stumbled again. Each time, however, the wolf was faster to correct. Twice he ran further to the flank of the running goat, and slowly redirected the animal toward the sedge brush, where the wolves waited.

The woman was far away from the pursuit now, and Blouvalk maneuvered the goat until it crashed into the thornbrush. *Nyeeaaah!*

The other three wolves sprinted toward the crashing sounds of brush, and quickly found Blouvalk gripping a hind leg. Kleinsperwer seized a shoulder, Swartwou closed his jaws on the snout of the goat, and Visarend eviscerated the animal. It sank to the ground, onto the rapidly expanding pool of red beneath it. By the time Blackthorn reached them, Swartwou was already pulling a limb free of the carcass.

"I do not understand." Blackthorn growled to himself. "Why did they not attack?"

"Come, old wolf." Blouvalk yittered to him. "You are surely as hungry as we are."

Visarend lapped Blouvalk's muzzle, and closed her jaws lightly on his snout.

***

The wolves laid next to the remains of the goat, the innards still steaming on the ground. After some assurances from Blackthorn that they were unlikely to be discovered in the dense brush, they decided to stay and rest, and make another final meal of the goat.

"Were there other goats on the farm, Swartwou?" Visarend twittered.

"I saw them on other farms we have passed." He rolled onto his back, one way, then the other, covering his coat with dust.

"This is why humans are here." Kleinsperwer chirped happily. "They are quite skilled at providing food."

"What?" Visarend chortled.

"It is like the feasts they brought us wrapped up when we lived in the cage." He licked blood from the fur around his mouth. "So much the better alive. We should find another cage where they provide goats."

The four wolves laughed to themselves as Blackthorn got onto his paws and padded away.

"Where are you off to, Blackthorn?" Visarend spoke nearly in a whisper in the midday heat.

"Patrol the area." He shook some of the gore from his head. "That human may yet be looking for us."

"I would think if that human meant us harm, it would have come."

"I am worried about this, Visarend." He stared off into the thick foliage at nothing.

"We needed to feed."

"Was it worth the risk?"

"Is a hunt ever devoid of risk?" She lapped his muzzle, but he did not respond in kind.

He sighed quietly, glaring into the dark. "I understand the decision is yours, how we hunt. I was hoping there would be a way to attack their animals without their notice." He shook his head. "These humans are always about. They are everywhere."

Visarend looked about, her brow furrowed.

"If there is a richness to the land, they shall take it all." A low growl rumbled in his throat. "They do not wish to be a part of the wild. Part of our world."

Visarend listened to the dark wolf, unsure what to think of this.

"We face danger from many enemies, but there is only one great marauder of our world."

"Humans?" Visarend looked in the same direction as Blackthorn, but saw nothing there.

"*Ja.* And with them came starvation as the antelope were slaughtered or driven away to make room for their cattle."

"And yet the human today was no threat to us. Perhaps not all are as capable as those you have faced."

"I am not sure what to make of why some are dangerous, others are not." He sighed. "I do fear them. Though we cannot run from this threat forever, I do fear them. The sagest course regarding humans is not clear to me."

"Off to hunt already?" Blouvalk had sidled up to them both.

"He is going on patrol, to ensure the humans are not after us." She turned to get back to the rest.

"I am unimpressed with these humans. I doubt they could find us given a season to search with."

"You thought that hunt brave, Blouvalk?"

"To the valiant goes the vantage." He stood taller still, head held high.

Blackthorn coughed. "Audacity is not its own reward. And if you know not your enemy, it is not bravery, but stupidity that drives you." He padded away, and the dense growth closed behind him.

"Perhaps we know these creatures better than you presume, black wolf!" Blouvalk returned to the goat, and to Visarend's side.

Blackthorn did not answer him out loud. *You may be right about that.*

Twenty-Three

Kwit-kwit-kwit... Kwit-kwit-kwit...

The swallow tailed bee eater sat perched on the bare branch of a dead bush. Keen red eyes buried in a black band surveyed the field. Its green plumage shook away the scant moisture of the night, its dramatic blue forked tail hanging below the branch. Flitting off its perch, he returned seconds later with a prize in its curved sharp bill. The bird swatted the partially crushed bee against the branch. The impact released a squirt of clear fluid. With the sting spent, the bird safely swallowed its meal, and flitted off again, one kill to be made every minute.

Blackthorn had shaken the dust from his coat, but did not prompt a morning rally. The other wolves were asleep. He padded off into the grass to patrol the area. Sniffing the ground, he found no trace of lions here. Not surprising, since humans tended to chase them away. Moving further from where the Pack slept at a brisk jog, he peered across the savanna. It was not long before he heard light pawfalls behind him.

"Off for a hunt this morning?" Blouvalk yittered.

"No." Blackthorn did not elaborate.

"Learning the area." Blouvalk nodded. "Would you be willing to show me how to survey a territory?"

Blackthorn regarded the other wolf, who looked him over evenly. "Have you decided to be an eager pupil today?"

"Every day. For every day could be the last."

"Very well, then."

They left behind the rest of the pack, padding through the dried grasses, threading between acacia trees and thorny shrubs. Seed pods littered the ground, flattened brown crescents laying in the dust, some torn open to yield darker brown rounded seeds.

"Tracks." Blackthorn indicated round impressions in the dust.

"Cattle?"

"*Ja*. And they have been through recently." A large dung midden lay nearby, dried in the heat and swarming with beetles. "Not terribly useful for us."

Blouvalk did not reply, sniffing the ground and following the hoofprints.

They traveled west, and from there traced an enormous semicircle from where the other wolves rested, arriving to the east. By not stopping for rest or hunts, they covered dozens of kilometers effortlessly.

The western portion of this patrol was taken up by a series of farms, each smallholdings tended by a single family. The farms were subsistence only, struggling to provide enough food to get by for the year. There were no tarred surfaces, the farms connected only to a dirt road, and to each other by footpaths trodden for decades by bare feet. The rocky soil supported small fields of maize, beans, and root vegetables.

Further to the east, the land became more wild, dominated by impenetrable thickets and partially dried rivers between gently rolling hills.

"Beyond this patrol is the area from where we came." Blackthorn peered to the east from atop a rock outcropping into the rising sun. "Wetter lands, and the danger of lions."

Blouvalk looked west. "Drier lands, and humans."

"We must return to the others." Blackthorn traced his steps back toward where the pack rested.

"Why would humans not take wetlands for themselves?"

"I suspect they have." Blackthorn sniffed the ground, detecting the urine markings he left earlier in the day. "Regions left to wild are not entirely so. Even dense thickets filled with antelope, as numerous as blades of grass." He sounded wistful for a moment before continuing. "Even these have roads, and vehicles crossing them. And every so often comes the thunder without the storm. I suspect they use the wild places to hunt."

"As dangerous as you make them out to be, it is a wonder anything is left alive."

"In some places, nothing is." Blackthorn picked up his pace, paws lightly hitting earth that flew beneath his feet.

Buttonquails hopped through the grass in search of seeds, freezing in place as the wolves passed. Their brown feathers were marked with black splotches and edged with white, melting into the foliage when motionless. Grasshoppers and crickets gnawed on the grasses, taking what nutrient was left in the depleted vegetation. Closer to the farms, scrawny dogs yipped at the departing wolves before quickly losing interest and returning to their piles of garbage. A pen of chickens clucked with anxiety behind a screen of wire. Blackthorn and Blouvalk veered away from this and back into the irregular and sprawling area between the farms. The humans had chosen their lands in a broad swath surrounding this central patch, too rocky for reliable food production. Into this rough land the wolves bounded, between hundred year old acacia trees and bald sandstone rocks.

The black, gold, and white shapes sprinted past, drawing the notice of an African rock python. Hidden in shadow under a shelf of rock, the dark brown and grey brown blotches camouflaged the five meter muscular snake from view. Its black eyes registered the presence of the wolves, and dismissed them as neither threat nor prey, and it continued to rest in wait. Expending little energy day to day, it slowly digested the remains of an impala calf eaten a week before, and could continue to wait for nearly a year for the next kill.

Blackthorn and Blouvalk returned to find the pack lazing in the sun.

"I wondered where you disappeared to." Visarend greeted Blackthorn with a lapping of his muzzle.

"I suspect you did not wonder too hard." Blouvalk bounded up to her effusively, and tongued her muzzle with excitement.

Blackthorn glanced at her before greeting the others.

Swartwou and Kleinsperwer scampered about the clearing, each trying to leap on the others' back with their forepaws. Eventually Swartwou won the exchange, bowling over the smaller wolf onto his back and mock-biting him with his gaping jaws.

"The sparrowhawk will have its day!" Kleinsperwer batted ineffectually with his forepaws.

Blackthorn laid down in the sun, a puff of dust erupting as he snuffed toward the ground. One ear twitched to flick away a biting fly.

He watched as Swartwou continued to torment Kleinsperwer, releasing a streamer of drool onto the smaller wolf's face. Further away, Blouvalk and Visarend spoke quietly to one another under the shadow of a wild fig tree. Vervet monkeys screeched above them while they ambled from one branch to another in search of fig fruits. After gnawing away the rich flesh of a fig, one of the older monkeys looked down at the wolves below. He peered carefully and dropped the spent end of the fig onto Blouvalk's head.

Blackthorn chortled to himself as Blouvalk shook his fur and ignored the monkey above.

"Do you feel more at ease, old one?" Kleinsperwer thumped to the ground beside him.

"In the interest of survival, it is seldom best to ever be truly at ease." Blackthorn rasped. "That was not your question, was it?"

"With us, I mean." Kleinsperwer turned over once, and turned back onto his belly, now coated with dust. "You seemed unsure at first about freeing us from the cage."

"I am still not sure. And likely never will be."

"I do not follow." The younger wolf's brow was furrowed.

"One cannot see all ends. And yet one must try, as a pack member, to foresee all possible hazards. Anticipate your deficits of knowledge, and fill them. See one's enemies coming, and evade them."

"Would you have left us, if you had known how difficult your task would be?"

"Perhaps."

Kleinsperwer looked to the ground, wounded.

"Thus far we have been fortunate, young one. And so I am glad you are here." Blackthorn nudged him with his snout. "Should disaster befall us, I will have wished I had never caught your scent. This is as it must be. One who feels no regret has never made a real decision." He surveyed the land around them as he rested. "In the end, all of one's efforts can be for naught."

"The mountain gave birth to a mouse." Kleinsperwer caught Blackthorn's quizzical look. "The greatest of plans comes to nothing."

Blackthorn regarded him blankly.

"The mountain is big, and—"

"I understand." He blinked away the dust from his eyes. "You are quite clever."

"You have a lifetime of experience. I have seasons of boredom and imagination."

"Mountain and... mouse." Blackthorn nodded, lost in thought. After a moment, he grunted with approval. "I would have freed you without regard to my concerns, sparrowhawk. However this transpires, it was worth the venture."

Coo - coo, co-kuk-coo coo.

A red-eyed dove flew steeply above them, flapped its wings, and glided back to its perch in an acacia tree. *Coo - coo, co-kuk-coo coo.*

"Hunting with you, teaching you. Learning from you." Blackthorn rumbled.

"An honor to be your student. Despite the danger."

"There is no life without danger." Blackthorn peered at the dove. "That danger stalks us, and will eventually bring us low. Each day is the only day we live, without expectation."

"And so hope is a stranger to us." Kleinsperwer whispered.

"Indeed. The veld is ours. Until it is not." He lowered his head onto his forepaws, but continued to watch the dove.

"Surely hope kept you alive before you found us?"

Blackthorn did not answer him, glancing toward where Blouvalk and Visarend stood, still deep in discussion under the fig tree.

"Blackthorn?"

He closed his eyes, and breathed slowly. Each exhale was longer than the next. For a moment, Kleinsperwer thought he had died, until he took another ponderous breath.

Twenty-Four

The following morning came with the *HA–DA!* blast of the ibis, shattering the calm. Blackthorn awoke to find Blouvalk was already up, and had trotted to Visarend, lapping her muzzle. Both were on their paws, and had began nudging the others awake. In a few minutes, all were running about, cavorting with jaws wide open, twittering with excitement, greeting each wolf and accepting a greeting in kind.

Blackthorn bumped into Visarend's side as they warmed up for the hunt.

"Are you ready, dark wolf?" Visarend's high pitched yittering was insistent.

"We are never ready, Visarend." Blackthorn gazed into her hazel eyes. "A lifetime expended in preparation for a great moment." He shook himself free of dirt. "Which moment will it be? And shall we be equal to it when it comes?"

"You sound like Kleinsperwer." She fixed her jaws on his neck, a light bite that did not break his hide, and she scampered off after Blouvalk, who was padding away to the north.

He watched them leave, tails tipped in white curving into the air, and his thoughts drifted to a den. Dark, smelling of damp earth, and the musk of wolf pups.

He hastened after his pack.

***

The wolves wound their way across the uneven ground, strewn with rocks and scrub. They bounced lightly on their paws with a steady pace, jaws hung open slightly to pant away the heat. Their poise was relaxed even as they moved quickly, filing between tangled thorny shrubs and stands of grass.

Blouvalk had taken the lead, his stark white back stripe like an arrow pointed into the veld ahead. He padded down a slight incline, his claws scattering gravel about before he thumped into a dry riverbed. There was little damp left in the sand, enough to hold the shape of wolf tracks.

Blackthorn looked down at the prints, mashed together in a chaotic series, claws all pointed in the same direction. He could not help but smile.

Their path led them under the shadow of wild date palm trees, growing in dense clumps along the river. The trunks jutted from the banks out over where the river flowed in the wet summers, then up to the crowns of feather shaped green leaves, tousled in the high breeze.

Barely audible *cheet cheet* calls came from the brush beside them. Fluttering above a thornbush was a red bird, the color of blood. The tar black of its face and chest were interrupted by a collar of crimson that bled into a hood and cape, striking against the drab color of the vegetation. The male southern red bishop flew off in search of food, while the more dull-colored female remained invisible in the grass.

A pair of small rounded ears atop a slender bullet-shaped head ducked into the grasses that lined the river, the tawny brown melting in with the dried foliage. The side-striped jackal browsed for insects and lizards in the brush, but watched the wolves with interest. Somewhere in the direction they were heading, there would be a corpse to feed upon. Whether it was wolf or prey did not matter to the jackal.

Soon the date palms were left behind, as was the river, as Blouvalk ascended the bank and headed north. The ground evened out, the trees grew more sparse and the ground less studded with boulders.

Blackthorn hastened to the front of the pack.

"Blouvalk, where are you headed?"

"In search of prey, dark one." His head was held high, hazel eyes surveying the land before him.

"One of the farms lays ahead. And more beyond them."

"Worry not, Blackthorn. You need not do all the hunting for us." He turned and regarded the old wolf with a nod.

Blackthorn slowed, watching Blouvalk as he padded forth.

"He seems quite keen. As though a rider drove him." Kleinsperwer nudged him as he passed.

"I am unfamiliar with a 'rider'." Blackthorn kept pace with the younger wolf.

"Growing up within our cage, we could see on occasion large beasts clomping past on heavy hoof, long-faced and magnificent. Like the zebra we happened upon not long ago."

"Brown in color, though." He nodded. "Horses. They are no longer wild, having been taken by humans to perform strange tasks on farms." He looked over to Kleinsperwer. "Riding, you call it?"

"The human rides." He displayed his teeth in a smile, rows of ivory. "The rest of us are beneath them."

"Rides. Very good." Blackthorn smiled in spite of himself.

"You are a most peculiar wolf."

"As you have so spoken without a growl, I will take that as praise." Kleinsperwer leapt as he ran, and snapped his jaws shut on empty air as a dragonfly zipped beyond his reach.

"Eccentric, indeed." Blackthorn grinned. "Your thoughts often drift from the immediate, to strange places."

"I am a leaf upon wind." Kleinsperwer slowed, his brow furrowed. "Do I endanger the Pack?"

"One must always focus on the task at hand." Blackthorn's mouth was agape in a laugh. "Never lose your eccentricity, however. It is a quality shared by some of the finest wolves I have known."

Kleinsperwer immediately resumed his bouncing gait, seeming to take flight with every step. With a leap over a thornbush, his lean body arced through the air.

"What say you, sparrowhawk? Will the veld one day be ours again?"

"It is ours as we run, free and without iron." Kleinsperwer was on his hind legs, and spun about in the air, thudding to the ground and almost losing his footing.

"Then forth to the wound that awaits."

"Is the wound for us, or our prey?"

"It matters not. If ours, a noble scar."

"What is noble about an injury?" The younger wolf's tongue lolled out as he galloped.

"There is nothing so redeeming as a scar." Blackthorn peered at the veld ahead, his torn ear flopped with each step. "A sign one has fought for their ground. Proof of life, and love, the causes that are all to us." Blackthorn prodded Kleinsperwer with his snout as they ran.

"Then I look forward to my scars, *Oom* Blackthorn." He

twittered happily.

"Run with me, this violent season. My brother always."

***

Before long, the pack reached the edge of a farm, the scattered grass and scrub abruptly ending at a margin of maize stalks. The wind had whipped up dust, and their pace slowed as their eyes became clotted.

"Bother this veil of dust." Blouvalk groused.

Kleinsperwer reared up on his hind legs and landed his forepaws on the other wolf's back.

"Patience, my fellow raptor." Kleinsperwer was shrugged off by the older wolf. "Veil of dust, of rain, or of ignorance. There is always a veil of one sort or another." He looked up to the sun, orange through the swirling dust. "Death finally lifts them all."

"You are tiresome as ever, little sparrowhawk." Blouvalk sniffed the air, and snuffed quickly as he choked on it.

Visarend shook her coat. "We should wait out this disturbance. Any hunt would be blind."

"Blind to us, and to our enemies." Blouvalk twittered, and he shot off into the obscuring wind. The white of his tail was barely visible as he sprinted through the field of maize.

The rest were on his tail quickly, although it was difficult to find him. Visarend and Swartwou both peeled away in opposite directions, following what appeared to be Blouvalk, but were scraps of leaf blowing about. The wind took hold of the trees, causing their crowns to waver. Branches were pulled past one another squealing, as the wind whipped about them. Gravel was in the air now, and every impact stung.

Blackthorn twittered to Visarend, his high pitched chirping calling her to a halt, and once he was by her side, they returned. Together, they fetched Swartwou before he became lost, bringing him back to the edge of the maize. Kleinsperwer had not moved, standing with his snout pointed toward the sun, eyes closed, ignoring the vegetation and stones that struck him.

"Stay close, my wolves. It will not be long." Blackthorn peered around him, eyelids pinched, through dust-flecked lashes until he could no longer stand to look.

The wind howled for a quarter of an hour, and the pack huddled in the arid storm. The sky darkened, but no rain fell. In the distance a tin sheet banged where it had separated from the roof of a shack. It banged over and over, incessant once it began, until with a brief shriek it stopped, followed by a muted thud.

As abruptly as the dervish erupted, it stopped, the dust settling, bits of gravel dropping to the ground. Leaves lazily stirred to a rest. Blackthorn blinked the grit from his eyes.

"Well. Now to find our—"

HOO!

Blackthorn stopped his thought, listening. His ears were erect, paws light and on edge. He darted away, leaving the field of maize behind, toward another farm. The wolves followed him closely, padding with urgency through the grass.

HOO!

Closer this time, and the wolves hurried. Blackthorn lowered his muzzle to the ground, releasing a hoo-call of his own in answer. Within minutes they had found Blouvalk.

The wolf stood, paws wide apart, raising his muzzle from the ground as he saw the others approach. His handsome black and gold face was covered with blood, fur standing on end and thick with gore and dust. He turned and padded back to a prone carcass. Hooves stuck out stiffly from the body, the off-white fur spattered with red. The belly was wide open, with entrails spilled. The head lay on the ground, tongue out, small horns curving to the rear. The goat was freshly dead, not even having drawn flies.

Blackthorn stood back while the others bounded up to the kill, each burying their snouts in the body cavity, gulping down organ and offal.

Blackthorn watched them devour the goat. He looked first one way, then the other, ears swiveling about. There were no sounds of dog or machine approaching them. None of the barking shouts that humans make when enraged.

"Come, old one! The meat is fresh." Blouvalk practically sang, his yittering resembling a songbird. Visarend lapped the blood from his muzzle, and the two were back to feeding.

***

Dusk found the pack resting under the arbor of a hairy bush-willow, the gnarled trunk leaning over as though about to fall, as it had for many years.

Swartwou lay on his back, legs splayed in the air, a round belly in the middle.

"Guh." This was all he had said since they dined a second time on the goat.

"You may have difficulty digesting that hoof." Blackthorn prodded him with his snout. "Take some grass, should there be any room in there."

"Did you know they would be unable to protect their goats?" Visarend lay next to Blouvalk.

"It seemed a reasonable guess." He licked a shallow wound on his forepaw, gashed against a rock during the chase. "We could barely see one another. How could they see us?"

"They will see easily enough that a goat is missing." Blackthorn rested at the root of the tree.

"If they value such things, they should keep a closer watch." Blouvalk smacked his lips, and laid his head on his forepaws.

"They just might."

"I understand you wish for greater caution, dark wolf." He spoke with his eyes closed, as though it were an extraordinary effort. "Caution, however, will not feed us. We shall stand our ground."

"The longer we linger among humans, the greater the peril. I can see there is no convincing you. You require your lessons in blood."

"The blood of my prey has been lesson enough, I assure you."

"We cannot make a stand against a superior enemy." He sighed. "It is for the alpha to decide." Blackthorn turned to Visarend, and gave a nod. "Not you. Not me."

Visarend regarded the rest quietly. She took a deep breath, lowering her head onto forepaws. With an exhale, she stirred the dust between her claws, and disturbed a beetle stumbling over the leaf litter.

"The risk of hunting around these humans is considerable. There have been few herds of antelope to cross our path, however." She looked to Blackthorn before he could speak. "I do not wish to move in search of them. Chasing prey seems as likely to lead us into danger as out of it. We shall hunt here."

Blackthorn exhaled his disappointment, and this did not go unnoticed.

"Blackthorn, you will see to our safety."

His eyes were open, onyx shining in the dim light.

"You will be our guard against the dangers that humans bring."

His eyes closed again, but he did not sleep.

Twenty-Five

The moon floated across the sky, driftwood on a bottomless ocean. Its brilliance was fading, as a hint of red seeped into the black of night. Twisted branches loomed from the darkness as dawn threatened to break, the horizon swelling into a hostile flare. Dim light splashed over the bushveld, and the katydid razzing began to abate.

Blackthorn watched this for an hour as the savanna transitioned from inky blackness to a translucent morning. Each shadow shrank before his sight, and the malevolent enemies of night seemed to disappear into vapor. As a cape turtle dove began its call, *kuk-coorr-uk kuk-coorr-uk*, he watched the wolves at slumber under the bushwillow tree. He stood well clear of them, lost in thought.

To the north, he could hear no sounds of human industry, the clank of metal or thrum of engine. Not yet. He knew they were there, and would soon begin their labors. He turned southeast, where the land grew wilder, impassible sedge and irregular ground. There, the lions dwelt. The range ruled by the pride was expansive, reaching out to ensnare wandering herds when possible. And the herds grazed as they crossed the land of the lion pride.

Lions are ever a threat, but a threat I can understand.

Turning back north, unease settled within him. His ear twitched, as though a carrion fly were taking a bite from it. He recalled long ago the hunter's bullet that went through it with a sting.

He tried to imagine how to approach a farm safely. Creeping toward a fence, body held low to the ground, ears flat. And then what?

When enemies can strike you from the far horizon, there is no way to avoid them.

He laid down again with a grunt. Thoughts began to drift again toward the southeast.

Your alpha has given you an order.

"An inexperienced alpha." His muttering did not wake the others.

Nonetheless.

He did not awaken the others, waiting for them to arouse on their own.

If you do not heed the rule of the alpha, what becomes of the Pack?

Blouvalk raised his head, shaking it free of dried grass, opening jaws wide with a yawn. Lapping Visarend's muzzle, he began the morning greetings. Kleinsperwer yawned as well, and planted both forepaws on Swartwou's side. Soon they were bouncing about on springing steps, tonguing one another's muzzles as the hunting rally began.

Visarend bounded to Blackthorn's side, and lapped his muzzle in earnest. Her eyes, the typical hazel color offset by a burning orange, glittered fiercely. Her wet black nose touched his. The black fur of her snout became a gold beyond the eyes save a black stripe between her large ears. Blackthorn nodded, his obsidian eyes reflecting her gaze. He swallowed his reservations and simply nodded to her.

"The hunt is on, Visarend."

***

Blouvalk found the way through the brush, flat areas of bare ground allowing the wolves to pass. They approached a thick wall of brush that grew along a dried rivulet. A stand of spikethorn trees stood tall, rounded crowns of green leaves concealing razor sharp spines. Between the spikethorn tree groves were growths of Kalahari yellowthorn, vertical branches festooned with short green, grooved leaves protected by spines of their own. A narrow stripe of hard, red dirt curved through the sedge ahead, and Blouvalk padded toward this.

"Our patrols have included this farm before." Blackthorn murmured.

"Yes." Blouvalk panted. "We have seen it from afar."

"Time to investigate closer, then." Visarend emitted a streamer of saliva.

As they neared the scattered yellowthorn, Blackthorn looked down to the ground, and a small object held his attention. A small cylindrical shape the size of a beetle, light brown in color, with grey on one end. A tiny tendril of smoke rose from the end, and as the dark wolf's nostrils flared, the spent cigarette seared his nasal passages.

He stopped, glaring at the smoldering butt. His breathing became deep and rapid, his pulse bounding. In the pit of his stomach, the gnawing began once again. Looking up, the last flash of white on Swartwou's tail passed behind a spikethorn tree.

Sprinting forward, he caught up with the wolf pack as they

entered more even ground beyond the trees.

"There are signs of impala." Blackthorn spoke quickly.

Blouvalk did not alter his gait. "What did you see?"

"Prints. Not long ago."

"Why did you not mention this earlier?" Visarend was now by his side.

"I was unsure, but I think we will find a herd not far from here."

"We are nearly upon the farm." Blouvalk indicated a distant fence line. It was barely visible between the yellowthorn strewn across the savanna, but he could make out the horizontal beams of wood held up by posts.

"It is safer to hunt impala." He rasped. A bull strode into view beyond the fence, horns angled straight out from its mighty head.

"Are you quite alright?" Blouvalk spoke, but did not turn to look at the old wolf, his eyes fixed upon the cattle. Near the bull stood a man, clad in brown clothing. He held something to his head, a small black shape.

The shape flashed with the powerful glint of sunlight.

"They are this way!" Blackthorn loped off, away from the farm, along the line of spikethorn trees. The wolf's change in direction was watched closely by the man on the farm through his binoculars.

For a moment, his heart pounded as his paws hit the ground, and he heard nothing other than the throb of his beating heart. Blackthorn relaxed slightly when he sensed a wolf beside him.

"Guide us to the hunt." Visarend yittered, and prodded him with her snout.

He could hear a series of footfalls behind him, the pads of wolf paws and claws that clicked on rocks. One set of paws was furthest behind, and remained so as they crossed the bushveld.

***

"Have you seen any more of those prints?"

Blackthorn sniffed the ground. His dark eyes darted around, wildly searching the path before him, and as distant as the horizon, for any sign of antelope.

"Any spoor?" Visarend was by his side, attempting to follow his gaze.

"I lost." He choked on his words. "I lost the trail."

"Perhaps if we find a body of water to follow." She offered.

Blackthorn grunted, fuming in silence. His pace quickened, as did his heartbeat.

"The sun disapproves." Kleinsperwer looked up to the blazing orange, his eyes closed against the glare. "It bids us to rest in the high of the day. Perhaps we should heed its advice."

"I am not sure of what you speak, Kleinsperwer." Swartwou intoned. "But I would like to lay down in the shade." He found a place under a towering apple leaf tree, the white of its trunk like a shaft of bone rising proudly into the air. He quickly found himself among company as the other wolves thumped down beside him. Visarend shook her head, deterring the biting flies. As each wolf laid down, they vanished into the tall grass. Even a few feet away, there was no way to see them.

"I will continue to look about." Blackthorn spoke to no one in particular, and padded away from the tree. As he left it behind, and went over a ridge, he broke into a run. Covering ground swiftly, he peered across the veld to the horizon, in search of a cloud of dust or moving shapes, any sign that would betray the presence of a herd. He kept sprinting, down into a low grass meadow, and up another hill. Cresting the rise, he found another empty field of dried grass. Nothing and nothing.

"Leaving us?"

Blackthorn spun about, his claws digging into the soil as he halted.

Blouvalk loped next to him.

"No. I—"

"You are still looking for impala."

"Yes."

"You never saw any sign of impala, I suspect." Blouvalk panted, his tongue lolled out.

Blackthorn glared at him.

"You have many fine qualities. The ability to deceive is not one of them."

"They are around. One needs only look." His dark eyes flashed in anger.

"As we have looked." He glanced back in the direction of the apple leaf tree where the pack rested. "Persist in this if you must, but we know how it will end."

Blackthorn snuffed his contempt.

"The longer you pursue this folly, the lower your estimation in her view."

"And what is your plan, then?"

"To return whence we came." Blouvalk stared, impassive.

"Where the humans have seen us." He grunted. "And may retaliate against your kills."

"I doubt that." He turned back toward the apple leaf tree. "In any case, defense against human danger is your concern."

Blackthorn watched the wolf leave, his dorsal white stripe undulating above the grass stems, the white of his tail tip fading into the heat and dust of midday. Eventually this melted into the nondescript brown of the grasses, and the savanna in all directions was still. Frozen in time, it seemed nothing was alive apart from the trees and grass in their infinite patience. For some of the acacia trees, living and slowly growing for hundreds of years, they could wait, one season after the next, for opportunity.

He closed his eyes, and could see the red through his eyelids as the sun burned. He felt a lightness in his body, unencumbered, able to run at top speed with no end. One step with his paw, toward the south, where the land grew ever wild, and he felt even lighter. Every tendon in his leg was sprung steel, prepared for the journey.

A glance back north, and he could sense in the distance the ordered fences and exotic weapons that worried him so. He searched the horizon for an answer, some telltale sign floating on the breeze or in the whispers of wind through the grass.

Indifference was all he could perceive, and all that nature would yield.

Every step back toward the north where the wolves rested, Blackthorn dragged a weight, invisible and heavy, gripped by every thorn that he passed.

***

Early afternoon, Blouvalk sniffed Visarend, bidding her to arouse.

Swartwou slowly turned over, his four paws lazily turning in the air, just visible above the grass tips. He stood with great effort, and lapped Blouvalk's muzzle. Kleinsperwer joined them, and Visarend stirred. After shaking dust from her coat, she began to greet them all, and the four wolves began the rally.

191

They were each still hungry after the morning passed without a meal.

Swartwou yipped and met Kleinsperwer, both standing on hind legs, forelegs entwined, muzzles clashing with excitement. They rejoined the ground in time to be met by Blackthorn, returning from his patrol to rejoin the rest of the pack. Lapping muzzles as well, he greeted each wolf in turn.

Visarend accepted his greeting, peering into his eyes, searching.

"We move—further east." Blackthorn met her gaze.

"Will we not return to the farms?" Kleinsperwer twittered.

"There will be more." Blackthorn's guttural call sounded optimistic. "There are always more humans to be found."

He bounded away before there could be a response. Visarend watched him quietly before sprinting after him, followed by the rest.

The sun made its languorous way across the sky.

Two hours passed, and the wolves crossed no herds, only dirt roads that led from nowhere to nowhere. Small isolated huts stood here and there on the grasses, next to fields planted with maize or beans, sometimes planted with nothing as fields were left fallow.

Blackthorn led them down a rise into a depression where a thicket of acacia and yellowthorn grew in a snarl. Distant, he noticed a vulture circling in the sky. And another.

Blouvalk galloped next to Blackthorn, but was unable to get the dark wolf to notice him. He cleared his throat to speak.

Blackthorn did not let him.

"Steady on, my wolves. There is something ahead." His ears folded back, nose in the air, sniffing, then lowering into his attack posture. The air became thick, the heat stifling.

He quickened his pace toward where the scavengers were descending.

A scent rose around them, and Blackthorn broke into a grin.

"I smell it as well." Kleinsperwer sniffed, then snuffed.

"It is close." Blackthorn slowed, easing his body through the thicket, thorns skittering across his gold, black, and white fur. He lowered his head to duck under some of the stiff branches. As the leaf-covered brush parted, the prone form of an impala was revealed.

The impala was a yearling, sprawled on the ground. Its neck was cinched tight beneath a thin wire. This hung from the stout branch of a yellowthorn bush. Eyes bulged sightless, tongue protruded from its slack mouth, opened in a silent cry.

A vulture hopped to a landing at the edge of the clearing where the impala died, but upon noticing the wolf pack, it stood a safe distance away.

"It has not been dead long." Blackthorn glared at the snare, repulsed by its presence. He ripped open the belly, spilling blue and grey intestines, dark with clotted blood. Black muzzles probed the cavity, and teeth ripped away muscle and organ to feed. They ate without a word, and rested as the sun descended, giving rise to a flame in the west.

Bellies filled, the wolf pack rested as the call from a fiery-necked nightjar rose. *Whrrrr-whrrr- whrrhrhrhr!*

Grass mantids stood sentry atop stalks of brush, awaiting prey with folded forelimbs as jagged as teeth. Grasshoppers sawed busily at the grass stalks, issuing trilling calls with their hind legs. A net casting spider prepared for the night's hunt near the dead impala. Spinning silk from its abdomen, it took hold of the non-sticky threads with forelegs, weaving a small net, barely larger than its own small body. It then hung low from a grass stem, looking down, waiting for an insect to blunder underneath that it would ensnare with its hand-sewn net. There it remained suspended, ever waiting.

"You have not patrolled, Blackthorn." Visarend looked to the old wolf in the enveloping darkness.

"Snares." He spoke the word with venom. "There will be more of them."

"We have withdrawn from that impala, back the way we came. Are we safe?"

"As long as we do not wander."

Have you encountered them before?"

He breathed heavily in the dim light, and a word gradually emerged as a creak. "Yes."

"Then you can avoid them."

"All so easy, is it?" He snapped. "Experience can conquer any dilemma?" His head raised off the ground, his graveled voice just above a whisper. "You bear the burden of leadership too lightly, Visarend. Perhaps our fortune has been too good, and the savanna too forgiving."

"Have you taken this tone with all the alphas you have served?" She stood, meeting his gaze. "I dare say you did not serve them long."

Blackthorn remained quiet, and laid back down. His body heaved once, and he breathed quietly.

Visarend settled down, looking up toward the moon, its glowing crescent providing little light to the bushveld below. She cast a glance toward Blouvalk, who watched them both.

Uneasy rest came to them through the night, the pack huddled a distance from the snared antelope. The thicket blocked their view, and the calls of insects and birds were a curtain of noise that would not allow them to hear a danger.

Blackthorn's ears strained to listen, and their owner got little sleep, on guard against enemies, real and imagined.

Twenty-Six

Dawn found the dark wolf already awake, his stomach tied in knots. The rest of the pack was still asleep. He resigned himself to hunting the farm, and here his schemes ran into a wall.

A wall, a fence. Waiting for the thunder.

His thoughts meandered from the straight lines and angles of fences and buildings and into the reassuring tangle of the wild. Lands filled with prey in herds, hyena clans, the realms of lions.

And somewhere, the land of wolves as well.

He recalled the long months searching for signs of his kind. The dearth of wolf prints across the expansive landscape was disheartening. He could remember every fruitless step.

There is the vast world remaining to search. Why do you wait?

Visarend and Blouvalk slept close to one another. Their forepaws nearly touched.

Is this worth the fight?

"The Pack is worth any fight." The words crawled from his throat without a thought. His gaze drifted to the south nonetheless.

These fools wish to stay put, when our itinerate nature is our salvation.

"I would not betray her."

Join fools, and you become a fool.

"She is no fool. With time and experience, she will be the greatest of hunters."

Soon they would arouse for the hunt. And his moment to slip away unnoticed would be gone.

You disappoint me in death, just as you disappointed me in life.

His eyes shut and his head lowered toward the ground.

How did you fail me, and the pups in our den?

Breathing heavily, slowly, a rattling from his muzzle was just audible. His head dipped further, his skull feeling as heavy as lead.

The snares were all around us.

Every muscle in his face locked, his head quivering.

And when the iron wire embraced me, you did nothing.

His head was nearly on the ground, tail low, legs trembling.

One hunting wolf after another found snares of their own. They came for me. They came to find me.

His teeth clenched, lips pulled away, a rictus of paralyzed rage.

And you did nothing.

"WHAT COULD I HAVE DONE?" Blackthorn released this as clattering howl, an abrupt blast through a throat unprepared for words.

As one, the rest of the wolves launched onto their feet, every hair of their fur on end, ears erect, paws as light as air and ready for the threat.

Kleinsperwer trotted over and lapped his muzzle.

"What ever is the matter?"

"An uneasy *droom* plagued my sleep." Blackthorn was standing as though about to fall over.

"What dream does one have when awake?" Kleinsperwer lowered his head to look into his black, marble-like eyes. "You were already standing."

He shook his head, struggling for some way to explain.

"The time for the morning hunt is upon us." Blouvalk sidled up to them. "The blood river, as you say." His hazel brown eyes twinkled with excitement. Swartwou joined them, and the hunting rally began in earnest.

Visarend greeted each member of the Pack. Licking of muzzles, rubbing briskly against bodies, each wolf received her attention. Each with the exception of Blackthorn, whom she only brushed past.

Blouvalk led them away to the north.

Weaving their way through acacia and spikethorn trees, they seemed to move all too quickly. Blackthorn felt pulled, as though in the current of a river.

He hurried to reach Visarend's side.

"Visarend, I must ask that we not go this way."

She ignored him, her steady lope covering ground quickly.

"There is a danger."

"As ever, there is danger." She snarled, but did not break stride. "We tried a hunt, in your fashion, and found only carrion to eat." She indicated Blouvalk in the lead. "Today we hunt the farms."

"Visarend—"

She loped ahead and took the lead next to Blouvalk.

"Humans can be counted on." Kleinsperwer joined Blackthorn's side.

"For what?" He regarded the young wolf with a quizzical look.

"To always have food, far in excess of their needs."

"They do not do so out of a kind heart."

"Indeed!" Kleinsperwer gushed. "And so the hunters shall take their measure." He fairly bounced on his feet.

"Be wary, sparrowhawk." His dark eyes narrowed. "They represent a danger to our *Volk*."

"I know the name." Kleinsperwer yittered. "Of our Pack."

Blackthorn sighed. "What?"

"*Maaier.*"

Blackthorn chuckled in spite of himself. "Reapers, are we?"

"*Reavers.*" His lips pulled back, serrated teeth glittering. "We take all we see, lords of the veld."

***

"The farm is not far." Blouvalk reviewed the other wolves behind him, before looking forward again. The ruff of his neck was tousled in the breeze.

"A human is ahead." Kleinsperwer twittered, a little too loudly.

"Quiet." Blackthorn could see a white shape through a thick layer of sedge, and padded closer. He poked his nose through yellowed foliage to see a *bakkie* parked on a dirt road. It was covered in dust, the clear windows clouded. The rear of the *bakkie* was uncovered, and he could see no equipment there. The cab seemed unoccupied. "A human... *thing*, in any case."

Kleinsperwer squeezed his narrow form through thorned branches and ambled toward the vehicle.

"*Kleinsperwer!*" Blackthorn rasped, glancing about fearfully. The young wolf approached the truck, and sniffed the rear bumper. His tail wagged one way with a swish, then back with another swish. He looked back to the rest. His tongue was lolled out, panting.

"I want to see." Blouvalk raced out to the *bakkie*, and Blackthorn did not bother trying to stop him. The two scampered around the vehicle, sniffing and investigating, taking particular interest in the tires.

Blackthorn looked both ways down the road.

"Kleinsperwer seems to have found something underneath." Visarend twittered.

The wolf crawled just under the chassis on his belly, white tipped tail still in the air. His body shifted, his tail dropped, and his hips shifted again. Suddenly he braced himself, his body shaking. The white frame of the vehicle began to lurch, back and forth, and the squeaking of the spring suspension echoed across the grass field.

"Always curious, his mind has never been one to be idle." She chuckled at the sight of the truck rocking back and forth.

"Indeed."

"Kleinsperwer happens upon some remarkable ideas. Many that never would have occurred to me." She looked further down the road.

"Should he learn the vagaries of the bushveld, he would make a formidable alpha." He padded forward to stop their play, but Kleinsperwer had already began to crawl from under the chassis. Blouvalk sniffed the air, and the two began to run down the road with Visarend and Swartwou close behind.

Blackthorn sniffed the dirt road that headed to the farm and followed them.

As the white tips of their tails disappeared down the path, two men came running from the grass. One pointed down the road at the retreating wolves, while the other took a device from his pocket and spoke into it.

***

The shade of the crowberry was scant, the short deciduous bushy tree having lost its leaves for the dry season. The shed leaves on the ground had been broken down into dust by various beetles over the past month. Five wolves passed beneath, not stopping for rest.

Blackthorn pulse quickened. He realized the pack had passed this way earlier, soon after they fled the lion pride territory. Blackthorn did not notice if humans had sighted them during that time, but one could never be sure.

This farm was more organized, larger, more signs of perma-nence. The fences were made of stout wooden beams rather than twisted cut branches. The paths were broad gravel ways meant to convey vehicles moving at great speed. There were more livestock loitering about, grazing on the grass. These marks of industry were concerning enough, but recognizing the land filled him with disquiet.

The treeline distant, the curving rise of hill beyond, a familiar riverbed. In his mind was a vast map, comprised of thousands of kilometers where his path had led him over years beyond counting. He could recall each tree, each rock, aardvark burrow, and human habitation. In his mind, the painted wolf wanders for good reason.

To remain beyond the reach of enemies.

Sights of the familiar filled him with dread.

As those enemies come to know my path, they come to know me.

He stood, staring, down the rise toward the farm, and spied a distant figure.

The figure that stared back stood on two legs, clothed in

khakis. It held a hand to its eyes, and Blackthorn knew he had been seen.

Another figure had joined it, coming from a hut.

"Visarend, the hunt should be deferred to another day."

"It will not."

"The humans know we are here."

"We will not starve within sight of food." Her voice did not waver, and she offered no opening for discussion. "Do what you must to counter their threats." She twittered to the others, and they roused for the hunt.

Visarend trotted toward the farm, Blouvalk by her side. The other two wolves were right behind them, and a twitter volleyed between them as she gave the order to attack.

Blackthorn followed them by several paces. As he watched, the two figures began moving. One ran off in the direction of the hut, the other held up a device. He appeared to be speaking into it, although he could not be sure at a distance of nearly a kilometer.

He glanced about wildly, looking for something he could not find. His heart raced, his mind swam. The humans were still running, one into the hut, the other toward a vehicle. Flailing, he puzzled through his memory, fixating on those encounters with humans. Alarmed, violent, cruel. His only response to their threats has ever been to run. Observing the figures as they scurried about, Blackthorn could not discern what they were doing.

I know not how to protect them.

I know not what is to come.

Despite his fear, he stayed with the Pack, and the four wolves began to separate. They descended on the farm, rapidly covering the distance, and closed in on a goat that was browsing in a pile of rubbish close to the house.

The goat suddenly looked up, stamped its hooves with a thump. A ball of paper fell from its mouth and it dashed away.

Swartwou darted after the goat, which pealed its call of fright. *Nyeeaaah!*

Visarend and Blouvalk closed in on the goat from another direction, cutting off escape. Before they could catch their prey, they scattered at a noise uttered behind them.

One man ran toward them with a stick, waving it wildly in the air. "*HAH!*" He screamed, over and over. "*HAHHH!*" His hoarse voice shook as he ran.

The wolves whirled about at the presence of the man, unsure what to do. They darted away, then stopped, and watched him. Kleinsperwer moved closer to the man, intrigued. He recoiled as the man shouted something unintelligible, but did not move away.

The goat sprinted off, hooves clomping on the hard ground.

"They will defend their animals!" Blackthorn snapped at each of the wolves' haunches. "*We must run!*" He collided with Visarend, and she quickly followed him, the pack racing away from the man with the stick.

Blackthorn's chest seared with pain as he bought every centimeter of ground with claw and paw, desperate to get away before he could hear the terrible clap of the gun. Cursing himself, he hoped only that they would escape.

A moment passed, and still he waited for the thunder as the pack raced down a dirt road.

The next few moments, he wondered why that stick did not strike him down. He turned back, and the man was running after them, but could not equal their speed. Kleinsperwer still lagged, and his lack of urgency was maddening. He called in an agitated twitter for the young wolf to hurry.

Neither he nor the others heard the truck coming.

Roaring around the bend in the dirt road, a *bakkie* ground on the gravel under its tires, now blocking the path of the wolves. A white truck covered in dust. One man was seated in the cab of the vehicle. Another was in the open rear, clad in khaki shirt and pants, the color of the dust on the road. One hand gripped the frame of the *bakkie*. The other hand held a larger stick. This weapon glinted with a metallic sheen.

Blackthorn froze. He looked to the man in back of the vehicle. Then back to the man, further distant, on the farm.

When he looked back, the man was pointing the great stick at him.

"*THE THUNDER!*" Blackthorn spat his anguished cry, and the wolves bolted off the road. Kleinsperwer paused to look at the truck, and followed the rest.

The thunder did not tear across the savanna. There was only a small, absurd 'pop'. And the wolves were away.

Blackthorn looked about, and could see all four of his companions. Blouvalk and Visarend overtook him while he glanced about, Swartwou bounded through the grasses, followed by Kleinsperwer.

As he ran, Kleinsperwer flagged. A bright red object bounced on his rump as his run slowed.

"The ground moves underneath me." Kleinsperwer slurred, his twitter caught in his throat. He stumbled to a halt, wavering on his feet.

Blackthorn sniffed him, and came to the red object. He nosed it, and it fell away onto the ground. One end was a light red tassel, the shaft clear plastic. The other end was a sharp point of bloodstained steel.

"The grass moves like water..." He sank onto his belly, his head swaying on his neck. "Am I swimming in a pool of it?"

"You have been poisoned." Blackthorn trotted around him, looking about in desperation, helpless.

"What is the answer from the veld?" His slur became more muffled.

"I am sorry, little sparrowhawk." Blackthorn croaked. He lapped the younger wolf's muzzle, but he did not seem to notice.

"The answer... is our *Volk*." He flopped onto his side, his skull conking on the ground. His body went slack.

An engine revved nearby.

"They are coming for us." Blackthorn's voice did not lose its urgency.

"What must we do?" Visarend twittered.

"Leave him. Or we will soon join him." Blackthorn stood close to her, peering into her hazel eyes. "They are upon us."

The *bakkie* was approaching, crushing thornbrush under powerful tires, engine roaring to propel it through the thicket.

"And abandon him?" Her hazel eyes flashed. "He is still breathing."

"He is dying."

Visarend glared blankly.

"You have never seen a wolf die." Blackthorn murmured. He laid a paw on the young wolf's shoulder.

"Breathing..." She panted, frenzied. "He is breathing..."

Another bush crumpled under the grille as the engine roared.

"We cannot help him. As alpha you will accept this."

She bared her teeth.

"And defend the survivors."

Rocks grazed against one another under the heavy tires.

"Away with us." She uttered this quietly, an apology, as she looked on Kleinsperwer one last time.

His breath was shallow, gaze unseeing.

The four wolves bounded away as the *bakkie* crunched over a yellowthorn bush, bursting into view. The khaki-clad man in the rear brought up the stick.

Again the inconsequential 'pop' reached their ears, but the tranquilizer dart shot harmlessly into a bush.

Blackthorn stopped running after a few minutes. "The engine has not changed its pitch." He turned. The men were not in the *bakkie*, instead squatting next to the prone body of the wolf.

"What are they doing?"

"Taking his body."

Kleinsperwer was hefted on a blanket, with a dark towel over his head. One of the men took a broad leather collar and clipped this around his neck, nestled into the brown ruff of fur. At this distance, he appeared dead. His body was gently placed in the rear of the *bakkie*.

"Do they... *eat* wolves?" Swartwou whispered.

Blackthorn glared at the men, his dark eyes narrowed to slivers of hatred.

"They eat the world."

One of them entered the vehicle. The other was speaking into a device held to his face, and he crouched in the rear next to Kleinsperwer. He wrote some notes on a clipboard. The engine revved again, and it backed slowly away into the brush, and out of sight.

Blackthorn stared at the grass where Kleinsperwer had lain. He stared at it, through it. His guttural rasp ratcheted with metallic noise. *"Bliksem. I curse you always."*

All was quiet. Even the birds seemed reluctant to call into the afternoon.

***

The Pack had moved further away from the farm into rough ground traversed by a dried riverbed, the area dotted with browned grasses and corkwood trees. Blackthorn had led them there, and the others stayed quiet, resting in their grief. None seemed to want to speak, fearful of the words that would come.

The dark wolf turned away, and began to pad toward the south. He could feel a deeper urge pulling him far from here, from the others. Blackthorn closed his eyes, and could see himself running, across vast lands of vibrant green. Alone.

After a moment, he turned back toward the other wolves, and stared at the ground.

"Is this a Pack?"

Blouvalk, Swartwou, and Visarend looked at one another, at Blackthorn, mostly at the ground.

"There is only the Pack. For us. In this country." He glared at them, and at his paws. "Death is with us. As ever it must be." His ears folded back, eyes closed, and he could smell the earthen den and the musk of wolf pups. "Wolves fight and die for one another, but it is only death that we can truly depend upon."

Swartwou laid down and whimpered.

"Kleinsperwer is gone. This wound shall scar. Remember it." He prodded the larger wolf with his snout. "Do not allow it to fester or destroy you."

"This wound shall ache. Every moment of my life." Visarend stared at the ground, at nothing.

"Grow accustomed to it. Pain is my closest companion." Blackthorn lapped her muzzle.

"You have taken Kleinsperwer's gift for strange ideas."

"I suppose I have." Blackthorn rasped. "Pain safeguards me against apathy, against recklessness." He walked in a circle and laid down. "The scar on my side." He angled his head toward his flank where the fur was thin, and a raised mark was visible along the lower margin of his rib cage.

Blouvalk and Swartwou stood with great effort in their sorrow, and gathered closer.

"I was hunting, a young pup with all the courage in the world. And none of the wisdom." He stood again. "A fool with teeth, and seeking a victim. Far to the north of here, a verdant grassland on the edge of a great marsh. Buffalo... eland... imposing kudu with crowns of spiral horns. The closest prey were lechwe."

"I have never seen those." Swartwou looked to the others, as though they potentially had.

"Lechwe are great antelope with powerful legs, splayed hooves that could leap through ponds with ethereal grace. Fast as birds, they dance across water." He indicated a boulder close by, two meters in height. "Imagine a leap over that, and greater still." He paced. "There were more experienced hunters among us, but I was not about to allow that to impede my bloodlust."

"Did you hunt alone?" Swartwou's ears were up. He seemed eager for the distraction of a story.

"*Ja*, alone. I was at least dimly aware of my limitations, and took care that none would see my failures. And so I stalked my prey. The lechwe seemed to laugh as they vaulted into the marsh away from my infantile attempt."

Visarend sighed.

"Not what a hunter like me would allow. I would not accept their contempt. I would have my *wraak*."

"What is that?"

"Vengeance. For slights suffered, and insults endured." He grimaced. "These things matter in the moment. And with time, forgotten, fallen as water from rock." He glanced at the others. "Back then, however, I would have my kill. None would presume to be beyond reach of my jaws."

A sparrowhawk flapped overhead with a *kew kew kew* call. The white underbody was invisible against the sky, and it vanished into the brush.

"The lechwe were truly shocked when this wolf crashed into the water after them. I was magnificent—the grace of a tree tumbling into a stream." He cocked a brow as he looked at the rest of the pack. "I nearly caught one."

"Truly?" Swartwou was on his feet.

"Truly. Only a move that stupid would have caught those graceful antelope off guard. And they leapt further from me. I swam out toward them, up to my ears in black water. The death threats streaming through my mind continued unabated, until I struck a solid object in the marsh."

"A stone?" Visarend wondered.

"If a stone were made flesh. It moved underneath me, lifting me and throwing me aside as though I were a field mouse." Blackthorn shook his head. "Courage gone, vengeance for-gotten, I swam for the shore as though the Rage were behind me."

Blouvalk glanced at him, dejected.

"Great jaws closed upon my side, and I was thrown from the water. As my stunned body spun through the air, I could hear a great guffaw, the deepest, most sonorous grunting I will ever hear, and it was veritably laughing at me."

Swartwou's jaw hung slack.

"After tumbling to the ground, I could feel my wound seeping against the mud. And yet I stood to see what it was. A hippopotamus."

"What ever is that?" Visarend was aghast at such a vision.

"Elusive to describe, other than an elephant that lives in the water. It tossed me as though batting aside an insect. Me, the supreme hunter, the *wraak* of the veld." He nodded. "An enemy had broken me. My greatest teacher."

"What do you mean?" Blouvalk cocked his head to the side, confused.

"Of humility and defeat. The penalty of failing to heed my limits." He locked his dark eyes with Visarend. "Above all, acceptance."

"One is to accept failure?" Her voice acquired an edge.

"Accept and learn, always. Else we abandon our leadership." He padded toward Visarend and lapped her muzzle. "The most important sign of a great leader? That many deaths have occurred under their watch."

"You cannot mean that." Her eyes were filled with anguish.

"Many, beyond counting. The longer your rule, the longer the Pack stays as one, the more numerous the fallen. Death will find us, no matter your decisions."

Visarend emitted a plaintive cry.

"Learn always, decide as best you can, and protect the survivors. One cannot expect more."

Far off, an engine revved again, as the *bakkie* drove off to some unknown destination.

"Have you ever watched a herd of your prey before and after

a hunt?"

Visarend did not speak.

"I have. When one falls to our hunt, the rest continue feeding." He lapped her muzzle. "They do not stop, and they do not mourn. They keep grazing. Neither apathetic nor stupid, they only hunger, and do as they must. As do we all."

Swartwou whined, with his head resting on his forepaws.

"No matter the loss, there is strength in our *Volk*. What our enemies have done, we shall learn from it." His voice softened. "And we shall learn from that blood without being consumed by it."

Blouvalk watched the ground before him.

"Our fur is matted with *bloed* of generations." Blackthorn intoned. "Of wolves dead long before we walked the veld, and of those in our Pack that we have lost. Learn from them, and we are bounded only by the horizon."

Visarend whined gently as Swartwou slumped to the ground. Blouvalk was silent.

Blackthorn's voice abraded the quiet of the savanna, in the dimming afternoon light.

"Blood endures. We *trek* forth."

Twenty-Seven

ncient eyes surveyed the rolling grasslands from a lofty perch on the trunk of a silver clusterleaf tree. The branches spread far and wide, as though the clusterleaf wished to embrace the veld to the far horizon. Silvery grey foliage was layered from the crown to the lower levels, and provided shade to the tree agama. The leathery skin of the agama was a rainbow, its head a brilliant blue through the neck and shoulders, to a green and brown of back and belly, and a light brown tail.

The male agama peered about with caution, all too aware its bold colors would attract more than females. Clawed feet held fast to the bark of the tree, and gripped tighter as a possible rival approached.

The rival was no agama, but a painted wolf, and he spotted the lizard with equally ancient eyes. Dark fur, in places thin and grey as ash, with only hints of gold and white across his side and back. Large dish ears swiveled about, ever seeking the sounds that would betray an enemy.

The agama knew the wolf could not reach him, but responded with the only show of force he could muster: press-ups. Pushing down and up with his forelegs, the blue head bobbed up and down on the trunk, showing all around his strength.

And with that, he retreated from view.

Winter was upon the land. Basins filled with summer rains had evaporated. Rivers gradually shrank, and the tributaries that fed those rivers gradually choked, the beds cracking as they dried.

Blackthorn returned his gaze to the veld itself, listening, waiting with the eternal patience of an aged veteran. The stand of clusterleaf stood on a rise that gave them an expansive view.

"This is an arid season." His voice resonated across the patch of grass. He looked behind to see the other wolves slowly making their way to his side.

"There is little scent in the air." Visarend sniffed. She stood at his side, looking about.

"Indeed." He smiled, serrated teeth glittering from an open jaw. "It will be some time before the rains return." He saw Blouvalk and Swartwou dragging themselves to the tree. They did not look at Visarend.

"We rest here. I roamed through this wild place before I found you." He exhaled heavily, and laid down, his aching joints flaring. Though some features of this land were familiar, he welcomed a return to nature. "The *trek* has been well worth it."

"To be away from humans?" Swartwou bit down on these words, looking toward Visarend, who only stared at the ground.

"Indeed. I shall never go near those invidious *bliksems* as long as I leave clawed prints on the earth." He looked at Blouvalk, who gave a nod.

"How far have you walked, Blackthorn?" Swartwou flopped to the ground.

"As far as you have, black kite."

"I meant over a lifetime."

Blackthorn closed his eyes. "Imagine our path since the farm. Now travel that many times each season, until the cool of winter nights comes and goes, once and again, and there again. And again and again." He opened his eyes to survey the world before him.

"I would die before I ever walk so far."

"The *trek* is in our *bloed*. Should the land be desolate, we journey to a new one. Should our enemies seek us, they will swallow the dust of our tracks. And in our new hunting lands, we shall endure, within the strength of the Pack." Blackthorn raised his head, closing his eyes for a moment before he continued. "Build our numbers, ever building. Within the Pack, we shall never be conquered." He was on his paws again, ignoring his pains. "And so we serve the Pack. Unto death."

"What do you mean?" Swartwou cocked his head to the side. The dark wolf did not respond to him, staring off to the horizon. Swartwou looked to the others, who only could answer with a shake of the head.

As the others rested, the sun began to set, and the tree agama again poked its blue head out to watch. Nightjars roused for their nocturnal flights.

Blackthorn remained standing, a statue, staring out to nothing, beyond the browned grasses. His last words of the day were whispered, but startled the others even so.

"*Unto death.*"

***

The following morning, Blackthorn bid the others to continue resting while he patrolled the area. Padding away from where they slumbered, he made a line away, far beyond sight, and made a vast circle all the way around to the same point near a large flat rock.

The land was sandy soil, uneven, rocky, punctuated by acacia and clusterleaf trees. A depression was carved into the ground, a rivulet from the past. He sniffed this, and detected a faint scent of impala. His brow softened, the furrow of worry clearing. On he marched along the great circumference of the wolf's wide patrol.

He came to a tall giraffe thorn acacia, hundreds of years old. The thorn-festooned tree was partially hidden underneath a series of oversized lobulated straw mounds, each built onto and around the branches of the acacia. The leafy branches poked out of the straw, as though struggling to reach sunlight again.

The mounds were alive. Fluttering everywhere were swift-moving ashen shapes. The sociable weavers had grey and white scaled feathers and milky-white chest and abdomens. The color was visible only for a moment as they appeared at holes in the mound, flitted off, and another returned with food or straw, disappearing into the holes. As he approached the tree, even at a kilometer distance, he could hear the swarming of chirping from the mounds, from a community of half a thousand weavers.

They were not the only tenants. Finches, tits, and innumerable other birds also roosted within the mounds. Vervet monkeys peered down at the wolf from perches higher in the tree. A mongoose foraged in the litter underneath the nests.

Blackthorn noted this hive of activity, and that it would be a place herbivores would visit and browse.

As he completed his circle, the sun was rising, as was the heat. He crossed a series of impala tracks, hoofprints of paired teardrops, all progressing in the same direction as a tangent across his patrol.

Approaching the flat rock where he began, he slowed his pace. Lanky legs slowed, paws dragged, and his sight was drawn to another set of prints in the sandy soil.

A central pad with four toe blots.

He placed his forepaw into the impression, and it was dwarfed by the larger lion print.

A bitter smile parted his lips. "So it must be."

Twenty-Eight

G *nu.*

Grunting, hoof falls, the fluttering exhalation of grazing beasts. Dozens of female wildebeest with their young ambled across the veld in the loosely associated herd that had gathered to feed. It was long since the rains had ceased, but isolated water sources persisted into the winter. Surrounding this water hole were growths of lush grass, clipped by passing antelope. Heads were down throughout the herd, lips pulling away tufts of green, molars grinding down the fibers. Those chewing stood with heads up, looking about for danger while others took their mouthful. In the air above the wildebeest herd flies buzzed incessantly, a persistent and annoying black cloud.

The rut had come and gone, the females had fallen pregnant, and were even more ravenous as they fed the growing generation within. In the summer males and females kept to different herds. In the winter between the rains, these aggregated around available pastures. The males were exhausted, from fighting over breeding rights, and from successful mating.

One male was more exhausted than most, having suffered the worse for the past rut. He was old and proud, having sired many calves over his lifetime. This year he was unable to beat back his rivals at the center of the wildebeest herd. Many times he ended up in the dirt, stabbed by the sharp curved horns, stamped by hooves. Each time he went down, he was back up to respond to the challenge. His black fur was now matted, worn thin, and marked with wounds.

He had, in the end, yielded to the younger, more able males, and resumed grazing near the edge of the herd. He took his share of the sweet grass, but no longer appreciated the flavor. It tasted as dry as the dust.

Days of feeding had passed for him, and he no longer noted the passage of time.

This morning, the pounding of hooves around and beside him were lost to the ringing in his ears from the traumas of the rut. He looked up to see the herd moving away, and moving fast. Suddenly, a twitter arose about him, and he turned to see them coming. The black, white and gold forms were closing in, and their fangs were at the ready.

He began to run, but his sprint was a fraction of what he was once able. The high-pitched chirping calls surrounded him, and he could feel teeth on his haunch. He lurched in the opposite direction, and attempted to turn to run away from the hunter.

Another set of teeth clamped on his other haunch, and with his momentum, the top-heavy wildebeest was toppled over. He crashed down, and could only bellow his protests to the hunters who brought him low.

The tear across his abdomen was only dully apparent to him, and his deep exhaustion sank further as he felt a cold wash over his body. He looked down through his flailing fore hooves at a crimson pool that expanded from beneath him, and his entrails pulled from the rent in his belly. His vision darkened, and he went into the deepest sleep.

For a moment he was young again, a newborn calf, ready to run with his mother on a grassland that was the whole world.

***

"You did well with the hunt, Visarend." Blackthorn ran a tongue over his lips, still tasting the blood that soaked his fur.

"The approach seemed just right." She laid on her side, her belly full of meat. "We did not need to chase him far."

"Indeed." He yawned, displaying serrated teeth. "The hunt was over before you launched the attack. You chose your target well."

"Will there always be an old or a sick individual to pursue?"

"There will always be a slowest prey. Each time we hunt, it begins with a probe." His voice rumbled, heard easily on the grass plain amongst the wolves. "We chase, and test the herd. We look for weakness, and exploit it. If we find no likely targets, the hunt will continue elsewhere."

"Was my approach adequate?" Swartwou rolled back onto his paws and stood.

"It was. You responded to the calls of your alpha, and kept your quarry from escaping."

"I doubt he would have escaped even if we walked to him." Blouvalk jested.

"Even so, assume no victory." Blackthorn uttered. "More than once an antelope faked an injury, only to flee swift as a bird once the chase was underway."

"Why would they do so?" Blouvalk canted his head to the side, perplexed at the notion of falsehood.

"I suspect they were guarding a calf, and wanted only to distract me." He chuckled. "It worked. Once."

He glanced across the grasses to the carcass of the wildebeest they had killed.

"What are you looking for?" Visarend came to his side.

"Hyena." He looked around, and got back onto his paws. "They would normally be upon that kill. They can scent the dead a day's run distant."

None spoke for a while as the morning bled away, the warm air blowing across the vibrant grass and the fur of the wild dogs. A dragonfly buzzed past, hovering before alighting on a tall stalk of grass. Its brittle wings were missing pieces, and the insect was barely able to fly. It was the last survivor of the summer.

"You have done well." Blackthorn finally broke the calm with his graveled voice. "All of you."

"Despite being so far behind in our learning." Blouvalk sounded terse.

"By any measure. Packs of our size struggle to make a kill, and you brought down a mighty wildebeest today. By any measure, you have done well."

The others did not speak, unsure of what to say.

"I have never been fond of having a pupil." The old wolf seemed to speak to no one in particular. "All too often they lack interest, or their mind is elsewhere. Or perhaps I have not the gift of being a teacher. Too short a temper, perhaps." He raked the ground in front of him with an idle claw. "And despite your internment, for nearly your entire lives, utterly wasted, you have countered the desperate challenge of the savanna. Kill or die—your answer has been most resolute."

"Even though—" Swartwou muttered.

"Even though Kleinsperwer was cut down." He paused, as a burning sensation rose in his chest, one he labored to ignore. He thought of the young wolf's body, prone underneath the blanket, before the men took him away. "The threat that humans present is implacable, and has taken far more hardened wolves than you." He turned to meet Swartwou's meek hazel eyes. "Do not bother with guilt. Learn, and *trek* forth."

Swartwou seemed to stand taller with that remark.

"I was content with solitude. No matter the grounds, I am capable of surviving. And solitude seemed to enjoy my presence." He lifted a lip, displaying his teeth for a moment. "The indifferent savanna was there to show me the fallacy." He thought of the hyena Kreun, and shook his head. "There is only the Pack for us." He was on his paws, and padded off.

"To where are you leaving?" Visarend was by his side, matching his pace.

"Patrol. I must find if there are more lion prints in our area."

"I am pleased you decided to stay with us. I presume you are ready, then?"

"For what?" Blackthorn noticed she was smiling in her inscrutable way.

"To accept your place in our pack."

He glanced back toward the others. "I am."

"Very well. I am ready, at long last." She lapped his muzzle, and brushed closely. The sensation of fur against fur was electric to him.

"What do you mean?"

She laughed to herself. "And I thought you were clever."

Visarend licked his muzzle again, and he returned the gesture.

"I did not think that..." Blackthorn stuttered, as understanding dawned on him.

"Now, my wolf, there is no need to think."

She led him away, into the tall grasses. He could feel his heart beating heavily, as though a great hunt were underway.

She presented herself to him, and they mated in the waving grass sea, heedless to all around them. His patrol forgotten, they whiled the afternoon away.

***

When they returned from the tall grass, Visarend and Blackthorn saw that the other two had not strayed. Swartwou promptly stood and padded over to Visarend, then Blackthorn. Swartwou lapped their muzzle gently in greeting, holding his head at a level lower than theirs. With his size, he stooped awkwardly to do so.

Blouvalk padded over and did the same, though he could not look Blackthorn in the eye. After licking the muzzle of his superiors, he lay down, on his back. Blouvalk looked to Visarend, who accepted this show of subservience, and he was back on his feet.

This gesture aside, they began the hunting rally. Their excited twittering and leaping, greeting after greeting, reached a fever pitch, and Blouvalk headed out to lead the hunt.

It was very brief, returning to the slaughtered wildebeest from the morning. The wolves tucked into the large antelope, now attracting flies. Pulling away hide and dismembering the corpse, they ate their fill as Blackthorn withdrew.

Smacking his lips, he met the gaze of another.

The brown spotted hyena stood close, daring the wolf to

leave the kill. His slight dorsal mane fluttered in the afternoon breeze.

Blackthorn grinned, revealing serrated teeth.

Swartwou stopped feeding as well, and chirped his alarm on sight of the hyena.

"Continue your feast. We will need every scrap of food we can preserve." He waited, and eventually the hyena strayed closer. And a little closer. Each time the male hyena paused, waiting for a response.

Blackthorn turned, surveying the surrounds, and found no sign of another enemy.

"*Aandag*, wolves."

At that, the others stopped eating and paid attention.

The hyena took a few more steps, now a few strides away.

"A new lesson is upon you." His lips pulled back, the white knives unsheathed. "Stay out of range of his jaws, and encircle him."

Visarend loped away first, and the hyena gave a nervous giggle as she took station behind him. The others took the sides. Blackthorn leapt forth, twittering his commands.

"Attack his hindquarters!"

Visarend buried her teeth in the rump of the hyena, and let go, giving a body length of distance as the male hyena whirled to face her. Blouvalk did the same, and the hyena gave a chattering cry. Its head was down, teeth bared, rump tucked in on the ground to protect his vulnerable underparts. Each wolf took a turn taking vicious bites of the backside, and shortly the hyena was bleeding heavily.

With a high cackle, the hyena bolted, managing to move quickly despite still dragging his rump close to the ground.

"And that is how you deal with one."

Blouvalk tittered, his face flecked with hyena blood. "And when more of them come?"

"No different, though a wolf must be cunning." He watched the hyena retreat, hindparts no longer tucked to the ground. "Even if they number greater than stalks of grass, they act as individuals. Working together, we can chase away one, then another. As their numbers mount, so does their confidence."

"Eventually they would overwhelm us, yes?" Blouvalk mused.

"Then you must run before you become their meal. But not before you exact a price for their theft."

A whooping call echoed across the plain. A barely audible whoop answered it.

"Come, it is time to finish eating. Now that the hyena clan know we are here, they will be our very shadow."

"Are hyenas smart?" Swartwou wondered.

"They are as canny as us." Blackthorn rooted inside the pelvis of the wildebeest, tearing away muscle and tendon. "Possibly more. Their power lies in numbers, their ability to think fast, and deceive when needed. Not to mention the terror they can inspire."

"I see nothing to fear from their kind." Blouvalk choked down a strap of hide.

Another whoop reached across the veld.

"If you are wise, you will know fear." Blackthorn looked in the direction where the hyena had retreated. "And they will be pleased to enlighten you."

Twenty-Nine

Several weeks passed, as winter dragged on into the earliest vestige of spring. Trifling rains visited the bushveld to relieve the drought. At first, the cloudbursts were brief, the water sucked away into invisible aquifers without a trace. Soon enough the rains were sustained, leaving behind mud and standing pools of water. What were in winter parched clay basins now supported creaking populations of frogs. Birds splashed down in shallow water to dip their heads in the cool liquid, allowing it to run down their backs with a shake that cleaned their plumage of dust.

A meandering flock of guinea fowl marched through the grass, heads bobbing as they took step after step. *Hek-eh-Keeeh! Hek-eh-Keeeh!* The squawking call joined the more subtle chirps of sparrows, the *wip wip wip* of common quails, and the trill of crickets.

Within days the scrub was embroidered in gold and green. Blades of grass thrust toward the sun as the land awoke from its dormant state.

***

Dawn revealed a crystalline latticework weaved across what

seemed every single stalk of grass on the savanna. Spider webs, degraded by the wind and the damp, clung to the tips, the remainders fluttering in the morning breeze. Drops of dew sparkled on the wisps of silk, the golden solar rays dancing as the yellow disk appeared on the horizon.

A subtle *thump* was felt more than heard across the grassland. The towering bird regarded the wavering grasses ahead, a naked head holding aloft large dusky eyes over a hard pink bill. The ostrich's black plumage fluttered, and it extended its broad wings with a flap. A single white feather was loosed to drift on the wind.

The male ostrich took another heavy step, and the head dropped low on its craning neck to scoop up seeds on the ground. The head lifted again, as though on the end of a puppeteer's string, to survey the field.

A handful of shapes appeared in its wide peripheral vision, and the ostrich knew there was a danger. It did not pause, continuing to pace across the veld, but no longer stooping for seeds. The brain was tiny, the size of an avocado pit, but this compact machine was no less able to calculate an escape, and know instantly that it would not be necessary.

"Have we seen that before?" Blouvalk wondered.

"You have not. Ostrich, common enough in these wild areas."

"We are to leave that one alone." Swartwou was not asking a question.

"Correct. The claw on its foot could open a wolf as wide as the morning."

The ostrich continued to watch them, its heavy footfalls in wordless communication with all around. Wolves were unlikely to hunt him. Wolves meant no hyenas, and no lions about, or at least none that would stay hidden. He dipped his head again, tapping the bill against the softened ground, swallowing the scattered seeds.

"Where do you presume the hyenas have gone?" Blackthorn asked any who listened.

"They last followed us at sunset in the direction of the river." Blouvalk called in his high twitter. "Could be anywhere."

"Also correct." Blackthorn was on his hind legs, and Blouvalk met him in midair, a light clash, and they were back on their paws. "Today you keep your snout low, and tell me the news of the veld."

He was down sniffing at the command, then sprinted ahead a few dozen meters, and sniffed again.

Swartwou was by Blackthorn's side, dipping his head low.

"Be his flank, and look out for prey."

The large wolf lurched forward, and was quickly by Blouvalk's side.

Blackthorn watched them go, as the two searched the ground intently. Then they were bounding off across the plain, pairs of large rounded ears bouncing just over the grass tips. His joints ached as they always had, but in his chest he felt a deeper, more elusive pang. A rat chewing its way out from the inside. His thoughts drifted to Kleinsperwer, and his eccentric musings. He wondered what strange new expressions the young wolf would have uttered.

Pawfalls behind him brought his attention back to the bushveld before his eyes. Visarend loped up behind Blackthorn, and touched noses with him. Each fall of her lanky legs seemed heavier than the last.

"It shall be soon." She breathed heavily.

"Come the night?"

"Not that soon. We have time to find a den." Her belly hung low, as though after a medium sized feast. Her teats were just becoming prominent.

"I agree." He sniffed her abdomen. "It should not be long before we find an abandoned aardvark burrow."

"I was not expecting the weight."

"New mothers never do." His grizzled laugh surprised her. "You hold a new pack within you—twice over our numbers at least."

"So strange." She grimaced. "That we will at a stroke have so many hunters to feed."

"Feed, yes. But hunters they will not be, not for a few seasons to pass."

She walked for a moment before stopping. "Blackthorn."

He stopped by her side.

Her mouth was open, but she could not speak. She seemed frozen in contemplation, staring to a far away place. Pupils dilated, and she breathed more heavily still.

He lapped her muzzle and met her wide eyes with his own. "Do not think upon it, Visarend."

"It is impossible not to."

"Do not." Blackthorn rasped. "What fortunes are favored by the savanna, we shall not know. And so we need not ask." He began to walk, and tugged on Visarend's shoulder with his jaws.

A rolling *coo-roo-coo* reached their ears as a rock dove took flight from a bare tree branch.

"Not all will survive." Her voice was flat, devoid of emotion.

"Perhaps none." Blackthorn kept his graveled tone even.

Visarend stood quietly, staring into the bushveld ahead. The grasses hissed with the winds.

"So be it." Her voice at first wavered, then deepened with resolve. "If no wolf is destined." Her eyes narrowed. "Should every pup of this litter die of starvation, or fall victim to hyena, I shall bring life to another litter." Her slaver dripped to the ground beneath her mouth as a low growl erupted within her. "And yet another." She lifted her lips into a snarl. "My pack shall be *Maaier*. And my first pup shall be named *Wraak*."

He moved closer to lap her muzzle, but she snapped at him, and he recoiled.

"Do not disturb my anger." She took a deep breath. "I love the way it feels." Her face was contorted with rage, and she loped ahead to catch up with the others.

Blackthorn watched her, and could only nod, and grin bitterly. "I could not agree more, my love." He followed her. "None are destined."

Thirty

A mosaic pattern of green and light brown grasses created a vast undulating curtain on the savanna. The shimmering background wavered with the slightest breeze now that the sweet grass stalks were in flower.

The antelope relentlessly devoured the greenery. Despite their best efforts, the seas of grass endured, now towering green shafts that held aloft the seeds for dispersal on wind. In the humid summer, all the plant predators were spoiled for choice.

Above even the tallest stalks stood a male reedbuck. Fawn brown shaggy fur covered his body, ending with a short tufted tail. He stood a meter at the shoulder, and advertised his strength with the erect posture. Thick ribbed horns jutted to the rear from his skull, curving up and slightly forward at the sharp tips.

His head dropped to take a mouthful of grass, ripped away from the tough growth at his feet. This was ground by powerful molars as he stood his full height, eyes wary for the approach of predators, or a female reedbuck.

His patience was rewarded with the approach of a familiar sight. Another reedbuck, nearly a meter at the shoulder and lacking the male's ribbed horns, stepped from the thick sedge.

She could see the male standing proudly in the field, and had been scenting him on the wind. Her triangular ears flicked away biting flies as she stepped closer. As the distance between them receded, her head dipped low, chin out. They sniffed one another, and she turned. He moved closer and sniffed her hindparts as they walked together in the mating march. She did not run off, which was a good sign.

Abruptly the march ended as he gave a sharp whistle, sounding as though blown harshly through a reed instrument, with such force his whole body shook. They both stotted with giant leaps, hindquarters held up, and repeated the whistling call.

The black, gold, and white hunters zeroed in on the male and gave chase as the reedbuck split off from one another. Two of the wolves darted in, closing the distance while the other two parted and went wide to cover the flanks.

The male reedbuck ended its stotting motion, breaking into a swift run. Hooves pounded the wet earth, slippery with the morning dew. The clawed paws of the wolves struggled to control their pace on the mud.

He powered forward, head angled low on a thick neck knotted with muscle, curved horns forward as the reedbuck charged. Hooves dug into the mud as he shifted direction, leaping two meters in the air over a line of thornbush.

The wolves held their heads lower still, missiles crashing through the brush, ignoring the bite of the acacia thorns. Blackthorn banked to one side to cut off the reedbuck's escape. Visarend fell behind, panting with the effort.

A high twitter erupted from the dark wolf, and the other two wolves pushed forward instead of following the reedbuck's direction. He snapped at the buck's flank, and the antelope was pressured back to its original direction, before the jaws of the pack. Swartwou was in striking distance, and nipped the haunch.

In a panic, the reedbuck stumbled, one hoof sliding on the slick mud beneath it. Blouvalk clamped down on the hind leg, and held on as the reedbuck desperately yanked the leg back, again and again, in an attempt to pull free.

Blackthorn ducked under the stamping hooves and took hold of the soft flesh of the belly, and gave a sharp pull. The reedbuck weakened instantly, and his struggles ceased. A cascade of bright red splashed under the buck. Swartwou gripped the side of the antelope and pulled him over. Visarend buried her head in the open wound and fed greedily. Unrooting the heart, she gulped down the rich meat and the blood that came with it, sensing relief from the pups that grew within her.

Whooop!

Blackthorn drew his head out of the abdominal cavity of the reedbuck and snarled.

"*Bliksem* approaches."

The spotted hyena grinned, and gave another deep *whooop!* He stepped gingerly, waiting to draw away the wild dogs before him.

"There is only one – chase him!" Blackthorn chirped his commands, and with Swartwou and Blouvalk, he pursued the hyena away. The head bobbed at the end of a long neck, his short legs carrying his heavy body with surprising ease.

Visarend continued to pull away organs and offal from the inside of the reedbuck. After three large swallows, she yelped, feeling teeth nip her hindquarters. She wriggled out of the reedbuck and whirled about, facing another male hyena.

He had moved in silently, and bared his fangs with a rolling chuckle. His head was held low on his awkwardly long neck, conical fangs dripping with saliva. One of his ears was notched, flopping back and forth on his head. He lunged forward, and Visarend withdrew.

She stood back from the reedbuck while the hyena stripped away the fine meat, scarcely pausing to breathe. Visarend stepped closer with caution, and the hyena sensed her presence immediately, clicking his teeth together within a centimeter of her snout.

Baring her fangs, she charged in heedlessly, gripping the thick hide of the hyena in her teeth. The hyena yelped, and exposed fangs of his own with an unnerved giggle.

Shortly, one wolf sprinted into view. On sight of the hyena close to Visarend, Blackthorn howled and charged.

The short mane stood on end, the spotted tawny coat shook and he whirled round to face the wolf.

Blackthorn stopped short. The dark wolf's voice was a guttural curse.

"*Kreun.*"

Kreun grinned widely, and cackled. He loped away, hindparts tucked in as the other two wolves gave chase.

"Feed, and feed quickly, Visarend."

She dove in and choked down the meat as fast as she could bear.

"They will soon be upon us." He pulled away the hide of the reedbuck's shoulder and attacked the muscle there while Visarend remained buried in the abdominal cavity. From his vantage point, he could see the approach of the first male hyena he chased away. This one gave a *whooop!* followed by a lowing call, mooing in a steady dirge.

Visarend pulled her head free and braced herself to give

chase.

"Ignore him." Blackthorn watched him for a moment before whirling round to face an enemy behind him.

Kreun cowered, shocked that the wolf could hear his approach.

"You have become quite good at what you do, craven beast." Blackthorn snarled. *"Shall my queen feed on you next?"*

He gave a high giggle and loped a respectful distance away.

"Where are those bloody *okes?*" He looked around for Swartwou and Blouvalk, but could only see more shapes rustling in the grass. Light brown with spots, one form after another. The lowing call began again in earnest, and only grew louder with time.

"Finish now, Visarend. We must yield this kill."

She pulled away again, her fur dark and matted with gore. They ran off with four hyena in tow, but they did not chase far, withdrawing to swarm over the body of the reedbuck.

Soon they found Swartwou and Blouvalk, chasing two other hyena.

"Leave them, you two! The kill is lost." Blackthorn barked to them, and they broke off their chase. As the four wolves loped away, they grumbled bitterly.

***

The horizon shimmered in the heat. Despite the warmth, the wolves lazed in the open, unaffected by the burning star overhead.

"What say you of the hyena clan?" Blackthorn shook his head, scattering the flies that worked on the blood in his fur. He rolled to his other side, but the flies shortly returned.

"They seemed to come from nowhere." Swartwou muttered.

"*Ja*, they were everywhere at once. We must assume they are tracking us, every hunt." Blackthorn turned over and was on his paws again. He had difficulty staying still when speaking. "And what of the two that you were chasing?"

"We nearly saw them off." Blouvalk snuffed.

"I think not." The dark wolf prodded him with his snout. "There is no doubt of your bravery, but they were not about to give way. They merely appeared to be on the run, counting on you to chase them."

"Those *domkoppe* meant to lead us away?"

"That is their game. Lure the hunter away, and take the spoils. They argue with one another, and there is no peace at a carcass between them, but make no mistake. They are aware of what they are doing. One clever hyena can keep an entire wolf pack busy, and will summon their clan until the numbers swing to their favor. While we chase them, and keep them running, they play for time. The kill shall be theirs. And after nightfall, they hold the veld."

"Are we not to chase them away?" Blouvalk grumbled. "Yield to them the moment they arrive?"

"No, Blouvalk, we must give chase, or they would harry us and bite us until we do. There is a balance a pack must strike. Short chases, eat what you can, while you can." He sighed. "Never mind. We have taken a decent share today. Rest while you may."

"You knew one of them." Blouvalk looked toward Blackthorn. "What did you call him?"

Blackthorn rumbled quietly.

"Kreun, was it?"

"Yes. I hunted with that *bliksem* in seasons past. Before I happened upon you." He rested his head on his forepaws. "He was alone then, as was I. Outcasts."

"Did a tragedy befall his clan as well?"

"No." Blackthorn glared at the soil before his nose. "He was likely expelled. Since then, however, he has risen in the estimation of his matriarch."

"Risen? How?"

Blackthorn mumbled something, almost to himself. The other wolves looked at one another.

"*Dief.*"

"What does that mean, Blackthorn?" Visarend righted herself with some effort, her belly protruding.

"Thief." He gave a nod. "He has become quite good at stealing kills. And his skills did not go unnoticed."

Thirty-One

"We divide our hunt today."

Swartwou and Blouvalk looked at each other, giving Visarend a wary eye.

"Blackthorn and I shall go to the south."

"Divided, we double our chances?" Blouvalk did not sound convinced.

"You and Swartwou will go further east, and make noise whilst you do so." Visarend issued her commands, pausing to yawn widely, displaying a curled pink tongue and serrated teeth.

"What herds are in that direction?" Swartwou took a few strides, looking about for the hunting rally, confused at the lack of enthusiasm in the air.

"Doubtful there are any. The day previous I found impala tracks leading to the south." Blackthorn lapped Visarend's muzzle.

She grinned, rousing herself for the hunt.

Kreun watched this from a distance, ensconced in shadows. He started for a moment as the wolf pack began yipping and scampering about with the licking of muzzles he had come to expect from a hunting rally. It seemed oddly subdued, however. Kreun observed the pack moving off to the east, with another male spotted hyena trailing them closely.

Kreun shook his head, his ruined ear flopping against his skull. He took up a slow loping pace, trailing all four wolves and the hyena tailing them by at least a kilometer.

***

The wolves padded quickly along a dirt path, twin ruts dug by some vehicle in the past year, now overgrown with grass. Blackthorn gave a slight chirp, and veered into dense thorn-brush. With visibility reduced to less than a body length, the pack split in two. Blouvalk and Swartwou continued onward, making noise as they cracked and crashed their way through the undergrowth in the direction of the rising sun.

Blackthorn and Visarend crept on through the sickle bush and acacia shrub further away, pausing as they heard the rustling of another large hunter move through the bush past them. There was no wind here, the air stilled against foliage that formed a wall. They scented nothing, but could hear easily the scraping of leaf and needle against fur.

Blackthorn pressed his body to hers, and she looked back to see the caution in his eyes. They waited, barely breathing. Skittering of thorns was all that rose above the wind through the higher branches, and a subdued rumble. The hunter moved on through the brush, and all traces of it vanished.

Once it was quiet again, they moved to the south.

"We will soon be free of this, and our hunt will begin in earnest."

Visarend nodded, increasing her pace to match that of her dark mate. Ears were folded back, eyes peering uselessly, seeing only grass centimeters away, blinking and closing constantly as thorns flicked close, ever threatening to stab them into blindness. They made maddeningly slow progress in the dim light of the dense thicket over the course of the hour.

They pushed through thornbush branches and abruptly found themselves breaking out of the sedge. The blinding white of the open grasslands faded to a golden dawn as their pupils adjusted. Dotted with giraffe thorn acacia, the vast plain of green grass stalks went on forever, broken only by a shallow river zagging across the veld.

"The promise renewed." Her voice sounded far away. Within her, she could feel the movement of a pup. The orange sun seemed to set her coat alight, white and gold wiry fur tousled by the breeze.

"Where will they meet us?" Visarend looked to the horizon.

"The small *koppie* to the south." He indicated a bald granite dome, its foot ringed by corkwood trees, nearly beyond their keen sight.

"Then we shall make a kill before our meeting."

***

Grass disappeared down the throats of the impala, beginning the long process of digestion. All morning they would clip large volumes of the fibers, down to the ground, and the grass would pile into four-chambered stomachs for rumination. When the sun climbed to the top of the sky, they would rest in the heat, bringing back up semi-digested grass for further chewing. All the while, their eyes were wide, taking in the signs of the morning, ears swiveling about in listening for alarm calls.

Grazing in the shade of a high hill topped by shining white stone, the impala were able to eat in some degree of relaxation. There were dozens of eyes watching. The impala took turns looking about. A resident gang of meerkats bulldozed through the dry bush, foraging as they went while experienced members stood tall as sentries.

Vervet monkeys browsed in the corkwood trees, ever watchful for movement. Their grey fur and white brow gave them the appearance of advanced age. Dozens of them were on the ground sifting through the foliage for seeds or nuts. When taking a break from browsing, lower ranked monkeys would groom the fur of more highly-ranked elders, always currying favor from the more powerful.

The browsing and grooming came to a halt as a cough interrupted the morning feed. All were stilled.

Another coughing bark, and the vervet monkeys as one scurried for the nearest tree.

Impala stopped grazing, heads up. The call alerted them to danger - but did not inform them of direction. They waited, silent, every nerve on edge, every tendon tight in preparation for what could be their last run.

A motion far distant, and an impala gave its own harsh alarm bark. The herd stood poised, but did not run, not yet. The call was for a predator, but one nowhere near enough to be a threat.

Every black globe eye was fixed on a shape that drew slowly closer. Up, then down. Up, then down. A round head atop a long neck, short ears. A shaggy brown mane down the neck.

Hyena. Another short alarm bark. Two impala paused to take more grass. Then a few more.

Two forms suddenly burst from the tall grasses closer to the herd - white knives unsheathed, and a high twitter breaking the calm.

Several impala gave more urgent coughing barks, but the

herd was already stampeding away from the threat. A thunder of hooves, and bodies launching themselves high over the grass in one leaping *pronk* after another that carried the impala several body lengths away from danger.

One yearling impala coiled for a leaping *pronk*, but was cut short. A wolf seized the impala by the side, and despite its lurching attempts to escape, it was anchored to the ground.

The other wolf gripped the throat, and the impala opened its mouth wide in silent protest. The head was pulled down, vanishing into the tall grass. The body was jerked aside, and toppled over. A hoof was visible for a moment above the grass tips, then this too disappeared from view.

"Hurry - take hold of its rear leg." Blackthorn rasped through teeth locked on the impala's throat.

"It is fighting us - it may regain its footing."

"Take hold and pull."

The two wolves pulled against one another, stretching the impala tightly between. For a moment, there was silence as its body hovered parallel to the ground, a taut string on an instrument, before a bleating *Hruh!* and the impala was pulled in two. Each wolf quietly went to work, choking down organs and muscle in great haste.

"We have time yet for Blouvalk and Swartwou to join us." Visarend paused, bringing her jaw close to the ground.

"No - eat quickly!"

She released a sonorous *HOO!* into the ground, a sound vaguely metallic, as though blown through a culvert.

"They can do without a meal. You cannot." Blackthorn returned to his, stripping away a sheet of hide to reveal the muscles of shoulder and rib. Serrated teeth made quick work of separating the muscle from bone.

A light giggle abruptly ceased their dining.

"*Kreun*." Blackthorn growled. He sprinted after the hyena, which loped off well ahead of the dark wolf. He returned quickly, and managed only a few bites before the hyena started to drift close again. He was off, chasing Kreun into the sedge, only to have him return as soon as the chase was stopped.

Visarend did not pause for a moment, gulping down solid organs and clotted blood as fast as her throat would allow.

A faint echo from across the veld reached their kill. *HOO*.

"They will be here soon." Blackthorn turned to lay by Visarend's side, glaring at Kreun.

The hyena wavered on his stout forepaws, shoulders rippling with muscle. His grin was steady and unpleasant, and he withdrew into the grasses.

Visarend pulled out the great length of the impala's intestines.

Kreun leapt out from hiding and fixed his jaws on the haunch of the antelope, ripping away a great section of meat and the lower leg. Blackthorn chased him, and the spotted hyena loped away, one hoof bobbing from the corner of his mouth.

"We have little time." As they continued to tear at the carcass, Kreun gave several *whooop!* calls from where he choked down sections of the impala leg.

Within minutes, distant whooping calls reached them, and the loping forms of hyena converged on where they had made the kill.

Blouvalk and Swartwou now appeared from the grasses.

"How did they find us so quickly?" Blouvalk fumed. He took only one mouthful of meat from the pelvis before two hyena shouldered their way onto the carcass. "We were leading some of them east - and if any were able to follow us so quickly, I will eat my own tail."

"Away with us, now!" Blackthorn gave an agitated twitter, and the four wolves fled. As they left the antelope behind, he looked up to see a lappet-faced vulture wheeling overhead. His gaze returned to the field, and to see the swish of a lion tail wavering over the grass tips.

"That is a pity." Blackthorn muttered. "Our every move is under watch."

***

The pack was quiet as they rested in the early afternoon. The purring *cuk-coor-uk cuk-coor-uk* of a cape turtle dove was all that could be heard over the buzzing of flies.

Blouvalk and Swartwou looked up to Visarend occasionally, considered asking a question, then thought better of it.

When she stood, the others were on their feet immediately. Her belly hung below, teats more distended now.

"It is time to move on. There will be no hunt today."

"I hunger..." Blouvalk whined.

"None today. We cannot fight both hyena and lions." She began to walk, leaving her prints on the light dust beneath the wild olive tree.

"I sense the hyenas will not be so easily left behind." Blackthorn gave her a nod. "I agree with you. You must seek a place of solitude for the den."

Visarend sighed. Her eyes were closed tightly.

He made his way to her side, and lapped her muzzle gently. "Moving again?"

"I can feel them. One of them."

"Perhaps they heed your command."

She opened her eyes at that, lifting a brow. "Was that in jest?"

"Of course, my love. Pups would sooner lift an elephant than listen to a word you utter."

She opened her jaws as Blackthorn did the same, and their mouths came together, a clicking of teeth in a playful gesture.

"The time may be short. To find a den, the edge of lion territory, and a place where hyenas will not pursue us." He grumbled. "We will not find the ideal in time."

She gave a nod. "Then we will find what is there."

Moving off into the grasses, Blackthorn padded to Blouvalk.

"Light on your paws, black kite. Listen for the hyena tracking us." He muttered quietly. "I suspect he is already on our trail."

Thirty-Two

Their progress was slow. Visarend was still unaccustomed to the effort of a wide patrol while carrying pups. Despite the visible strain, she did not complain. Blackthorn noted that she almost never made a sound. Even as she panted, she would not call for them to rest.

The wild opened before them on their travels. The arid scrub of winter had transformed into a near-wetland with the rains. Bare brush that had appeared dead in the dry season was covered with a riot of greenery. Birds seemed to be everywhere, endlessly browsing for seeds. The indigenous birds of the savanna were joined by seasonal travelers from Europe. Any disturbance would send a flock of birds boiling into the sky, chirping madly until settling on another tree to continue the business of gathering food.

Insects filled the air. Mosquitoes took to wing to hunt down warm-blooded animals within range. Citrus swallowtail and meadow white butterflies flitted about, moving from flower to flower in a hunt for nectar. Wasps buzzed through the air, hunting for beetles in the leaf litter or undergrowth. A mammoth wasp, pitch black apart from her brilliant yellow head, found a suitable beetle larva in the soil after following its tunnel into the dirt. She seized the larva and pierced the flesh with her paralyzing stinger, and laid an egg on the surface. The larva itself was unharmed by the sting, but would soon be devoured whole once the wasp larva hatched.

As the wolves padded across the rough ground, they found only more rough ground, always more trees, and yet more thick brush.

"Glorious. It seems never to end." Swartwou mused.

"It ends all too quickly. Before a wolf expects, we run headlong into a fence. A road. And then the places where humans live never seem to end." Blackthorn never took his dark gaze from the distance.

"That Kreun is following us." Blouvalk sounded disappointed.

"I never doubted he would." Blackthorn rumbled.

"Our prey evade us, and our parasites cling everlasting."

"I never doubted *they* would."

"Day and night." Blouvalk muttered.

"What?" Swartwou trudged, one paw before the next.

"Day and night, a hunt, rest, another hunt, rest. The endless routine of a wolf."

Blackthorn scoffed. "There is nothing routine about lasting the night. Yes, our days run together like the roads of humans – hunt and slumber. Yet there is no repetition." His eyes flickered about, studying the scrub before him for threats.

Swartwou glanced behind them for any sign of pursuit.

"Every day is my first, fresh as the scent of new growth in spring. Every hunt is the first, marked by the first kill. Each drop of vital blood spilled is the first... and may yet be the last. Each breath quick and savored, each clawfall as urgent as a beat from the heart."

"Words of your mother?" Visarend moaned.

"She taught me to relish the pain of living. It reminds a wolf of the alternative."

"A wise matriarch." She sniffed the air, nostrils flaring.

"If our world were a mountain of the gathering storm." He glanced at her. "The wolf is ever on the windward side of it." He gave a smile, and they continued on.

***

"Halt, all of you."

Her twitter was both urgent and quiet, and the others almost did not hear her. They could, however, scent immediately her anxiety, a subtle hint of fear.

Blackthorn looked back to her, and then to the ground she stared at.

She stood on a path along a line of boulders and the smaller rocks that had broken off over time. Among the rocks were scattered finger-thickness bluish green stems lined with rubbery teeth. Some of the stems had begun to bloom, dark maroon in color and emitting a scent of decay. Corpse flies buzzed about these flowers, alighting on what seemed rotting meat, laying eggs, and carrying off the pollen to the next flower.

In the wet soil next to the clump of polished star plants was a lion print. Fresh and wet on the muddy ground.

Blackthorn trotted over and sniffed it. The pads created deep impressions with high ridges that had yet to break down as prints do over time.

"We are in their midst." Blackthorn gave this as a deep rumble, and the other wolves held themselves low, heads low, ears flat, ready for the attack.

Cautious looks. Sniffing the air. The grasses were tall, and were able to conceal a lion even if it stood straight. Further on were shrubs of sweet thorn acacia and isolated bushwillow trees.

"There is a hint of the freshly dead on the air." Blackthorn rasped. "And not from one of those carrion flowers."

Swartwou had his snout high in the air. "I can smell it too."

"A good sign." Visarend whispered. "If there is food, they may be too busy to hunt us."

Blackthorn gritted his teeth, and gave her a look that suggested otherwise. He crept forward, in the direction of the paw print. He lowered his snout to the ground, and looked over his shoulder. He had found another print. Creeping forward, ever slower, every tendon drawn as taut as a bow string.

"You hear that?" Blouvalk twittered, barely audible.

"No." Swartwou held his head even lower.

"Precisely. Even the insects are muted." A glance at a nearby acacia tree appeared devoid of movement, not even a browsing sparrow.

Blackthorn held himself low to the ground, and hooked his head around to motion to the others. They gathered themselves close to him, and crept one paw before the other. Each footfall came with a pause, and cautious glances about for a swish of lion tail or a glaring golden eye. None breathed except with great reluctance. Ears folded flat. Bodies were held low to the ground, eyes wide as they peered through the grass stalks that parted as they inched forward.

Blackthorn issued a short, sharp grunt, glancing back at each member of his pack. Cautiously, they raised their heads to glimpse through the line of high nile grass before them.

"*Yoh!*" Swartwou uttered in spite of himself. The other wolves glanced at one another with curiosity.

"That is... unexpected." Blackthorn intoned.

They looked down over a slight depression in the landscape, where a clump of red bushwillows had taken root, their crowns high and heavy with green elliptical twisted leaves. Creamy yellow flowers sported their spiky blooms, and drew the insects in great numbers. What drew the attention of the wolves, however, was the lion stuck high in a tree.

A lioness perched in awkward fashion on a thick pale branch that rose off the central trunk of the bushwillow tree. Her hind-parts were wedged where the branch jutted off, her forepaws resting on the limp body of an impala draped over the branch. The lioness's face was fixed in an expression of serenity, in-congruous with her struggles to balance upon the branch. Her claws pricked against the bark as she adjusted her precarious footing.

Below two other lionesses paced, looking up at the prize impala. One reared on its hind legs, forepaws with claws raking against the trunk considerably out of reach of the dangling hooves. Further from this, the male lion reclined in the sun, content to wait for gravity to do all the work.

The lioness in the tree bent lower her head, ripping free a hunk of meat from the impala's hip, quaking violently for a moment before returning to a still form, gulping down the bite of meat.

"That one is going to fall." Swartwou chuckled. "And it will be spectacular."

"Her pride, so to speak, will be bruised, but any fracas will be short lived." Blackthorn muttered.

"Why?"

"That male will bound in the moment meat touches ground, and the rest will scatter before him."

"Lions do not share a kill?" Swartwou was offended by the notion.

"Lions fight over every scrap. The male eats first. Then the lionesses that actually made the kill will have a turn. Then, if there is anything left, the cubs." He angled his head higher, looking into the more distant brush. "Lionesses did not kill this one, however. At least they would not have been able to pull it into a tree."

The wolves followed his gaze and saw a spotted form crouching in the thicket. A leopard glowered at the impala prize, now hopelessly beyond its grasp. She grimaced, exposing her fangs, her long whiskers dancing in her frustration. Slinking away, she vanished further into the brush to hunt elsewhere.

"I suppose Kreun is watching this as well?" Blouvalk looked about.

"With dead prey around? Certain as dung beetles on *kak*." Blackthorn glanced behind him, though there was no immediate sign of the hyena.

Blackthorn froze suddenly. He felt the wind shift, and before he could utter a warning, he heard a growl from the male lion.

He looked up, and the blond-maned male was on his feet, looking in their direction.

A resounding *Roh-unngh* reached them, and Blackthorn took a step back.

"You wish to cross claws with me..." The resounding growl of the male lion reverberated across the savanna.

"Prepare to flee." Blackthorn's ears were flat against his skull.

"From him?" Blouvalk looked on with curiosity.

"GEVAAR..." His roar reverberated off the rocks. The lion shook himself, his light mane ruffled against his back. "Such

a small wolf pack."

The male lion suddenly took his glare from the wolves as another noise caught his attention. Under the red bushwillow tree, the impala had slid away from the branch and thumped to the ground. The two lionesses set upon it, while the one in the tree continued to shudder, fearing the drop to the ground. The lionesses had no time to enjoy their prize, and scattered as the male pounced on the dead meat. Gevaar gave another low growl.

"He seems to have forgotten us." Blouvalk canted his head to the side.

Blackthorn shook his head. "I doubt that."

The lionesses paced a deferential distance away while the male tucked in, tearing away the hide to expose the ribs. He ate lazily, taking more time to look around than actually eat.

A frenzied scratching of claws on bark disturbed the uneasy calm.

"*GRAH!*" The male suddenly scrambled as the body of the lioness crashed to the ground, an inelegant thud that crushed the already mutilated kill. The male charged back in, and struck at the lioness that had flattened his meal. She bled from the claw marks across her snout, sniffing in anger, ears pulled back. She struggled to move aside, and the male struck again, laying part of her face wide open. Clambering back to her feet, she limped as quickly as she could, pulling the dead weight of a broken hind leg after her.

WHOOOP!

The sound caused the entire pride to jump, and the uninjured lionesses padded toward the source.

Five spotted hyenas crested a nearby rise, watching the scene below with a strange mania. Their blood red eyes stared, jaws agape, giggling and cackling as they closed in on the male lion and the stolen impala. Hunched and powerful foreshoulders trudged forward, each hyena issuing a whooping call. These were answered with more distant *WHOOOP!* calls in kind.

Within minutes, the hyena were clustered around the male, still draping a forepaw over the dead impala, staring with an aloof manner at the hyena clan. A steady lowing call rose, enveloping the savanna. The low pitched mooing from the hyenas filled the wolves with unease as it resonated through their spines.

Finally one of the female hyenas dashed forward with a high giggle. As she advanced toward the male lion, he got up on all fours and walked away, releasing one last low growl over his shoulder as he departed.

"Kreun is among them." Blouvalk indicated one of the males reaching in for a small share of the meat.

"He probably led them here." Blackthorn grunted. "We must be off."

The wolves slunk away, taking care to look for signs of the lions as they left. Visarend sniffed the ground with care, but found no additional cat prints. They padded away with some haste, and heard no further growls. The savanna behind them was marked with whoops and cackles.

"Was that the great threat of a lion?" Blouvalk mused.

"All predators flee before a determined hyena clan." Blackthorn set his jaw, wondering almost to himself. "Although the male seemed less concerned than most about defending his territory."

"He barely mattered." Blouvalk looked back toward the sound of hyena whooping. "Useless at hunting, useless at maintaining a kill."

"Nonetheless, we take care. Report any lion prints we see." Blackthorn watched the ground before him, deep in thought.

"With good fortune." Visarend panted. "We may leave behind the hyena clan that has pursued us."

Thirty-Three

There was no kill that day, nor the following day, and no ground that seemed safe for a den. At one point Swartwou halfheartedly scratched at a depression in the ground, though the scent of hyena on the dirt repelled him. There was only a brief, abortive chase of a common duiker to pass the time. There was little desire for a kill in any case, despite the hunger, knowing hyenas would quickly steal it.

Swartwou leapt away from their trail and crushed a scrub hare under his paws. He brought this to Visarend to tear apart and consume. The pack stopped while she scarfed down what little meat there was.

"How many lions are in a pride?" Swartwou licked the blood from his lips.

"Lions can be alone, or in a group as large as the hyena clan. The stronger and more aggressive the male, the larger the pride he can hold together." Blackthorn laid down on the ground for the moment, resting his aching joints.

"Not a very large pride then." Blouvalk sniffed the ground.

"No, it was not." Visarend spoke between swallows.

"Less than impressive, they were." Blouvalk padded about, rustling amid the grass.

"I was impressed." Swartwou twittered. "I never saw a

lioness take flight before."

The wolves laughed among themselves while a spurfowl fluttered its wings, flushed from a thicket by a pursuing Blouvalk. After it landed again far away, the wolf shook his fur free of grass and burrs.

"Come, our search continues." Visarend was back on her feet, the carcass stripped to the bones.

***

"I am guessing that... *thing*... is beyond our abilities." Swartwou admired the immense rhinoceros before them.

"Your judgment serves you well. You would as soon devour a mountain."

The rhino lumbered with what seemed languid ease, stepping slowly around a squat bush. The wide lips swept a broad swath of grass into its mouth, ripped free of the ground and quickly swallowed. The grey of its thick hide was spattered with water from the last rain in the morning. The horn, sharp as a spear, curved up from its snout for a meter. Funnel ears swiveled one way, then the next, seeking out signs of danger.

"Does it even know we are here?" Blouvalk edged closer.

"You will not know for sure until you are one with the earth beneath its feet." Blackthorn nudged him back before he moved any closer.

Swartwou rejoined them, panting. "That hyena is still on us. Are we any closer to finding a den?"

"*Bliksem.*" Blackthorn shook his head. "That decision can only come from the alpha." He dipped his head toward Visarend.

She breathed heavily, and did not answer them.

255

***

Toward evening, Visarend gave orders to the other three to feint a hunt. Blackthorn led them away, noting quickly that Kreun was indeed behind them. Their path took them across the expansive plain, about thick scrub and groves of acacia and bushwillow. After the first hour, he no longer was able to sight the male hyena.

"Do we still have a hyena tail?" Swartwou grinned.

"We are alone." Blackthorn exhaled. "Their sense of smell is greater even than our own, so he may yet find our path."

They ambled past a knot of yellow eriosema shrubs, the silvery green stalks now showing off dangling clusters of butter-colored flowers. Ground mice darted in and out of the foliage, busy with gathering the seeds that would stock their buried larders for the winter to come.

"We press the distraction further. With good fortune Kreun or other hyenas will pick up our false trail further from our matriarch."

After another two hours they doubled back as the light dimmed, and the sun dipped below the horizon to the west.

Dusk swiftly melted into the dark of night, enveloping the savanna in its resolute embrace. The moon above was a crescent, still bathing the veld in a slight, pale light.

Blackthorn sniffed the trail that Visarend had left, urine markings at regular intervals. Leading through the brush, there was one final, more pungent urine marking near a mound topped with an acacia shrub. Near the base of the thornbush, a hole yawned open to a downsloping passage.

Pausing for a moment, he rasped into the dark interior.

"Visarend?"

"*Welkom.*" Her hollow voice echoed to him.

"Quite a large aardvark hole, this." Blackthorn gestured for the benefit of the others. The rise of katydid calls rang in his ears. "The earth is dry, no scent of death or disease."

"She should be well protected in there." Swartwou sniffed the opening.

"Well enough, though we will still need to watch for hyena and jackal." Blackthorn sat, scratching his ear. "She may give birth soon. Then, my friends, the hunting is ours. The need of the pups will be relentless. And the lives of the pack are hefted onto your back for the duration of the season."

"Then we hunt with dawning light." Blouvalk spoke loudly, over the din of the calling insects.

Swartwou affirmed this with a nod, and flopped to the ground to rest until morning.

Blackthorn stood on the threshold of the den. In all directions, the grassland was level, with tall stalks of herringbone grass and squat bushes.

He started for a moment, then stood watching into the darkness.

A pair of crimson eyes, retinas glowing with the moonlight, regarded him from across the veld.

"*Vervloeks.*" Blackthorn cursed.

Thirty-Four

Shards of pale yellow crept across the savanna, between stone and tree. Stretching forth across the veld, one blade of dawn crossed the paws of hunters. Mottled gold and black, sporting pale claws, they were displayed on the wet dirt of the clearing. Their slender figures stood, lithe and capable, staring across the flat grass plain. The den was behind them, and within the alpha had yet to awaken. Her hunters were poised, ready for the attack before the cool of night began to seep away.

"What know you of gambits, Blouvalk?" The dark wolf still resembled a shadow in the early morning.

"Less than I would like." His white dorsal stripe stood out from the dim. "My plan, however, I will see done."

"Very well, Blouvalk." He twittered to the others. *"Ever taut, my wolves!"* Blackthorn nudged him with his snout. "So this hunt begins." He bared his teeth. "And for our prey, it shall indeed be the last."

***

Hammer of hooves, followed by a *pronk* over brush, the impala fled. Within a few body-lengths sprinted a stout wolf, the largest of the group. Ears were flat to the skull, head held low, streaking swiftly through thornbrush. He just managed to keep pace with the swift impala, followed by a wolf on either flank. If the impala strayed to one side, a flank would charge forward, returning the impala to a straight course.

"Toward the river!" Blouvalk called, and Blackthorn pushed forward, forcing the impala to turn in that direction.

Blackthorn paused to look over his shoulder. Distant, he could see the loping form of Kreun. As soon as he was spotted, he shrank into the foliage.

Down the long rise, the grass grew wild, waving in the morning breeze. It grew thicker down by a river that snaked through the bushveld, a wild zagging course crafted over millennia as water bit through rock. Cropping the vegetation with machine-like industry was a great white rhino, as broad as a road, and as heavy as the vehicles that used it. Its thick hide was grey and dusty, resembling the great dinosaurs that once stalked the grasslands of a bygone era. Each lumbering step brought its ponderous head closer to another clump of grass that was ripped free of the earth.

Drawing away from the shadow of the rhino was a smaller form, the young calf of the mother. It stepped gingerly, unsure of itself, comfortable only when the scent of the mother surrounded it.

The mother snorted, nervous for reasons it could not understand. The shifting wind brought news of a pursuit. There was a thudding sensation felt through the ground. A danger was coming.

The mother ignored the grass for a moment, and turned to face the coming disturbance. Nearly blind, she could only see vague shapes, the slight rise of the land, the tall smudge of a tree, and behind her in both directions the wide, slow flowing river.

By her side, she sensed the presence of her calf, and the calf could detect her nervous demeanor, and was unsure what to do. Running from an unseen enemy could end up blundering right into them.

She did not back up – the river had crocodiles, this she knew.

The thunder of hooves drew closer. More faint, claws across ground.

She gave a low grunt which her calf understood, hugging close.

The impala appeared over the rise, headed directly for the rhino mother. Three wolves were close behind it, their lean bodies powering forward.

The great head of the mother lowered, horn pointing directly at the approaching threat.

And suddenly it was over.

There was a thud and a scrabble of hoof against hard ground, and the light flutter of wolves talking amongst themselves. And then nothing.

Her sensitive nose sniffed the breeze, and all that was present was eviscerated antelope, bowels ruptured and open to the air. The calf started to pull away, and she grunted again, prompting the calf to adhere to her hide like a tick.

Just a trace of wolf musk lingered in the air, carried on currents to nowhere. It was strong, but faded quickly as the wind picked up.

She was loathe to forego good grazing time, and needed to keep up her milk production. The rhino mother returned to the grass, uprooting a tussock with broad lips. Molars worked the rich grass into a paste. A step forward, and she repeated this. The work of processing relatively indigestible fibers was never truly done.

A new scent crossed her path, and she immediately rumbled her alarm to the calf. *Whump*, as the calf smacked into her side, and pressed close. This was a different scent, less offensively pungent than wolf, but with a rancid edge to it. And she knew the source was a danger to her calf. Her horn lowered again. Ripping noises reached her sensitive ears, both funnels trained toward the noise of tearing meat. It was close.

A stamp on the ground by a foot, causing a reverberation like an iron ingot slammed into the earth. The ripping stopped for a moment, and resumed. Tearing, swallowing of flesh.

Abruptly they stopped as twitters rose again, coming from beyond the impala kill. Now the rhino was becoming agitated, not knowing from where the attack would come - but why would wolves bother her? Wolves have no interest in rhino calves. In any case, she would ensure these would not have an interest for long.

"*Welkom*, *Kreun*." Blackthorn yittered this with a ear-splitting peal.

Kreun shrank against the ground next to the impala carcass where he had been feeding.

"Found our den, *ja?*" Blouvalk growled. "Hoping for some fat wolf pups to feed your matriarch?" His jaws were bared, drool cascading onto the ground.

Swartwou jumped forward and clicked his jaws shut near to Kreun's sensitive nose.

Kreun recoiled, his fangs bared, hindparts tucked in as he backpedaled. He was nearly sitting in the impala's open body cavity.

"*GET OUT OF THERE.*" Blouvalk lunged, gripping a section of his face. He held fast, the conical killing fangs of the hyena close to his throat.

Blackthorn planted his jaws on the hyena's haunch, and Kreun twisted away from both of them, tumbling end over end. Swartwou was on the other side of him, and the wolves reformed a wall of fang and claw between him and the impala.

Kreun backed away, turning to run, and another bite was delivered to his tender rump. He turned to face his tormentors, his head held low, desiring to appear as pathetic as possible.

"*Craven you are.*" Blackthorn rumbled with his low voice. "But once free you will plague those pups with your every breath." With a howl, he thrust forward, missing Kreun's shoulder.

"Press forward!" Blouvalk twittered his command, and the three wolves harried him further from the impala.

Kreun stumbled further back from the jaws of the wolves, whimpering as he went, teeth bared, head low to the ground. He stumbled back, and further back, pressed by the painted wolf pack.

He gave a nervous giggle as he retreated.

Pounding, pounding upon the ground.

Suddenly, the wolves heard a meaty thud, a slight cry from Kreun, and the hyena was halted as though he had struck a boulder.

Kreun's eyes were wide with disbelief. His mouth gaped as he was lifted entirely off the ground, a horn spearing his body through the lower part of his rib cage, his legs wheeling helplessly. His mouth was stuck open with a silent scream, a river of blood pouring from his throat, but not a sound with it.

The legs wheeled more slowly, the head spasmed, then hung slack. Dead before he hit the ground, he was slung indifferently to the side from the front horn of the mother rhino.

She held her head low again, awaiting an attack.

The wolves drifted away from the mother rhino. Light paws clattered on gravel and leaves as they padded away, pausing to devour some of the meat that remained of the impala kill, and they were gone.

The calf nudged its mother with its nub of a horn, whining softly. The mother was uneasy about allowing the calf to suckle, but knew there was no stopping a calf when it needed milk. She would allow it to feed for now, but it was best to keep moving. This place would soon be visited by vultures and their incessant chatter. For one carcass, and then the other.

***

The hunters returned to the den to find Visarend resting outside the hole. She lay in the sun on the mound that housed the den, just outside the shade of a giraffe thorn acacia that grew as a tangled shrub. The ancient plant would continue rising into the blue sky, and in decades would be a tree, nourished on the rain of the wet season and the nutrients that accumulated in the soil from the many visitors to the abandoned aardvark hole.

"How fared your errand, Blouvalk?" Visarend stood, holding her head towards the golden sun.

"If the hyena clan learns the location of the den, it will not be from that *oke*." Blouvalk bounded up to her, and she met him on hind legs, boxing with forepaws before they returned to all fours.

She lapped Blouvalk's muzzle tenderly.

Blackthorn and Swartwou lapped her muzzle as well, and this prompted the regurgitation of what they had consumed of the impala. Visarend devoured this as it fell, leaving only a stain on the ground.

"You have done well." She nodded, lost in thought. "The challenge of the veld we have answered. Despite our loss."

Swartwou was downcast, even after the successful hunt.

"He would be pleased." Blouvalk intoned. "Kleinsperwer surely would have had something eccentric to say."

"Death has come to know us." Blackthorn rumbled. "And work on our behalf."

The rest were quiet for some time. Above, a cape turtle dove purred. *Cuk-coor-uk.* The thorns scraped against branch and bark as the wind stirred the flat crown of the acacia.

"*Maaier.* My Pack is so named. Death will come to know it well." Visarend's voice rasped. "We shall not yield another wolf to the veld." She shook her head, her features contorted. "Not another of my *jagters* will fall under my sight."

"Your hunters stand at the ready, Visarend." Blouvalk seemed to stand taller even than Swartwou. "Fear is for those who stray into our territory." He glared at the veld around them. "This hyena has received a bitter rebuke. Who shall be foolish enough to join him?"

Thirty-Five

Rain pelted the bushveld below, the surface of temporary pools now alive with dancing globes of water. Insects waited out the deluge under the umbrella of leaf or flower petal. A herd of impala grazed in the open on the vibrant green grass, quiet as they waited for the irritation of the rainfall to cease. As the orange sun rose higher in the sky, the showers tailed off and the clouds dispersed.

Male impala rams shook their heads free of moisture, their horns rocking right and left, the jaws ever working to chew down the grass.

Female ewes wandered amid the herd, taking turns watching the horizon for danger and eating more vegetation. The herd numbered a few dozen, and was sprawled across a wide space of savanna that gradually descended down to a languid flowing river. The temporary artery of water had gushed forth with the rains, and would eventually wither and vanish in midwinter, leaving behind dried plates of mud. For now, it carried water away from this veld, eventually merging with greater rivers to the south.

"These good lands will bear us well." Blackthorn admired the view from under the shadow of a waterpear tree. Branching wildly in a tangle, the rounded leafy crown was heavy with new green fruits.

"The *Maaier* pack is at the ready." Visarend lapped his muzzle. "Blouvalk has taken to your teachings well."

"The teacher is only a somewhat older student." He returned her gesture.

She urinated lightly on the ground, marking the territory. Blackthorn stepped forward, and carefully urinated on the same spot as Visarend.

"Perhaps our markings will be followed by others looking to join a pack." Visarend mused.

"We will need a few more hunters. We will soon lose our best."

Visarend opened her mouth for a moment before realizing he meant her. She snuffed at that, and padded along the river. The waterpear trees stretched further down the river.

"How much longer can you run the hunt?"

"Until I birth my pups, I shall not miss a single *jag*."

"Would that you could hunt even then." He touched noses with her. "We would never know hunger."

Swartwou and Blouvalk joined them.

"The herd is close." Blouvalk twittered. "The *bloed* river closer." He was on hind legs boxing Visarend, who joined him on hind legs despite her protruding belly. Forepaws batted head and shoulders in play, and for a moment they appeared to dance before they returned to the ground. The rally began as the wolves lapped one another's muzzles, the excited twitter rising. As their enthusiasm reached a fever pitch, Visarend loped away from the river toward the grazing herd of impala.

She twittered her orders to the others. Jaws were parted, teeth revealed, in the way wolves smile. She trotted off into thick brush.

The males bounded in another direction, around the wall of sweet thorn acacia and through a stand of bushwillow trees. Their paws produced little sound on the moist leaf litter, but above, they could hear the chattering begin.

None were within sight, but higher on the branches vervet monkeys clung tight to the bark, and they had not missed the threat below. A squawk erupted from one, then another, and the entire group joined in. Blackthorn glanced up, and looked to the others.

"We must hurry—the word is out."

The wolves accelerated, and the nattering intensified. Each tree they sprinted under had more monkeys in them, and the jarring noise was infectious.

"Forward to the killing field." Blackthorn growled, and the wolves ran faster still. Heads low, ears flat, lean bodies flexing along the spine, claws clinging to ground. Every muscle was tight, engaged, sinewed legs pistons, propelling the hunters toward the impala herd grazing before them.

The impala coughed, and alarm barks were made throughout the group as the monkey babble galvanized them.

When the wolves burst from under the trees, panic seized the antelope. Dozens bolted when they spotted the pairs of dish-like ears bouncing amid the grass tips. Hooves thudded into the dirt, and the antelope instantly reached maximum speed. Muscular forms launched themselves into the air in the soaring *pronk* with antlers held high.

Their speed rivaled a bird in flight, designed by evolution to outrun their killers. Leaping forward, traveling several body lengths with every *pronk*, the impala declared their vigor. Rapidly they matched the pace of the wolves, set to outdistance them as they thundered toward the sweet thorn acacia thicket.

When that thicket parted, Visarend leapt out, fangs bared. The impalas stopped short and divided, a wave breaking upon a rocky shore.

She was not distracted by the chaotic display, focusing on one group of antelope and pressing them close to the sedge, denying them escape. Despite her pregnancy, she managed a swift pace and matched every evasive movement her prey could manage.

Salvation lost, they split away in a manic dispersal, every impala choosing a random direction to flee. In this choice, seconds were wasted.

Seconds were all she needed. Visarend charged in and clamped her jaws shut on the rear of a ram, holding fast. The impala was anchored, and unable to raise a hind leg to kick his captor. He could only rear up, forelegs in the air, but to no avail.

The male wolves mobbed their prey and pulled it over to the ground, Blouvalk gripping the snout, Blackthorn the foreshoulder. Swartwou took a mouthful of belly and slashed aside, and blood welled. The intestines poured out in writhing blue coils that Swartwou held and pulled, and the impala bled out and died within moments.

Impala pounded the earth heading away from the kill, seeking distance from the fallen. Abruptly the fleeing herd stopped, and dispersed once again in a frenzy, splitting in two further away past the acacia sedge.

Between the departing crowds of impala stood a lion.

Blackthorn stopped devouring meat. He sensed fear in the air and looked up from the body cavity of the carcass, his fur slick with red.

"The kill is lost."

The other three stopped feeding.

A roar reached them from across the veld. *"Gevaar calls."*

"Step away from the prize." Blackthorn rasped to the wolves.

Blouvalk padded a short distance from the impala, glaring at the male lion. His fur was matted with clotting blood.

"Where are your lionesses, Gevaar?" He yittered toward the approaching form. "Have they wised up and went hunting without you?"

His blond mane shimmered in the morning sun, like waving grass on the savanna. Bounding, he closed in on the wolves.

"You are right." Swartwou twittered to the others. "He is alone." He padded forth. "So comes the thief, unable to kill a grazer on his own!"

"Caution, Blouvalk." Visarend moved forward. "We can hunt again elsewhere."

"My friends, we must run." Blackthorn's voice was on edge.

"From this lazy *oke?*" Swartwou coughed. "He can take off and kill his own meat."

Visarend watched them carefully.

"Do not doubt his strength, my love." Blackthorn moved closer to her.

"Let us see how he reacts." Her eyes were locked upon Gevaar.

Blouvalk shot forward, bounding across the grass, ears flat and lean muscles working to their limit. The white stripe of his back danced as he powered toward his adversary.

Gevaar snarled, and slowed his approach. Tail whipped from one side to the next, awaiting what was to come.

The wolf banked around him, twittering as his claws sank into the earth. The lion turned, following the arc, and recoiled for a moment as the wolf snapped his jaws not far from his shoulder. He returned to join his pack, by the side of his alpha.

"I doubt his ability to stand against hyena." Visarend nodded to Blouvalk.

"His great enemy that we destroyed, and fed to the vultures." Blouvalk's voice rose into a high cackle that resembled the hyena that was killed.

"Harass him, but give him ample room to withdraw." She glanced at Blackthorn, and he nodded back to her. Her belly, low with pups, swayed beneath her.

The lion's stout body rose and fell as his paws struck ground, propelling him forward, golden fur glowing.

The distance between them diminished to nothing, and hunter met hunter.

Gevaar growled as he dashed toward the wolves. Blouvalk and Swartwou broke to the sides, jaws bared, while Visarend ruff-barked at their enemy.

"Do you wish to join the dead, *bliksem?*" Swartwou's head was held low, ears down, lips pulled back in a grimace of rage.

"Grin as you wish. Your throat will have a smile to match." His fangs dripped saliva, powerful jaws working as though already holding his foe.

"We shall see the back of this one." Visarend showed her teeth.

Blackthorn said nothing, heart pounding.

Blouvalk rushed in and clicked his jaws on the hip of the lion, and Gevaar whirled about, snarling.

"None are as fast as we, foul beast." Blouvalk's jaw hung open, releasing a streamer of drool.

Gevaar raised a paw, and set it back down. His roar was muted, swallowed.

Swartwou twittered to his rear, jumping far back before the

lion rounded on him, holding his head lower as he growled at the wolves.

Blackthorn bounded closer to Swartwou's side.

"Give him distance." His graveled voice was clipped.

"He shall give us all the distance in the world." Visarend snarled. "The *Maaier* pack shall stand, and give no ground."

Blackthorn twittered urgently to Swartwou to move aside, opening a path of escape for the lion. His obsidian eyes never left Gevaar's paws.

"My call echoes across veld and season." Gevaar took a step back. *"My cubs... weaned on cruelty, with an endless taste for vengeance. They shall come for you all in time."* His lips were pulled in a smirk as he took another step back. *"You shall have no sleep in the night."*

"Back away, my wolves." Blackthorn urged.

Blouvalk sneered. *"Voetsek, vermin!"*

The veld was silent.

The lion took another step back. His eyes opened wide and he thrust forward, hind legs digging furrows into the wet ground. A wide paw swept across and struck Blouvalk on the shoulder.

The wolf was stunned, rolling aside from the glancing blow. The next paw came down on his haunch, and he was on the ground, white stripe flecked with blood. His hazel eyes were wide with fear.

Blackthorn snarled, and snapped his teeth near the broad face of the lion to draw his attention.

Gevaar ignored him, and parted his jaws stepping toward Blouvalk where he lay.

His throat erupted in a roar as teeth sank into his shoulder and he turned to see Visarend clamped down. Taken aback, Gevaar bellowed, his long conical fangs dripping with saliva.

Visarend let him go, unleashing a scream as Blouvalk retreated to safety. *"Voetsek – now and always!"*

With a sudden burst of speed Gevaar lunged forward and swept across with a mighty paw, and struck Visarend on the head. She moaned, wavering on her legs.

Blackthorn thrust forward and bit Gevaar on the haunch, but could not stop him.

The lion shrugged him off and struck again with a titanic clout, and Visarend went down, her lean body spun about. Disregarding the wound on his side, Gevaar pounced upon her, closing his powerful jaws on her neck and crushing the bones within. He lifted her wholly off the ground with a fierce whip of his head, and her limp form flew several meters before thumping to the ground.

Blackthorn's jaw hung slack as he stared at her body. When he turned toward Gevaar, the lion's paw was coming for his head.

He cringed, jumping back a body length, evading the blow, turning to dash away. Gevaar was close behind, bounding toward him, a golden wall of muscle, wide nose snorting his anger.

Swiftly Blackthorn outpaced the lion, and Gevaar rounded to face the other wolves. Blouvalk and Swartwou had moved back, staring at Visarend with numb shock.

Gevaar trotted past where Visarend lay, overlooking her. He stood next to the fallen impala and roared, sending a chill through the spine of every animal that roamed the veld.

"GEVAAR CALLS."

Distant across the expanse of the plain, two lionesses were inbound.

Blackthorn panted, his chest burning with every heave. Near

the impala, by a tussock of grass, her body laid still. He could make out her face, hazel eyes blank, sightless.

A moment before those eyes burned with life.

The chest did not rise with a breath. Her swollen abdomen did not move. Blackthorn could not tear his gaze from her belly, and from the pups that would never run from the earthen den into the morning sun.

Gevaar relaxed, and licked blood from the antelope's hide before taking a hunk of meat from the haunch. The lionesses settled close by, and waited patiently for their turn at the impala. They would not move for the rest of the day, possibly the next. They scorned Visarend's corpse.

Blackthorn's mind raced. "No... she could..." He began to pace forward, toward her prone body.

Gevaar stood at once, his heavy breathing starting to wheeze into another territorial roar.

The dark wolf backed away. He stared at her, looking for signs of movement that were not there. Pulse bounding in his ears, he cried in anguish, his jaws locked open in a silent howl. Burning with a desire for pain, he imagined leaping to his death from a mountain crag, racing into the lion pride to waiting fangs, impaling himself on a sharpened stake from eye sockets to belly. His mind raced and reeled.

Chest heaving, his throbbing head slowed, and stopped.

His breathing gradually calmed, and a cold settled into him that took hold.

The male lion returned to his meal, his apathy toward the wolves restored.

"Blackthorn, we must go." Blouvalk muttered. The dark wolf had not noticed Blouvalk had crept to his side.

The three shared blank stares before they padded off, together.

The male lion ripped away flesh from the impala carcass, his guttural call still resounding across the land.

White tip of tail vanished into the dense brush. As the branches cracked beside him, Blackthorn turned, wet eyes glittering in the sun, to look back one last time. A whisper echoed in his ears.

Do not disappoint me.

Thirty-Six

Night.

Katydids gave their razzing call, punctuated by the *Whr-whr-whrwhrwhr!* of the fiery-necked nightjar. A civet foraged in the dark, stepping with great care, one paw before the next, always on wet leaf or ground. The slender body was black spot and stripe coloration on brown, with dark circles around its eyes, utterly invisible even in moonlight. Its head was held close to the ground, ears angling about for sounds, sniffing as it went.

It searched among the rocks, moving gradually to avoid making noise with its claws on stone. Another sniff. Approaching an overhang on a large boulder, it struck forward, and nipped its prey. A brown house snake, coiled within a cleft in the rock, spasmed with its injury, a hole torn in its side. Another lightning fast strike and the civet had grabbed the snake near the head and tossed its long, lean body away from the boulder, where it writhed on the ground. Before the brown snake could move back to shelter, the civet pounced, gripping the snake in its jaws and whipped it back and forth in a violent death shake, snapping the bones in several places. The killing bite that crushed the skull was instinctive, but its prey was already dead.

Rapidly, the civet bolted down the meat after tearing aside the skin of the snake, leaving little behind apart from bone. The moment the meal was finished, the civet continued its careful walk, disturbing none of the undergrowth.

In the grass nearby was a wolf lying on its side. His dark coloration of mostly black with splotches of gold allowed him to melt into the darkness. The only sign of life was the occasional heaving of his chest, and the light sound of exhalation. Eyes as dark as asphalt were open, staring at nothing. He lay alone.

Swartwou and Blouvalk lay elsewhere, somewhere. Blackthorn was not sure. The day before passed in silence as the three wandered in a daze, noticing prey, looking at them, through them, never attempting a hunt. Words turned in his mind, but became ash on his tongue. He looked up to Blouvalk once, but their eyes never met. Hours passed, and in the dusk they each collapsed in grass, somewhere, alone.

They had not spoken a word since leaving her behind. There was nothing further to say.

As the sun rose, there was no twittering or excitement about the hunt to come. When Blackthorn finally stood to look around the surrounding savanna, he saw little of interest. He padded up to a rock outcropping, topped with grass and dirt, and surveyed the area. Scattered bushwillow trees, scattered rock and boulder, far away water birds taking to wing.

Across the grass sea, another form rose to look about. Black, white, and gold fur with large dish-like ears marked a familiar figure. The dorsal white stripe made clear it was Blouvalk, but somehow he seemed alien, someone else entirely. He eventually turned to notice Blackthorn.

When their eyes met, Blackthorn felt a longing to join him, with sniffing and lapping of muzzles, boxing one another on hind legs, exchanging the greetings of a fellow wolf. An ache bore into his stomach, a longing to be with one's own kind on the vast savanna.

Blouvalk turned and began to walk.

As the morning passed, the sun climbed gradually overhead to bathe the veld in a golden glow. In the late dawn, the great wild sprawled before Blackthorn, with no other wolves in sight.

He looked down, feeling a weight as though struggling to pull down a wildebeest, simply to remain standing. Claws clicked on the rocks as he made his way back down to the damp ground. The bronze grass wavered in the dawn where he stood. Looking down, he moved his paw aside. A wolf print in the wet earth, four toes with matching claw marks.

He wondered how long it would be before he saw another.

***

Sere lands shimmered in the heat, and nothing seemed to be moving on the scrublands at midday.

Kudu crouched in the shade of giraffe thorn acacia, within sight of a lion pride. The antelope looked toward the predator, knowing it would be safe until sundown. The boiling heat would render the hunters lethargic and unwilling to pursue the effort of a kill.

Even birds perched unmoving on branches in shade, waiting out the day.

A single lone figure trundled slowly across the bushveld. The wolf did not seem to mind the temperatures, the antelope beneath the trees, or even the presence of lions.

Blackthorn took one step at a time, ears up, tail held high, panting constantly. He thought little beyond the effort of walking.

To the south, one paw before the other.

Thirty-Seven

The land became drier toward the south, and the flat arbors of giraffe thorn acacia were scattered across the savanna. Baobab trees appeared more often here, the top of their broad trunks terminating in root-like branches that carried green leaves.

Days blurred into weeks, and Blackthorn was immersed in silence. He kept the sunrise on his left, the sunset on his right. His only reason for choosing this was to ensure he never returned to the familiar. The wild remained open before him, yet he felt no comfort. He barely seemed to notice as his path converged with a highway.

The black ribbon reached far into the distance, just wide enough for cars to pass by one another, each on their left side of the road. White stripes painted on the center of the highway were faded. Blackthorn sniffed, still detecting the acrid smell of tar, dried years ago. A paw laid on the road was withdrawn quickly, the surface baking in the heat.

He padded alongside this human pathway, lean form bouncing with each step, his pace tireless. On one side of the black surface, a railing sprouted from the ground, a red and white striped petrified vine. Snaking alongside the endless highway, it then abruptly disappeared into the ground. Shortly after this, the road widened, and appeared darker, the white stripes more bright. He paused, somewhat more nervous. Road signs of green background with white lettering began to appear more frequently, and seemed more neat and well maintained.

Cars whooshed by hourly, and Blackthorn left the roadside to reenter the grass and brush. In spite of his fear, he was drawn toward the signs of human habitation.

In the distance, he could make out huts, and occasionally cement dwellings. A green sign by the side of the road read "Ngoma" with a number beside it.

Each structure he passed, he peered in that direction. Green rain barrels, small kitchen gardens, mangy dogs lingering just outside the doors. No chain link fence animal enclosures were in view. Blackthorn continued looking for cages that may hold a captive wolf. He found none as he continued his never-ending lope.

Will I forget the appearance of wolf tracks?

A cream colored building sat by the tar ribbon, and the edge of the road was marked by a black and white striped curb. The road itself merged with a surface of bricks, where several white *bakkies* were parked. A flag was stirred by the minimal breeze, a diagonal stripe of red separating fields of blue and green.

Beyond this, the road stretched between metal guardrails and a white walkway on either side of the road. The land itself dropped away to the river below.

Blackthorn peered down the bank to the river, which was swollen from the rains. Toward the center of the waterway, the water appeared black, listlessly flowing to an unseen place beyond the horizon. On the far bank, a crocodile rested with its jaw wide open in the heat. He snuffed, and returned to the road as a car zoomed past. While another car approached crossing the bridge, he noticed none of the vehicles taking the walkway. He hastened across this to the other side of the bridge, claws clacking on the steel. On the other side he quickly moved away from the speeding cars and back into the grasses.

Even near the human buildings of the border post, he saw no pens that could contain trapped animals. Enemies seemed everywhere.

Does it matter if I lose heart? Will the way of the painted wolf be lost over time?

South, he continued, enduring.

Will I forsake the language that brought me this far, the dialect of the veld that my kind holds dear?

He left the road behind, left the signs behind. The stink of gasoline faded as the twisted branches of acacia shrub and waving tall grass concealed his lithe form. His black fur, with touches of gold and white amid the darkness, melted into shadow and foliage.

My Volk. Hunters all, we once roamed the land entire.

The wind stirred the leaves and branches above him as he walked in the shade of giraffe thorn acacia and jackalberry trees.

Shall my Volk give way to the rest of the world?

Sharp thorns skittered upon bark. The savanna provided no answer.

South of the Chobe river he disappeared into the wide open wild.

On this side of the river, he noticed one tree after another uprooted, torn from the ground, ripped open. Larger acacia trees seemed robust enough to resist the pruning efforts of the elephants here. Beside the river were stands of trees, Natal mahogany, fever berry, and the occasional sausage tree. The riverine forest provided lush stands of green. Thinning groves gave way along the river to bleached white skeletons of dead trees, mostly termite resistant leadwoods.

A family of elephants luxuriated in the river, the titanic matriarch submerged to her belly throwing a splash of water over her back with a trumpeting blast. The other female elephants stood in shallower water, minding the calves. Hippos floated in the river further down from the elephants, only ears and eyes visible above the waves. On the shore, lechwe grazed on the rich grass while a monitor lizard basked in the sun.

Blackthorn's thoughts drifted to a place he had been dreading. Her voice echoed in his mind.

What is the wild?

He saw her, behind the chain link fence, her paw hanging on the iron.

I knew we were not alone.

He could smell the scent of dank, moist earth within a den.

No wolf is destined.

His eyelids clenched shut as his head ached.

My pack shall be Maaier. And my first pup shall be named Wraak.

His own voice echoed: *Unto death.*

Blackthorn opened his eyes and the voices faded into the splashing of the elephant herd in the river.

Do not disappoint me.

"I shall not." He was unsure whether he spoke aloud, nor did he care. "I shall not lose heart in *die trek*."

There was no response from the veld, and none was expected. Blackthorn knew his was the only answer that mattered.

The herd continued its bath, the vultures wheeled upon the thermals above, and the land watched them all with disinterest.

"The path takes us." His graveled voice rasped. "As it takes us all.”

Epilogue

The torn, ragged wound in the abdomen of the impala calf yielded a pool of blood that had flowed into the grass before clotting. Alone, he was unable to dismember the kill, making the process of eating more difficult. Simply tearing the meat was work, as any pull would merely drag the body across the ground. His canine teeth scissored meat from bone with frustration.

There is only the Pack.

Days had passed since he crossed the bridge. At long last, his hunger had returned, and he was able to make a kill on his own. The pain of the past was dulled as he enjoyed the savor of the meat.

A shadow crossed him, and he looked about with alarm. A white-backed vulture circled overhead, and was soon joined by another.

A giggle startled him.

Blackthorn looked behind him, and saw a hyena approach. A male, small in stature for a hyena, but still twice his size, strode closer with broad foreshoulders. The head was held low in apparent supplication.

"*Sharrre?*" His shallow chuckle grated, jaws parted.

Blackthorn growled and charged straight at him. The hyena

recoiled, tucking his hindparts low instinctively, backpedaling. Though his teeth were bared as well, the hyena ran off, giving a resounding *WHOO-OOP!*

Blackthorn returned to the kill and devoured what he could before a larger hyena troop arrived to assume control of the remains. He left them very little, anticipating hard times ahead.

His search continued with a full belly, and he padded on, ever deeper into the wild country.

Dark eyes scanned the ground continuously, sniffing as he went. Urine was sprayed as travelled, marking the ground. Ever deeper into the savanna, he searched.

Passing a series of towering termite mounds, he nearly missed it.

Stopping, he padded back, looking down. Despite himself, a smile was allowed to creep across his face, and he gave a long, relaxed exhale.

A wolf print in the sandy soil.

THE END

Author's Note

As in the first book of the series, *Wait a Season For Their Names*, this novel was written to reflect as accurately as possible the behaviors of the African Wild Dog or Painted Wolf. The species name has been a moving target for decades now: African Wild Dog, Cape Hunting Dog, African Painted Wolf, Painted Dog. Even textbooks aren't unanimous in naming the species.

I stuck with African Painted Wolf because 'dog' suggests it is a feral dog that everyone can be comfortable with shooting on sight. Rangers and hunters were given a bounty on shooting them until the mid 1980s. I do occasionally also mention 'Wild Dog' for variety's sake in the text, but overwhelmingly call them 'wolves'. It is more appropriate name for something of the wild.

In addition to my experiences with these complicated and elusive hunters, the following sources have been essential to understanding more about their tactics, movements, and family structure. Other resources have been useful to get the correct details on plant life, herbivores, and everything that makes an ecological system work.

The mistakes are mine alone.

The African Wild Dog - Behavior, Ecology, and Conservation by Scott and Nancy Creel c2002

Running Wild - Dispelling the Myths of the African Wild Dog by John McNutt and Lesley Boggs c1996

Painted Wolves - Wild Dogs of the Serengeti-Mara by Jonathon Scott c1991

A Window on Eternity by E.O. Wilson c2014

The Behavior Guide to African Mammals by Richard Estes c2012

The Safari Companion by Richard Estes c1999

African Wild Dogs on the Front Line by Brendan Whittington-Jones c2015

The Antelope of Africa by Willem Frost c2014

The Field Guide to Insects of South Africa by Mike Picker c 2004

Sasol Birds of Southern Africa by Ian Sinclair, et al c2014

Snakes of Southern Africa by Johan Marais c2004

Field Guide to Trees of Southern Africa by Braam van Wyk c2013

Organizations protecting and researching the African Painted Wolf:

Painted Dog Conservation – painteddog.org
    Peter Blinston, managing director

Endangered Wildlife Trust – ewt.org.za
    Dr. Harriet Davies-Mostert, head of conservation

Wildlife ACT – wildlifeact.com
    African Wild Dog monitoring and research

African Wild Dog Conservancy – awdconservancy.org
    Dr. Bob Robbins, director

African Wildlife Foundation – awf.org

African Wild Dog Conservation Malawi – wilddogconservation-malawi.org

African Wildlife Conservation Fund – africanwildlifeconserva-tionfund.org
    Dr. Peter Lindsey, Africa director

If you have enjoyed reading this novel, I would be immensely grateful if you were to post a review on Amazon. They do help, and spread the word about the books, therefore improving sales and thus the contributions I make to the organizations protecting this endangered species.

About the Author

About Alexander Kendziorski

Alex is a practicing physician in the United States with interests in carnivore conservation, community health, and South African history and politics. He is transitioning to living and working in South Africa to be a part of the changes taking place, and to continue working with wildlife conservation and community health education.

All proceeds of this novel will go to wildlife groups working to protect the African Wild Dog/Painted Wolf.

You can connect with me on:

🌐 https://amzn.to/2UhHjL9

Also by Alexander Kendziorski

Wait A Season For Their Names
Oh, my African Painted Wolves, do not be anxious to claim your pups. Wait a season for their names.

And hope you survive a season to claim one.

For a painted wolf mother, the hostile savanna is a place where daily survival may be the only victory. An escape from gnashing teeth or human predators carries no guarantee of tomorrow.

The matriarch Aalwyn, her new litter of pups, and her mate Grootboom, the cunning antelope hunter, battle for survival through Botswana, Zimbabwe, and Mozambique. In this wildlife odyssey set in an ever-changing world, no one is safe.

What fate lies in store for Aalwyn and her family? Discover the answers through animal eyes in a well-written, gripping epic for fans of *Watership Down* and *White Fang*.